MW00782414

THE GHOST
WHO LOVED DIAMONDS

The Ghost of Marlow House

The Ghost Who Loved Diamonds

The Ghost Who Wasn't

The Ghost Who Wanted Revenge

The Ghost of Halloween Past

The Ghost Who Came for Christmas

The Ghost of Valentine Past

The Ghost from the Sea

The Ghost and the Mystery Writer

The Ghost and the Muse

The Ghost Who Stayed Home

The Ghost and the Leprechaun

The Ghost Who Lied

The Ghost and the Bride

The Ghost and Little Marie

The Ghost and the Doppelganger

The Ghost of Second Chances

The Ghost Who Dream Hopped

The Ghost of Christmas Secrets

The Ghost Who Was Says I Do

HAUNTING DANIELLE - BOOK 2

BOBBI HOLMES

The Ghost Who Loved Diamonds
(Haunting Danielle, Book 2)
A Novel
By Bobbi Holmes
Cover Design: Elizabeth Mackey

Robeth Publishing, LLC

robeth.net

ISBN 978-1-949977-01-1

To Mom, for being my most
dedicated beta reader and loyal fan,
also because she loves diamonds.

ONE

Tilting the rearview mirror down slightly, Cheryl looked at her reflection. Despite the long car ride, her makeup required minimal repair. Lipstick tube in hand, she used the tip of her pinkie finger to wipe away stray mascara from the corners of her eyes before applying the lipstick.

Cheryl readjusted the mirror again to get a better view of the young man standing by the side of her car, filling its gas tank. She wished her home state of California had the same law as Oregon, which didn't allow consumers to fill their own gas tanks. It was a job she loathed. Fortunately, since crossing the border into Oregon, that was one less thing for her to worry about.

Placing the cap back on the lipstick, she tossed the tube in her open purse sitting on the passenger seat and then removed a neatly folded piece of paper from the handbag's side pocket. Unfolding the paper, she reread the Internet article printed out from her computer at home. If she had never stumbled across the story, she wouldn't be sitting in her car right now, in some little Oregon beach town that she had never heard of before.

"Dani, Dani," Cheryl said aloud, her eyes focused on the article. "Just what are you trying to pull?"

The gas attendant stepped up to the driver's side of the car—its window down—and said, "All filled up. It took the entire forty bucks."

Cheryl looked up at the young man while she refolded the paper and asked, "Do you know where a place called Marlow House is?"

"Marlow House? Why sure. It's only a couple blocks from here."

"THESE JUST ARRIVED," Lily announced. Wearing worn jeans and a faded blue T-shirt, her red hair fastened atop her head in a lopsided ponytail, she stood in the kitchen doorway, holding a floral arrangement of red, white, and blue roses. Danielle glanced up from where she stood at the counter, measuring ingredients for a chocolate cake into a large stainless steel mixing bowl.

"Those are lovely!" Danielle said. "Who are they from?" She did not attempt to see for herself but continued with her task.

"Marie Nichols. Did you notice the little American flags?" Lily walked into the kitchen, tilting the vase slightly to give Danielle a better view. "I left the card on the entry table. Where do you want me to put it?"

"I don't know, where do you think? Maybe on the entry table?" Danielle shrugged.

"Okay." Lily turned back to the doorway.

"What did the card say?" Danielle called out.

Lily paused and looked back at Danielle. "It was just wishing you luck on the grand opening. Said she was looking forward to it."

"Did she say anything about her lovely thief—I mean grandson coming with her?"

"No, but I'm sure he'll be bringing her."

"I guess there's no way of avoiding that." She sighed and picked up a wooden spoon from the counter. Danielle thought of Marie's grandson, Adam, and how he and Bill Jones had once broken into Marlow House. She began beating the cake batter with a tad more zeal than was necessary.

When Lily returned to the kitchen a few minutes later, she found Danielle preparing to pour the batter into cake pans.

"So what do we need to do?" Lily grabbed her vintage apron from the kitchen table. It was a recent find from a Frederickport yard sale. The apron, with its colorful strawberry print, appealed to her elementary school teacher sensibilities. She would be wearing this one in the classroom, when school started in the fall. Her students would love it. Tying the apron around her waist, she watched Danielle, whose dark hair threatened to slip from its haphazard bun.

"I have a list around here someplace." Pouring the batter into the cake pans, Danielle attempted to blow escaped strands of hair from her eyes as she glanced around briefly, searching for the misplaced list. She didn't see it.

Lily looked around the room and spied a piece of paper on the floor under the kitchen table. She picked it up. Looking over the list, she said, "Before we tackle the next item, why don't we break for lunch?"

"Sounds good to me." Danielle opened the oven and moved the filled cake pans from the counter to the oven's middle rack. After closing the oven, Danielle took the list from Lily and looked it over. "What do you think about bringing that croquet set down from the attic and setting it up in the backyard? It might be fun, give people something to do? Old fashioned."

"It might be fun," Lily said as she grabbed the loaf of bread from the counter. After making them each a sandwich and a glass of iced tea, she sat at the table, waiting for Danielle to join her.

"You still picking up the necklace in the morning?" Lily asked as she sipped her tea.

Danielle glanced up from the list. "Yep." She joined Lily at the table.

"I hope you know what you're doing. Wearing a piece of jewelry worth more than a million bucks—with all those strangers in the house—seems a little risky to me."

"I wouldn't be getting the press attention without it."

"I know. It just makes me nervous."

"Don't worry, Lily. Remember, Officer Morelli plans to be here to help keep an eye on things." *Not to mention Walt—there's no way he'll let someone walk out of Marlow House with the Missing Thorndike.*

"I admit I feel a little better knowing you aren't taking any reservations until after the party. I don't think I'd like the idea of strangers being here overnight when the necklace is in the house."

"Well, don't worry. It goes back into the safety deposit box on Saturday morning, after the open house. And then on Monday or Tuesday, the buyer will be here to take it off my hands. So you can stop worrying," Danielle said.

"Are you sure the bank is going to be open? After all, it is a holiday weekend."

"I checked. They're always open on Saturday mornings, and they told me they'll be open until noon."

Lily started to say something but paused when she heard the doorbell. "I wonder if that's Ian." Lily glanced at the clock on the oven. "He's not supposed to be here for another hour."

"Maybe it's more flowers," Danielle suggested as she stood up.

"I'll get it. You eat your lunch." Lily jumped up and headed for the front door. Danielle sat back down and took a bite of her sandwich.

When Lily opened the front door a few moments later, it wasn't Ian standing on the porch but a buxom blonde Lily had never seen before. Escaping cleavage spilled from the woman's snugly fitting white spandex halter top. Speechless, Lily's eyes traveled down the woman's body to skintight satin slacks in hot pink. The woman's stiletto heels were the same shade of pink. Next to her feet on the porch was a suitcase. Lily's gaze darted back up to the stranger's face, and she looked into blue eyes—blue eyes lined in black with purple glitter shadow covering each lid. Lily thought the woman—who she guessed to be about her own age—might be quite lovely if she scrubbed off the heavy makeup and toned down the purplish lipstick.

"I'm afraid we aren't open for business yet," Lily said, glancing again to the suitcase.

"We?" The woman laughed. "I'm here to see Dani." Not waiting for an invitation, she picked up the suitcase and pushed her way past Lily into Marlow House. Once in the entry, she dropped the suitcase on the wood floor and looked around the dark-paneled entry hall.

"And who should I say is here?" Lily asked, clearly annoyed as she shut the front door and faced the intruder.

"I'm Dani's cousin, Cheryl, and who are you? The housekeeper? If so, you really need to improve your people skills, or you're going to run away the guests," Cheryl scolded.

Lily stood speechless for a moment, unable to grasp the fact this was Danielle's infamous cousin, Cheryl. From what she understood, Cheryl was Danielle's only living relative. Both women had lost their parents in the same airplane accident when Danielle was still in college. Though Cheryl was Danielle's only remaining relative, the two women had never been close.

"Well, what are you waiting for?" Cheryl asked.

"Excuse me?" Lily blinked her eyes, coming out of her momentary stupor.

"Go get her! And you might as well take my bag up to my room. When you're done with that, you can get me something to eat, I'm starving." Cheryl wandered over to the mirror hanging on the wall behind the roses and looked at her reflection. After pursing her lips, she combed her fingers through her hair.

"Danielle's not expecting you," Lily blurted out. "We don't have any rooms ready."

Cheryl turned from the mirror and faced Lily. "Don't be silly. Dani will have room for me. I am family, after all."

"I'll get Danielle," Lily muttered, heading to the kitchen.

"What about my suitcase?" Cheryl called out.

Lily glanced back briefly, muttered something under her breath and continued on to the kitchen.

"You've got to get out here," Lily said the moment she walked into the room.

"What's wrong?" Danielle stood up from the table.

"You have a visitor. One who expects to stay here."

"I don't understand. Did you tell them we aren't accepting reservations yet?"

"I told her we didn't have any rooms ready yet."

"She?" Danielle frowned, heading to the doorway.

Cheryl was no longer standing in the entry. They found her in the parlor, inspecting a porcelain figurine.

"Cheryl?" Danielle asked in disbelief. Cheryl looked over at her cousin, smiled, and set the porcelain figurine back on the table. "What are you doing here?"

"That's a fine greeting," Cheryl scolded. "And in front of the help."

"Help?" Danielle glanced over at Lily, who just shrugged. "Lily doesn't work for me. She's a friend. I'll ask again, what are you doing here?"

"Isn't it obvious? I've come for the open house." Cheryl plopped down on a chair and kicked off her shoes. Wiggling her toes, she briefly admired her recent pedicure and the pink nail polish that perfectly matched her shoes.

"What do we have here?" Walt asked a second later when he appeared in the room. Of the three women, only Danielle could see or hear him. Curious, he circled the newcomer as Danielle watched them both.

"You can't stay here. We don't have any rooms ready," Danielle told her.

"Don't be ridiculous. After all, Aunt Brianna was my aunt too." Cheryl leaned back in the chair, crossing her legs over its armrest.

"Who is she?" Walt asked.

"This is really not a good time, Cheryl. We're getting ready for my grand opening."

"Yes, I know all about that. Something you obviously failed to tell me about."

"Why would I? It's not like we keep in touch anymore," Danielle said.

"And whose fault is that?" Cheryl asked.

"Why are you here, Cheryl?" Danielle asked.

"Obviously to straighten out Aunt Brianna's estate." Cheryl jumped up from the chair.

"I don't know what you're talking about, Cheryl. Aunt Brianna left this house to me, what is there to straighten out?"

"She was my aunt too." Cheryl circled the room, inspecting and touching the parlor furnishings. "My attorney thinks I have a solid claim on the estate. Aunt Brianna was old, forgetful. Leaving me out of her will was obviously an oversight." Cheryl turned and faced Danielle and Lily.

"From what I remember, you barely knew Aunt Brianna," Danielle said.

"So? It doesn't change my relationship to her—which is identical to yours."

"Not exactly. I actually had a relationship with her. You were simply the great-niece of her husband."

"Oh, blah, blah, blah…that is not going to hold up in court, Boo."

"Don't call me that," Danielle snapped.

"Dani Boo, Dani Boo, Dani Boo." Cheryl giggled.

"I take it that's some childhood nickname?" Walt asked. "She's the cousin you mentioned?" Walt sat on the back of the couch and watched Cheryl. Lifting his hand with a flourish, a lit cigar appeared between two of his fingers. He took a puff and continued to watch the unfolding drama.

"You can't stay here," Danielle insisted. "None of the rooms are ready for guests."

"She's staying here." Cheryl nodded to Lily, who stood mute, listening.

"Lily is my friend; she's helping me get Marlow House open for business."

"And I'm your cousin." Cheryl paused and sniffed the air. "I smell cigar smoke! You lied! You're already open for business. You have a man staying here!"

"No, Cheryl, it's just Lily and me." *And Walt,* Danielle silently added.

"Don't tell me you've taken up cigars." Cheryl snickered.

"Don't be silly, neither of us smoke cigars," Lily said.

"I can definitely smell cigar smoke," Cheryl insisted.

"What do you want?" Danielle asked.

Cheryl considered the question for a moment. "For starters, I want to see the necklace."

"The necklace? It's not here. It's in a safety deposit box at the bank. But you aren't serious about all this, are you?"

"We'll let the courts straighten all this out. There's plenty of money for both of us, no reason to be greedy." Cheryl smiled. "Now come on, we are cousins, Dani. It has been absolutely ages since we've gotten together for a little family reunion." Cheryl surprised Dani by giving her an enthusiastic bear hug. Danielle passively accepted the hug, flashing Lily a weak smile over Cheryl's shoulder.

TWO

"You're letting her stay?" Walt asked Danielle when he appeared in the kitchen thirty minutes later. He watched as she removed the cakes from the oven and set them on a cooling rack on the counter.

"She is my cousin. I couldn't very well throw her out on the street." Danielle glanced up to the ceiling, wondering what Cheryl was doing in the room she had given her on the second floor.

"I don't suppose you kicked Lily out of her room," Walt teased.

"Of course not. I gave Cheryl the Red Room."

"Charming how you've named the rooms according to color." By his tone, Danielle didn't think for a moment that he found it charming.

"She wasn't thrilled she had to put her own sheets on the bed. I told her she was welcome to stay for a couple of days—until we get this straightened out with our aunt's attorney—but while she's here, she shouldn't expect me to wait on her."

"Apparently, she doesn't share your—gift." Walt leaned casually against the counter, smoking a thin cigar. He watched as Danielle grabbed the baking cocoa and powdered sugar, preparing to make cake frosting.

"No. Yet she did smell your cigar." Danielle nodded toward the lit cigar in his hand.

"As can Lily—and Joanne—and..."

"Yes, I know. I'm starting to think the main reason you smoke those things is so people will sense your presence."

"If that's true, it's not working. Lily credits the scent of smoke to this old house, hardly flattering or encouraging for me." Walt waved his hand and the cigar vanished.

"All I know is that I have a ton of things to finish before the open house, and the last thing I need is Cheryl getting in the way!" Danielle angrily slammed a clean mixing bowl on the counter.

"Is she really your only living relative?" Walt asked.

"Cheryl's mother, Susan, was my father's sister. Cheryl had a younger brother, Sean. Uncle Carl, Cheryl's father, was a private pilot and had his own plane. One weekend, when I was in college, my parents went flying with Uncle Carl and Aunt Susan. Sean was with them. The plane went down. They were all killed."

"That's horrible."

"I thought you were indifferent to death," Danielle said.

"Not indifferent exactly. Just not overly sympathetic to hear someone has passed—considering my situation. Yet that doesn't mean I can't appreciate the severity of losing touch with so many family members at once. You were never able to see them again—like you can see me?"

"Nope." Danielle shook her head. "I assumed I'd see them at their funeral. When that didn't happen, I held onto my parents' ashes for over a year, expecting them to make some sort of contact with me—let me know everything was okay."

"But they didn't?"

"Nothing. I finally spread their ashes at the beach where we used to spend our summer vacations. I've come to believe a lingering spirit is not necessarily attached to a body or ashes. If that was the case, you would be hanging out at the cemetery with your wife."

"Please, spare me that thought!" Walt cringed.

"Anyway, after that, Cheryl was the only family I had, except for Aunt Brianna and Uncle Harry. Of course, they lived in Europe. I suppose I might have some distant cousins out there, but I never knew my grandparents, other than Dad's mom, and Dad's only sibling was Aunt Susan. Mom didn't have any brothers or sisters."

"Are you Cheryl's only relative?"

"No. Her dad had a brother and sister. What I remember from the funerals, the sister had two sons. I'm not sure how close she is with them."

"Do you think she has a valid claim?"

"You mean on the estate?" Danielle asked.

"Yes. I'm wondering, will she become a permanent member of this household?"

"Even if she had a valid claim—which I don't think for a moment is the case—this is just Cheryl doing what she does, being a pain. She would never move in here and help me run a B and B. Not her style."

Walt arched his brow. "I did notice she dresses slightly differently than you."

"She's never gotten over her beauty pageant days."

"Beauty pageant?"

"Aunt Susan started putting Cheryl in beauty pageants when she was just a toddler. Mom dragged me to one once, but from what I heard, I threw such a fit she never tried with me again. Of course, I don't remember it." Danielle smiled at the thought of her younger self refusing to walk the runway.

"Beauty pageant for little girls?"

"Oh yes. Cheryl loved the makeup, the frilly dresses, the attention. She continued the pageant circuit as a teenager and young adult. Running an inn isn't something she would want to do. Trying to get money from the estate—that is an entirely different matter. But you know what really irritates me?" Danielle asked angrily.

"What?"

"After the plane crash I was approached by an attorney who tried to get me to sue my aunt and uncle's estate—which Cheryl had inherited. They were well off, much more so than my parents. When all was said and done and my parents' estate settled, I think I had just enough money to pay for college and buy a car. After Cheryl settled her family's estate, I heard she had over five million dollars."

"I'm not sure I understand."

"The plane crash was due to pilot error, and I probably could have walked away with a healthy chunk of her estate had I taken her to court—which I refused to do. And now—now this!"

"It will work out, Danielle. Remember, you have me on your side." Walt gave her a little wink.

"Maybe you should give her the same treatment you gave Adam and Bill." Danielle giggled.

Before Walt could reply, Lily entered the kitchen and announced, "She wants something to eat."

"Lily, I told her we aren't going to wait on her. I thought you were going up to the attic to get the croquet set?"

"Damn, I left it in the hall. I got it, but when I was coming back downstairs, she called me in her room."

"Please, don't call it her room." Danielle cringed.

"Okay. She called me into the *Red Room*. She wanted to know where the kitchen was. Wanted to get something to eat."

"So why are you here and not her?" Danielle asked.

"You should see her room!" When Danielle scowled at her choice of words, Lily rephrased her sentence. "You should have seen the Red Room. She was only in there five minutes and had already unpacked—throwing her things everywhere. Rearranging the furniture. The place is a fricking mess!"

"Hmmm..." Danielle wrinkled her nose. "I forgot what a slob she could be. Her bedroom was always a disaster. She didn't know how to use a clothes hanger. Mom never understood how Aunt Susan put up with it."

"I just figured if she destroyed that room in a matter of minutes, what would she do to the kitchen? Getting her a sandwich seemed less work."

"I better call Mr. Renton and get this thing straightened out before she destroys the house or has us waiting on her hand and foot."

"Well, if she's still here when you have the open house, something will need to be done with her room. You can't show off the house with it looking like that!" Lily insisted. "I can't imagine what it will look like in a couple of days!"

"No reason for you to make her lunch. She's my problem." Danielle reached for the loaf of bread.

"You don't need to make her a sandwich." Lily snatched the bread from Danielle and tossed it back on the counter. Turning to the kitchen table, she removed the uneaten halves of sandwiches from the plates on the table.

"What are you doing?" Danielle asked, watching Lily set the two halves on a clean plate.

"Our sandwiches are stale now. Cheryl did interrupt our lunch. No reason for these to go to waste."

Danielle laughed. "You're evil."

"No, evil would be throwing these out." Lily giggled. "I'll make us fresh sandwiches after I take these to your houseguest."

"I'll miss Lily when she goes home," Walt said, watching Lily leave the room with the plate of food and glass of milk.

"Me too. Wish she could stay here, but she has her job and family back home," Danielle said after Lily was out of earshot. She tossed the two partially eaten sandwich halves in the trashcan and began making fresh sandwiches for Lily and herself.

LILY MADE her way up the staircase, careful not to spill the milk. She cursed herself for filling the glass too full, which forced her to gingerly take each step. Once she reached the top of the staircase and stepped on the second-floor landing, she picked up her pace. When she got to the doorway of the Red Room, she found Cheryl on her hands and knees, looking under the vintage cherry wood dresser.

"Did you lose something?" Lily asked, walking into the room. She set the plate and glass of milk on the nightstand.

Cheryl looked at Lily and then stood up. Glancing at the glass of milk, she asked, "Don't you have any Diet Pepsi?"

"No. There's no soda in the house."

"Well, take it away." Cheryl waved her hand dismissively at the glass of milk. "Bring me some ice coffee. With extra cream. You do have coffee, don't you?"

"I tell you what, if you want something else to drink, you probably should go down and make it yourself." *I hope I don't regret saying that. But how much of a mess could she actually make getting a drink?*

"Oh, fine…leave the milk. I guess I have to drink something." Cheryl flounced to the bed, sat down, and picked up the plate. Wrinkling her nose, she looked at the sandwich halves and gave them each a little poke with one of her fingers.

"Did you lose something?" Lily asked again.

"What do you mean?" Cheryl looked up from the sandwich.

"You were looking under the dresser."

"Oh, that." Cheryl laughed. "I figured if Dani found a million-dollar necklace in this house, there's bound to be other treasures."

"I don't think so," Lily mumbled and turned to leave the room.

"Lily…your name is Lily, isn't it?" Cheryl asked.

Lily paused at the doorway and faced Cheryl. "Yes."

"Is my dear cousin still seeing ghosts?"

THREE

"Seeing ghosts?" Lily asked, stepping back into the bedroom.

"Oh, she hasn't told you?" Cheryl sniffed the sandwich and took a bite. "This bread is stale."

"Sorry, it's all we have," Lily lied. "What do you mean seeing ghosts?"

"How do you think she got her nickname Boo?" Cheryl asked before taking another bite and washing it down with a swig of milk.

"I had no idea anyone called her Boo."

"Boo or Dani Boo. I gave her the name. Cute, isn't it?" Cheryl smiled at Lily, showing off a milk mustache. "Although she never liked it much."

"Sounds like Dani Pooh. Can't say I'd like that either if I was her."

"No, Boo, as in spooky ghosts—not pooh." Cheryl shook her head at the idea.

"So why do you say she sees ghosts?"

"She's really never said anything to you? I guess you're not that close of friends." Cheryl took another bite of the sandwich.

"We're good enough friends. Are you going to tell me what you're talking about or not?" Lily asked.

"Okay." Cheryl sighed, still unaware of her milk mustache. "When our grandmother died, Dani insisted that Grandma's ghost talked to her at the funeral. Of course, she was just saying that to be mean to me."

"I don't understand. Why do you think she was being mean to you?" Lily had never heard the story before.

"She was always jealous of me. Although, I can't say I blame her. I did get all the attention, what with the pageants and all." Cheryl shrugged.

"Pageants?"

"It's not like it was my fault I was such a beautiful child. Poor Dani just couldn't cut it at the pageants, so she had to stand at the sidelines and watch me get all the attention. I did feel sorry for her, you know. But it was mean of her to make up that story."

"I'm afraid I'm not following you." Lily was totally lost.

"Dani tried to make me think Grandma's ghost talked to just her and not me. As if Grandma loved her more."

"Did Dani say your grandmother loved her more?" Lily asked.

"No. But making up that story about Grandma's ghost, like Dani was special or something, like she was better than me because Grandma picked her and not me. Of course, I knew she was lying."

"Kids can be imaginative." Lily wondered if Dani had made up the story to spite her annoying cousin. If so, she was going to have to tell Dani she appreciated her originality.

"She didn't get in trouble that time. Of course, I called her on the lie. What got her in trouble was when that classmate of hers got killed and she told his parents his ghost talked to her. That's when I started calling her Boo."

"I can't believe Dani would do something that cruel, even when she was a child. Dani is a very kind person."

"I'm sure all her time in therapy helped. Her parents sent her to a shrink to straighten her out. They couldn't very well let her go around telling people she talked to ghosts." Cheryl tossed the crust from her sandwich onto the plate and wiped her mouth with the back of her hand, removing the milk from above her lip.

"I don't know about any of that. But the Dani I know—and we have been close friends for years—has never talked about ghosts."

"I just figured since she's living in this big old spooky house, she might fall back into old habits." Cheryl pulled her bare feet onto the bed and stretched out. "I think I want to take a nap. It was a long drive. You can take this away." Cheryl waved her hand at the plate and glass on the nightstand. "And close the door on your way out."

Annoyed, Lily walked toward the bed and picked up the plate and glass. Without saying another word, she left the room and closed the door behind her.

"WHAT TOOK YOU SO LONG?" Danielle asked from the kitchen table. "I made you another sandwich."

Walt stood nearby, casually leaning back against the counter.

"Thanks." Unaware of Walt's presence, Lily walked through him and set Cheryl's plate and glass in the sink and then sat at the table with Danielle. "I was talking to your cousin. She told me why she gave you that nickname." Lily picked up her sandwich and took a bite.

"She did?" Danielle stopped eating and looked across the table at Lily. "What did she say?"

"Just that when you were a kid, you made up some stories about seeing ghosts. No biggie. When I was a kid, I had an imaginary friend, Rupert. He went everywhere with me. Drove my parents nuts."

Danielle set her sandwich on its plate and took a sip of iced tea.

"Sounds like your dear cousin just spilled the beans. Will you deny the stories?" Walt asked.

"So it's true?" Lily asked after a few moments of silently eating her lunch.

"I suppose it depends on what she actually said," Danielle said quietly, not wanting to lie to her friend.

"She told me you claimed to see your grandmother at the funeral. Said you did it to spite her."

"She's crazy. To Cheryl, everything was always about her."

"Well, I wouldn't blame you if you had. She seems to have a high opinion of herself. Was she in beauty pageants or something?"

Looking at Lily, Danielle cocked her head to one side. "She told you about that?"

"Mentioned being in pageants and how you were jealous of her because of it. Which definitely does not sound like you." Lily laughed at the idea.

"My aunt started her in them when she was a toddler."

"Oh my god, you mean like *Toddlers and Tiaras*?" Lily cringed.

"Pretty much."

"I hate those things. Something about little girls putting on makeup and dressing up like that makes me think of pedophiles. Little girls should dress like little girls, in my opinion. Last year I had a couple of my students show up in class wearing heels. I mean, what the hell, who lets their second grader wear heels?"

"Not sure she wore heels back then. I don't remember that." Danielle shrugged. "Of course, back then, people seemed to think pageants were cute. At least my family did. If I had been more cooperative, Mom would have loved for me to do it. You'll have to remember, we were just entering our teens when Jon Benet Ramsey was murdered and kid's pageants came under such scrutiny. Before that, I don't remember hearing anything negative about them."

"Oh, I don't know about that; in my family beauty pageants were scorned. Heck, when my mother was in college she picketed the Miss America Pageant. Something about objectifying women."

"Yeah, I love your mom." Danielle grinned. "I guess we really were raised differently."

"So tell me about the ghost stories," Lily said.

"Ghost stories?"

"What are you going to tell her?" Walt asked.

"She told me about you claiming to see your grandmother. Which, by the way, is a great prank. And if she was as annoying as a child as she is as an adult, I hope you scared the pants off her. But the other thing—well, it just didn't sound like you."

"Other thing?" Danielle pushed the partially eaten sandwich around on her plate.

"She said you told the parents of some kid who was killed that you spoke to their dead son. That doesn't sound like you. I can't believe you'd do something that thoughtless. Even as a child. What really happened?"

Danielle closed her eyes for a moment. She opened them and looked across the table at Lily, who was staring at her.

"What would you say to me if I told you I really did see my grandmother's ghost…that my classmate came to me, asking me to reach out to his parents. Tell them he was okay. Would you think I was a liar—or crazy?"

Speechless, Lily stared at Danielle, noting her friend's serious expression.

"Oh…this is going to get interesting…" Walt murmured.

"Dani," Lily said at last, "I've never known you to be a liar, and I know you aren't crazy."

"So what would you think?"

"If you told me you really saw their ghosts, I would have to believe you. I mean, it's not as if I don't believe those kinds of things are possible. After all, Mom saw my grandma after she died."

"What?" Danielle wasn't expecting Lily's casual acceptance.

"Well, it's not something I go around telling people. They'll think I'm making it up or accuse my mother of being wacko. Mom is perfectly sane—okay, maybe she is a little wacko." Lily laughed. "But I believe she saw Grandma, and I believe you."

"Lily, I can see ghosts."

"You told her, you actually told her," Walt mumbled. "Will you tell her about me?"

"Why haven't you ever told me about it before?" Lily asked.

"Because when I told my family, they thought I was nuts."

"Cheryl said they sent you to a shrink."

"Yep. That taught me to keep those kinds of things to myself."

"When Mom told me about seeing Grandma, she asked me to keep it to myself. She said people wouldn't understand," Lily said. "Did you ever tell anyone else?"

"Just Lucas."

"Did he believe you?"

"Honestly? No. I don't think so. He acted like he did, but I got the feeling he was humoring me. He once said something about my overactive imagination. Said that's why I was so good in marketing."

"I imagine that hurt your feelings."

"It wasn't that exactly. But we were married, and I felt I needed to share everything with him—even my secrets. I thought that's what married people did."

"So did you…well…did you ever see anyone else…like Lucas?"

"I never saw Lucas." Danielle fidgeted with her glass.

"So tell me about seeing your grandma. I love those kinds of stories. Mom said her mother came to her the night of the funeral, because she was having such a hard time accepting her death. Grandma told her everything was okay, that she was with Grandpa now and told Mom to be happy. That everything was going to be all right."

"I guess it was sort of the same thing with my grandma. I had never known anyone who had died before. I don't think I understood the finality of the situation. She just showed up at the table."

"The table?" Lily asked.

"The service was at Grandma's church. Afterwards, they served food in the fellowship hall. Cheryl and I were at this table with our parents—but they had gotten up to talk to some friends of Grandma's. Cheryl left me alone for a minute to grab a cupcake off the refreshment table. And Grandma just showed up. She was sitting there in the chair next to me. We talked; she told me she was happy, that she would be watching over me and to remember how much she loved me. She told me to be happy for her. That was pretty much it."

"And you told Cheryl?"

"Yeah. I guess I wasn't the sharpest kid." Danielle laughed ruefully. "I thought she would think it was cool, but she just got mad at me. Called me a liar. When our parents came back to the table, she told them what I said. I don't know…I don't think my folks or Cheryl's were overly concerned at the time. I remember being upset that they didn't seem to believe me."

"So what happened with the classmate?"

"Unlike Grandma, who only visited once, he kept popping in my room. Telling me I needed to get his parents a message. He just wanted them to know he was sorry. He'd taken his bike out when he wasn't supposed to and ended up getting hit by a car. He was frantic to apologize to them. I'm afraid that didn't work out so well."

"I can imagine." Lily shuddered. "Have you ever seen any other spirits…since then?"

Danielle didn't answer immediately. Finally, she nodded her head.

"When? Who?" Lily asked anxiously.

Walt leaned back against the counter, looking from Lily to Danielle. With a wave of his hand, a lit cigar appeared. He took a puff and listened with curiosity to what Danielle might reveal.

"Maybe it would be best if we dropped this subject," Danielle suggested, glancing over at Walt.

"No, come on, Dani! I want to know. I love this kind of stuff! I still can't believe you never told me about this."

Danielle glanced from Walt to Lily.

"Do you smell that?" Danielle asked.

Lily took a deep breath. "Smells like cigar smoke. Funny how that smell comes and goes. I didn't notice it a minute ago."

"That's because he wasn't smoking a minute ago," Danielle explained.

"Who wasn't smoking?" Lily glanced around the kitchen.

"Walt Marlow."

"Walt Marlow?" Lily frowned.

"Yes. He smokes cigars."

FOUR

Silently, Lily stared at Danielle, her brows drawn into a frown. It took her a moment to register what Danielle was saying. Lily's expression shifted from confusion to surprise and finally to amusement.

"Oh, you almost got me!" Lily laughed heartily. "Walt Marlow, right…" Lily stopped laughing a few seconds later when she noticed Danielle's serious expression had not changed. Mirth wasn't tugging on the corners of Danielle's mouth—there was no sign of suppressed laughter.

"Oh my god…you are serious, aren't you?" Lily said after a few moments of silence.

Danielle nodded her reply.

Glancing around the room, Lily asked, "Is he here now?"

"Yes. Over there." Danielle pointed at the counter near the sink.

"Hello, Lily," Walt said, taking a puff off his cigar.

"He just said hello," Danielle told her.

Slowly, Lily stood up and faced the section of the counter Danielle indicated. Making her way to the spot, she stopped a few feet before reaching Walt. She sniffed the air.

"Yes, the cigar smoke is strongest here," Lily observed.

"You're taking this rather well," Danielle said.

"It's not like I hadn't wondered." Lily reached out and waved her hand from right to left. Walt leaned back away from Lily but not before her hand moved through his face twice.

"Tell her to stop." Walt scowled, waving Lily away with his free hand.

"He doesn't like that. You just smacked his face." Danielle chuckled.

"Oh, I'm sorry." Lily jumped back, looking at where she believed Walt would be standing. "Did I hurt him?"

"Of course not. He can't feel anything. He doesn't actually have a real body."

"Now that hurt." Walt glared at Danielle and then disappeared.

"Nice to meet you, Mr. Marlow," Lily said.

"He's not there anymore."

"What do you mean?" Lily looked at Danielle.

"I think my crack about him not being able to feel hurt his feelings. Or maybe it was because I said his body wasn't real. Either way, he took off in a huff."

Lily sniffed the air. "I can barely smell the cigar anymore." She rejoined Danielle at the table.

"So you believe me?" Danielle found Lily's acceptance of the situation a bit unnerving.

"Since I first got here…well, I sort of felt something. And then there was Sadie."

"Sadie?" Ian had rented the house across the street from Marlow House for the summer. Sadie was his golden retriever. The dog, like Danielle, could see Walt.

"The way Sadie acts when she comes over here is strange. She barks at nothing. But it's not nothing; is it? She was barking at Walt Marlow."

"Yes. It appears Sadie can see him."

"They've become friends, haven't they?" Lily asked.

"How did you know that?"

"The way she wags her tail at nothing…I guess it wasn't nothing. Or how she likes to hang out alone upstairs in the attic when she's here. But she wasn't alone, was she?"

"Sadie has become attached to Walt. It's amazing how they communicate with each other—it's like they can read each other's minds."

"I've read animals are sensitive to the supernatural," Lily said.

"Are you saying you've been wondering if this house was haunted all along, because of how Ian's dog was behaving?"

"It wasn't just Sadie. The thought first crossed my mind when you screamed bloody murder that first day we arrived. Remember, in the bathroom? You saw him then for the first time, didn't you?"

"Yes, but at the time you asked me if I had seen a mouse."

"I couldn't very well ask you if you'd seen a ghost. How would that have sounded? And then there was the cigar smell—coming and going."

"Why didn't you ever say anything to me?" Danielle asked.

"Oh, right. *Hey Danielle, I think your house may be haunted.*"

"But when I first told you, just now, you thought I was kidding."

Lily shrugged and said, "Well, it's one thing to have a feeling about something that's out of the norm—and another to have someone come right out and confirm it. For a moment I thought you were pulling my leg, but then I realized you weren't kidding, and it all sort of made sense to me."

"You know, you've met him already," Danielle said.

"I have? What do you mean?"

"In your dreams. Dreams are a way some spirits communicate with the living."

"Hmmm, I'm not sure how I feel about that—Walt Marlow popping in and out of my dreams."

"You believe me?" Danielle asked.

"I rarely remember my dreams. And if I do, I typically forget them shortly after waking up in the mornings. Those dreams, the two with Walt Marlow, were quite vivid. Some parts were a little blurry, but basically I can still remember them." Lily glanced around the room. "Is he still gone?"

"He's not here. At least I can't see him."

"He likes you, you know," Lily told her.

"Well, I like him too." Danielle shrugged.

"No, I mean he likes *likes* you," Lily whispered. "It was obvious by the questions he asked me."

"Lily, the man is a ghost," Danielle scoffed.

"I'm just saying." Lily shrugged. "Why is he here anyway? Is his spirit trapped or something?"

"Trapped?"

"Well, I figure when people die, they go somewhere. When Grandma came back to say goodbye to my mother, she was on her way somewhere. Walt Marlow died, what, almost ninety years ago, and he's still here."

"Eighty-eight but..."

"Oh, that's why you wanted to prove he didn't commit suicide! You did it for him!"

"Yes, he couldn't believe he killed himself."

"You mean he didn't know?" Lily asked.

"No. He couldn't remember what had happened. I'm pretty sure it was because he was knocked unconscious before he was strangled."

"And he showed you where he hid that necklace, didn't he?" Lily asked.

"Yes. I was worried we were going to have more break-ins once Ian published his story and people knew Walt may have taken the Missing Thorndike."

"Wait a minute...when you first showed us the necklace, you were so sure it was fake. I wondered why. He told you the stones weren't real, didn't he?"

"He thought they were fake."

"Why?" Lily asked.

Danielle paused a moment, reluctant to break Walt's confidence. "I really can't say, Lily. I promised him."

"You can't tell me?"

"It's a long story, and I promised Walt I would keep his confidence. Let me talk to him first. Please understand. All I can say is he did believe they were fake. It came as quite a surprised to discover they were real."

"Gee, I can imagine. Especially considering they were hidden in his attic for a century. But I still don't understand..."

"What, Lily?"

"Why is he still here?"

"I suppose he's not quite ready to leave yet. For one thing, he'd like to find out how the necklace he stole—the one with the fake gems—turned out to be real."

The doorbell rang, interrupting their conversation. "I think that's Ian," Lily said as she glanced at the wall clock.

"She took that rather calmly," Walt said when he appeared a few moments later, after Lily left the room to answer the door. "Thank you for keeping my confidence, but you can tell Lily about the necklace. It might make things easier, especially if we're to find out how those stones turned out to be real."

"You left abruptly."

"How do you know what I can or cannot feel?" Walt asked.

"I'm sorry if I hurt your feelings. But I meant your body can't feel physical pain in the way a living person can."

"And just how do you know that?" Walt challenged.

Danielle stood up, facing him. "Well, can you?"

"No…but…" Walt stammered. "But how do you know that?"

"Let's just say I've picked up a few things since I first started seeing ghosts."

"Oh my god…now you're talking to yourself!" Cheryl called out from the doorway. "And you're back to that nonsense about seeing ghosts!"

Danielle groaned and turned to face her cousin. Cheryl had changed her clothes and now wore a short cotton dress; its hemline fell just inches down her upper thigh. Judging by the pink straps pulled up through the neckline of the dress and tied around Cheryl's neck, Danielle guessed her cousin was wearing a bikini and the dress, its pink and orange floral print reminiscent of the sixties, served as a cover up. Danielle didn't see how the garment could be used as just a dress; Cheryl would be showing the world her derrière if she leaned over just slightly.

"I knew you were standing there," Danielle lied. "I know you were telling Lily stories about me." Danielle sat back down at the table.

"I think I'll leave you ladies to fight this out," Walt said before disappearing.

"The way you say stories, it sounds like I made stuff up. You did tell us you saw ghosts." Cheryl walked into the kitchen, sniffing the air. "There it is again…are you sure you haven't taken up cigars? Not exactly ladylike."

"I don't think it's necessary for you to gossip about me with my friends. We've all done embarrassing things when we were children. I don't feel compelled to tell everyone I meet about the embarrassing things you did when you were a child."

"Oh, boohoo, Boo." Cheryl giggled. "Boohoo, Boo…now that's funny."

Danielle shook her head. "Whatever…"

"It's not like I tell everyone I meet. I can't recall the last time I even thought of you, much less talked about you. I just thought your friend might find the story amusing. And anyway, you don't have anything embarrassing to tell about me."

Danielle started to say *what about being in pageants all your life* but stopped herself. As much as Cheryl annoyed her, Danielle had no desire to demean her cousin. Cheryl was proud of her years in the pageant circuit, whereas Danielle compared the accomplishment to first-place winner in a food-eating contest. Danielle loathed food-eating contests.

Cheryl nodded toward what was left of the sandwich Danielle had been eating. "I hope you don't plan to serve those hideous sandwiches to your guests. If you do, you won't be in business a month."

"What are you talking about?"

"Lily brought me a sandwich; it was barely edible."

"What is it they say, beggars can't be choosers?" Danielle smiled sweetly.

Cheryl made a grunting sound and started to turn back to the doorway.

"Are you going somewhere?" Danielle asked, noting the straw purse in Cheryl's hand.

"I tried to take a nap. But I couldn't sleep. So I decided I'd go check out the beach."

"You might get chilly. The beach is a little cooler here than what you're used to. You might want to put some jeans on and grab a sweatshirt."

"I'll be fine. But thank you for worrying about me." With a flounce, Cheryl walked toward the doorway. As she stepped out of the kitchen, she called out, "Try not to talk to yourself too much!"

Danielle could hear her cousin's laugh as Cheryl made her way down the entry hall to the front door.

FIVE

Ian sat quietly on the small sofa in the parlor of Marlow House, listening to Lily rattle off the list of things that needed to be done before the open house on the fourth. He had hoped she would join him for a walk along the beach, but he doubted that was going to happen this afternoon. She was dressed more for cleaning house—wearing her strawberry-print apron and tattered denims and T-shirt—than for a leisurely stroll along the seashore.

He wasn't paying close attention to what she was saying and hoped there wouldn't be a quiz when she was done. But he enjoyed watching her talk and move—she was a bundle of sexy enthusiasm. She had secured her red hair into a casual side ponytail, and he resisted his temptation to remove the rubber band and watch the hair tumble down.

Sadie lay curled up on the floor by his feet. She had already lifted her head a few times since they had arrived and had let out little whimpers, seeking permission to dart from the room and up the stairs to the attic. He didn't know why Sadie acted this way at Marlow House—she had always been so obedient. Ian wondered if perhaps there were mice in the attic. That might explain why she found the top floor of Marlow House so fascinating.

Reaching down to give Sadie a reassuring pat, Ian noticed something tucked under the sofa next to his foot. He leaned down and reached for the item, picking it up. It was a hot pink stiletto high-heeled shoe. The moment Lily noticed what was in his hand, she stopped talking and faced him.

Smirking, Ian turned the shoe over in his hand, inspecting it. By its size, it was obviously not Lily's. It was much too large. However, he would love to see Lily wearing a pair of these—in her size, of course. He wasn't sure how he felt about the color.

"Danielle surprises me," Ian said with a chuckle.

"Danielle?" Lily asked.

"Well, these obviously aren't yours." Ian glanced down at Lily's small dainty feet.

"Oh, my shoes! I forgot I left them in here!" Cheryl stood at the parlor doorway, staring at Ian.

"This is Cheryl, Danielle's cousin. She just arrived today. The shoes are hers." Lily walked to Ian and reached down, snatching the shoe from his grasp. In the next instant, she retrieved the second shoe from under the sofa and then tossed the pair at Cheryl, who was not prepared for the missiles hurled in her direction.

Cheryl's straw purse fell to the floor as she fumbled with the shoes, catching one while the second shoe hit her in the shoulder before falling to the floor. Glaring at Lily, she leaned down and picked up the fallen shoe and purse.

Ian stood up and glanced from Lily to the new arrival.

"Are you okay?" he asked Cheryl.

"I think so." Cheryl's instantaneous transformation from brassy to timid did not go unnoticed by Lily. "I'm Dani's cousin, Cheryl. And you are?" Cheryl flashed Ian a beguiling smile as she walked into the parlor. Ignoring Lily, she set the purse and shoes on a table by the sofa and put out her hand to Ian, who accepted it.

"Nice to meet you, Cheryl. I'm Ian, Ian Bartley. I'm renting the house across the street for the summer. I didn't know Danielle's family had come for a visit." Instead of a handshake, Cheryl gently squeezed Ian's hand, lingering a moment before finally releasing her hold.

"Actually, I'm Danielle's only family." Cheryl moved a little closer to Ian, looking up into his face. She gave him her entire attention.

Lily silently observed the pair, annoyed at the dopey smile plastered on Ian's face as his gaze drifted from Cheryl's eyes down to her prominent bustline. Its cleavage peeked provocatively from the low-cut neckline of the cotton shift. Instead of being insulted by Ian's wandering gaze, Cheryl stood a little straighter, arching her back to give him a better view. Lily resisted the temptation to reach over and give Cheryl a good smack and Ian a kick in the shins.

While focusing all of her attention on Ian, Cheryl failed to notice the dog by his feet—who was now lifting her head up curiously at the new arrival. Cheryl took a step closer to Ian, and her foot landed on Sadie's front paw. Sadie jumped up and let out a yelp. Cheryl in turn let out her own cry of surprise and jumped backwards, looking down at the dog.

"Oh my god, a dog!" Cheryl blurted out, staring down at Sadie as if the dog had three heads. Ian immediately dropped to one knee to comfort Sadie while Lily rushed to his side.

"Is she okay?" Lily bent down and ran her hands over Sadie, who seemed to appreciate all the sudden attention and rewarded Lily with a wet lick across the face.

"She's fine," Ian said, glancing from Sadie—who was now wagging her tail—to Cheryl.

"Are you sure? It looks like she really crushed Sadie's poor paw." Lily glared up at Cheryl.

"Oh my god, I barely stepped on her. I can't believe Dani has a dog in the house. What about the guests with allergies? The dog hair?" Hands on hips, Cheryl looked down at Sadie and Lily, who both sat on the floor while Ian stood over them.

"What, you don't like dogs?" Lily asked.

Before Cheryl could answer, Ian said, "I hadn't considered that—with Danielle getting ready to open this place, she really doesn't need to contend with dog hair. And some people are allergic…"

"She's yours?" Cheryl's expression of disdain quickly vanished.

"Yes, this is Sadie," Ian introduced.

"Oh, she's so cute," Cheryl cooed. Leaning down, she awkwardly patted Sadie's head.

"She doesn't like her head touched like that," Lily said when Sadie shied away from Cheryl's touch.

Cheryl ignored Lily and leaned over again, giving Sadie another quick pat before standing back up.

"What are you guys up to?" Cheryl asked sweetly, her eyes still on Ian. Taking a few steps back, she sat on a chair facing the sofa, where Lily and Ian now sat side by side.

"I'd hoped to convince Lily to take a walk on the beach with me, but it seems she and Danielle have other plans, with getting this place ready to open for business."

"The beach? That's where I was headed. But I'm not sure how to get there. If you don't mind, I'd like to tag along with you," Cheryl asked.

"The beach is just across the street," Lily told her, pointing west. "Not exactly hard to find with the big ol' Pacific Ocean out there."

"Aw, come on, Lily, it's the least I can do for Danielle. With you two so busy getting this place ready for the open house, I don't imagine she has time to show her cousin around. I'll be happy to walk her down to the beach." Ian patted Lily's denim-clad thigh while flashing Cheryl a smile.

"The beach across the street doesn't allow dogs," Lily reminded him.

"I guess I'll have to drop Sadie at my house first."

Cheryl stood up and snatched her straw purse from the table. "Oh, thank you, Ian, I really do appreciate you taking the time. And I'm sure Dani and Lily will be glad to get me out of their hair for a while." Cheryl flashed Lily a smile.

Ian stood up and patted his thigh, signaling Sadie it was time to leave.

"No, Ian," Lily blurted out.

Ian looked curiously at Lily. "What, Lily?"

"Sadie can stay here," Lily said quietly. "No reason to leave her alone at your house. She's fine here with us."

"Are you sure? Cheryl has a point about the dog hair and allergies, and once Danielle starts taking guests…"

"No." Lily stood up. "Sadie is fine here. She's not a problem."

"Well, now that that's settled, I'd really like to pee before we go. Is there a downstairs bathroom?" Cheryl asked.

Inwardly Lily cringed at Cheryl's choice of words. *I'd really like to pee—seriously?* Lily thought. She walked to the doorway and pointed to the powder room door.

Cheryl smiled at Ian then hurriedly made her way to the bathroom.

"You don't like her much, do you?" Ian asked, wrapping his arms around Lily and pulling her close.

"Gee, how could you tell?" Lily halfheartedly attempted to pull out of his embrace before leaning back against his chest and allowing him to wrap his arms around her waist. He rested his chin atop her head.

"First clue was the way you hurled the shoes at her. Considering those heels, that might be considered attacking her with a deadly weapon."

"And you thought those were Danielle's gaudy shoes?" Lily scoffed.

"You failed to tell me Marlow House had its first houseguest. But obviously, you're not thrilled with Danielle's cousin. Why?"

"For one thing, she plans to challenge Dani for half of the estate." Lily turned around in Ian's arms so that she could face him. Wrapping her arms around his neck, she pulled his face to hers and brushed a kiss over his lips.

"She is? Interesting." Ian brushed a second kiss over Lily's mouth.

"I saw the way you were checking out her boobs," Lily whispered.

"Hey, you can't blame me. They were…well…practically in my face." Ian gave her a little squeeze.

"You didn't have to offer to take her to the beach."

"You can go with us, you know. I'd rather spend the afternoon with you."

"No, I have too much to do."

"She might try to take advantage of me."

"Well, you're a big boy. I don't have any claim on you." Lily nipped Ian's lower lip.

"Ouch!" Ian ran his tongue over the injured lip. She hadn't drawn blood. "Are you jealous?"

"Not my style." Lily hugged him a little tighter.

"Could have fooled me," Ian whispered into her ear before nipping her earlobe.

Lily pulled back and looked into Ian's face. Narrowing her eyes, she said, "You were trying to make me jealous!"

"I wanted you to spend the afternoon with me. I was jealous of Danielle."

"Oh my!" Cheryl called out from the doorway, surprised at what she was seeing.

"You ready to go?" Ian asked, still holding Lily in his arms.

"Umm…yes…I mean…are you two…?"

"Are we, Lily?" Ian asked, looking down at the woman in his

arms, a mischievous grin on his face. When Lily's only response was a blush, Ian said, "I'm quite mad about redheads." Ian gave Lily a grin. He dropped a kiss on her nose before releasing her.

"Lily, when you and Danielle are done doing whatever you have planned today, go out to dinner with me tonight, okay?"

Lily glanced from Ian to Cheryl, who stood silently in the doorway, a perplexed expression on her face.

"It's a date, Ian. Have a nice walk. I'll take good care of Sadie."

"I know you will." Ian reached out and gave her ponytail a playful tug as he prepared to leave.

Lily and Sadie followed Cheryl and Ian to the front door and said goodbye one final time. Ian and Cheryl made their way down the front walk to the street. For a moment, Lily considered changing her mind and going with them, but she really didn't want to spend time with Cheryl, and she figured if Ian decided he was interested in someone like Cheryl, she wouldn't want him anyway. When Ian and Cheryl reached the front gate, Lily closed the door and went into the house to find Danielle. Sadie raced off ahead of her, charging up the stairway to the attic.

SIX

Danielle was just getting off the phone when Lily entered the kitchen.

"Did she leave?" Danielle asked.

"She went with Ian to the beach," Lily said.

"Ian? You let her go with Ian?"

"Well, I don't exactly own him." Lily shrugged. "Although I admit, the idea did make me uncomfortable at first."

"It should. I never told you, but she hit on Lucas at our rehearsal dinner."

"You're kidding?" Lily glanced at the door, wondering for a moment if she should get down to the beach.

"That was before Lucas's wandering days—at least I think so. He was pretty horrified, and she claimed she'd had too much to drink and it was all a misunderstanding."

"Has she always been like that?" Lily asked.

"Cheryl and I are only a month apart. Growing up, our families did a lot together, and I think our parents—our mothers particularly—thought we should think of each other as sisters. In their minds sisters were supposed to share everything—and I'm afraid Cheryl took that message to heart. Of course, only when it applied to what I had. When we were teenagers, I hated it when she'd come over when I had a boyfriend at the house because she'd shamefully flirt with him."

Lily grabbed a plastic tumbler from the cabinet and started making herself a glass of iced tea. "I can't imagine my sister ever flirting with one of my boyfriends. Violation of the sister code."

Danielle leaned back against the kitchen counter and watched Lily. "I guess since we were cousins, there was no code."

"So did your parents ever say anything about how Cheryl behaved around your boyfriends?"

"They never saw it." Danielle shrugged. "I think the hard part for me back then, by the time Cheryl was fourteen she was already built like Marilyn Monroe, while I barely had any boobs and looked more like a little girl. I'm afraid the boys lost interest in me pretty quick once Cheryl set her sights on them. Of course, once they dumped me, she really wasn't interested in them. One time I said something to her, and she told me if I was dating a guy who would drop me so quickly over the first pretty girl who flirted with him, he was the wrong guy for me."

"No wonder you two are so close."

"It wasn't just the boyfriend thing. When she came over to our house, she thought it was perfectly acceptable to borrow my things without asking. If I tried to complain, my mother told me not to be so selfish—Cheryl was family."

"Did you ever do that with Cheryl's stuff?"

"No. But since she was always bigger than me, even though we are practically the same age, Aunt Susan always gave mom the clothes Cheryl outgrew. So in Cheryl's mind she was already sharing her stuff with me. Fact was, I hated it when I had to wear one of her hand-me-downs. By the time something actually fit me, it was not only out of style, but it also wasn't really age appropriate."

"Were you guys together a lot when growing up?"

"Pretty much. Our families took vacations together. Every summer we'd get a place at the beach for a few weeks. I remember Aunt Susan would always let Sean, Cheryl's little brother, bring a friend along. But our mothers wouldn't let us invite friends; they said we had each other."

"Didn't your parents ever see how you two didn't really get along?"

"Oh, to them it was because we were more like sisters—at least in their minds. And you know, sisters fight. They would laugh about our squabbles. In some weird way, they found it endearing. I know that sounds odd, but I think that's how they rationalized our relationship while maintaining this fantasy that we were as close as sisters."

"Sisters that didn't like each other, I guess." Lily shrugged. "I wonder how Cheryl felt about it all."

"You mean being stuck with me, like I was with her?"

"Yeah."

"I assumed she hated it too. By the way, I just got off the phone with Mr. Renton."

"He's back in town?" Lily asked.

"Yes. And he said if I'd come over to his office now, I could talk to him."

"I thought you wanted to take Cheryl with you."

"No. I'd rather see him first without her. Cheryl has a way of wrapping men around her finger, and while I haven't met Mr. Renton in person yet, I assume he's a man."

"Well, if you're lucky, he's gay," Lily teased.

"That would be nice." Danielle smiled.

"I'll stay here and work on that to-do list. Plus, I'm dog sitting for Ian."

"I thought I heard Sadie rush upstairs."

"She's probably with Walt…yikes, I almost forgot."

"Does it bother you, being alone in the house with…with a ghost?"

"No, not really," Lily lied.

"Well, don't worry about Walt. He's a good guy." Danielle glanced at the plate with Lily's second partially eaten sandwich of the day. "You never finished your lunch."

"I sort of gave up on the idea of eating. Anyway, Ian asked me out to dinner tonight, so I'll go with a healthy appetite and order everything on the menu—a payback for him taking Cheryl to the beach."

"I guess that means I'll be alone tonight with my dear cousin."

"Sorry, afraid so."

"Oh well, maybe Mr. Renton will have good news for me, and I'll be able to convince Cheryl there's no reason for her to stick around."

AFTER DANIELLE LEFT for Mr. Renton's office, Lily went back

upstairs to retrieve the croquet set she had left on the second floor outside the Red Room. The set, including the mallets and balls, were crammed into a large canvas bag she had found in the attic. Alone in the hallway, she heard what sounded like Sadie running back and forth in the attic overhead. Looking up at the ceiling, she stood silently and listened. What was going on up there?

Cocking her head ever so slightly, her attention focused on the sound overhead, she heard Sadie let out a bark then run across the length of the attic and then back again. Sadie barked a second time and repeated the series, running back and forth across the attic before coming to a stop and barking.

Curious, Lily left the croquet set on the floor and walked to the staircase leading to the attic. With her hand on the banister, she trod lightly, not wanting to alert the attic occupants of her arrival.

Just as she entered the top floor, a tennis ball hurled by her head and smacked the wall as Sadie raced in her direction. The dog snatched the ball in her mouth just after it hit the floor and bounced up. Turning from Lily, Sadie raced back across the attic and dropped the ball in the far corner. Sitting down, the ball on the floor before her, Sadie looked up and barked, her tail wagging excitedly.

Motionless, Lily stared across the room. Sadie's playmate was not rushing to throw the ball, much to the dog's disappointment. Sadie stood up and barked again.

Is he watching me? Lily wondered. Clearing her throat, Lily mustered her courage and said, "Hello Mr. Marlow."

There was no response, although she didn't really expect one. She hadn't been able to see or hear him before; there was no reason she would be able to now just because she was aware of his presence. She took several more steps in Sadie's direction. The dog continued to wait for Walt to toss the ball.

"I think Sadie's getting impatient. I don't mind. You can throw the ball if you want," Lily said, her voice shaking.

She took two more steps toward Sadie when the ball seemed to rise on its own from the floor and then flew across the room and hit the wall. Sadie was already racing for it and once again grabbed the ball in midair before it hit the floor for a second time.

"Holy crap…" Lily muttered, her eyes wide in disbelief. It was one thing to say you believed in ghosts, it was quite another to bear witness to paranormal activity. Lily gulped nervously. Her heart felt like a war drum beating wildly in her chest.

"You two have fun!" Lily called out, her voice no more than a squeak. She turned to the attic door and raced from the room.

Walt leaned over and picked up the ball from the floor. Sadie sat down and looked up at him, her tail wagging.

"I believe we may have frightened poor Lily," Walt told Sadie as he stared at the doorway. He could hear Lily's footsteps racing down the wooden stairs. He tossed the ball across the room again. Sadie raced for it.

"I must say," Walt said aloud, "I would rather not have frightened her. Wasn't a bit satisfying, like with those two thieves."

When Sadie returned with the ball and dropped it on the floor, Walt leaned down and looked Sadie in the eyes.

"I think that's enough for now, girl. Why don't you go downstairs and check on Lily."

Sadie continued to stare at Walt, her tail wagging. She barked once.

"Go on. We can play later." Walt pointed to the doorway. Sadie let out another bark, then turned from Walt and raced from the room, heading downstairs to find Lily.

Lily was just going out the kitchen door to the backyard, the canvas bag with the croquet set in her arms, when Sadie raced into the room.

"Where's your friend?" Lily asked nervously, glancing around the kitchen, sniffing the air. There was no hint of cigar smoke.

"You want to come outside with me, Sadie, and help me set this up?" As if Sadie understood the question, the dog raced out the doorway to the backyard, pushing Lily to one side.

Momentarily losing her balance, Lily awkwardly held onto the canvas bag as she shifted her weight and repositioned her hands to get a better grip. One of the wooden balls rolled out and hit the floor with a loud cracking sound. Lily cursed and leaned down to get the ball, without setting the bag down. She was afraid if she did, the rest of the balls would tumble out. Unfortunately, before she could snag the errant ball, it rolled under the kitchen table.

Trying to juggle the load, Lily attempted to reach the ball with her toe and nudge it in her direction. When that proved impossible to do because of the bulky and heavy bag in her arms, she cursed again. Preparing to set the bag down and let all the balls roll out, she stopped when she smelled it…cigar smoke.

Glancing around the kitchen, she wondered where he was. Then she saw it—the wooden croquet ball rising slowly from under the table—floating effortlessly in the air—coming toward her. Yet it wasn't hurling in her direction, as had the tennis ball earlier. She watched, mesmerized as the croquet ball returned to the canvas bag, slipping inside with the rest of the set. Lily stood there a moment, her heart again pounding.

"Thank you, Mr. Marlow," Lily said at last. Swallowing nervously, she flashed a weak smile and turned to the door leading to the backyard. When she reached the door, she paused a moment and turned back to the kitchen.

"I think I understand why I found this croquet set scattered all over the attic after the break-in. You threw it at them, didn't you? Like you tossed the ball for Sadie a few minutes ago." Lily's smile broadened. "Wow, I bet they wet their pants when you pelted them with the croquet set." Lily giggled at the thought. "Good work, Mr. Marlow. Good work."

Lily flashed a final grin before turning back to the door and going outside with Sadie.

Walt walked to the kitchen window and looked outside, watching as Lily tossed the bag on the lawn and removed the croquet set. When Lily and Danielle had first arrived, the backyard was overgrown in bushes and trees, and the lawn was a wild jungle of wildflowers and weeds. The gardener Danielle had hired tamed the yard in a matter of days, returning it to the way Walt remembered—back when he was still alive and sharing the home with his bride, Angela.

Smiling, Walt watched Lily arrange the croquet set while Sadie ran around the yard, chasing birds and barking at the croquet balls that lay silent on the lawn. When Lily had left the kitchen minutes earlier, she seemed less nervous than she had been in the attic, and that pleased Walt. He had no desire to frighten the residents of Marlow House—at least, not Danielle and Lily.

SEVEN

Cheryl studied Ian as they crossed the street. She liked tall men, and he had that going for him. She wondered if he intentionally wore his T-shirt a size too small to show off his impressive abs. If so, she had no complaints. It was a nice view. The Cubs baseball cap needed to go. She assumed his hair was short, although she couldn't be certain because of the cap.

After Ian and Cheryl reached the sidewalk in front of his rental, Cheryl asked, "Is it always this cool here?"

Ian's gaze swept over Cheryl; she was now shivering. "You're cold. You want to go back so you can grab a sweater?"

"I didn't bring a sweater with me. Didn't occur to me the beaches would be so cold up here this time of year."

"I've a sweatshirt you can use." Ian nodded toward his house.

"If you don't mind." Cheryl smiled up at him.

"Sure, come on. It'll probably be huge on you, but it will keep you warm. Lucky for you, I just washed it."

Still smiling, Cheryl followed Ian up the walkway to his house. Her smile vanished when he headed toward his car parked in the driveway instead of the front door.

"What are you doing?" Cheryl asked when Ian unlocked his car's trunk.

"Getting you that shirt," Ian explained as he opened the trunk.

Cheryl stepped closer and looked into the back of his car. Inside were two laundry baskets filled with folded clothes.

"You keep your clothes in the car?" Cheryl frowned.

"No." Ian laughed and grabbed a sweatshirt from one of the baskets. He handed it to Cheryl. "I took my clothes to the Laundromat. Just haven't gotten around to taking them in the house."

Cheryl glanced up at the house and asked, "The rental doesn't have a washer and dryer?"

"Sure it does. But it's quicker to take them down to the Laundromat and do them all at once." Ian slammed the trunk shut.

"So we aren't going into your house?" Cheryl sounded disappointed.

"I don't see why. You going to put it on?"

Cheryl glanced down at the blue sweatshirt in her hand. *Men can be so dense sometimes*, she thought. Here she had given him the perfect opportunity to get her into his house, where they could be alone—and he was totally clueless. She wasn't stupid. She saw how he had looked at her when they first met, the way his eyes seemed incapable of looking away from her breasts. Some women might find that insulting, which she could never understand. To her it just meant the man had fallen under her spell, and if she wanted something from him, he would be willing to give it to her. She wasn't sure what she wanted from Ian yet, but she found him very attractive, and according to what she had read online, he was something of a celebrity. Some of his books had been made into television documentaries; *How cool was that?*

"Here," Cheryl said as she handed the sweater back to Ian.

"What? You don't want to try it on? It's clean, I promise."

"I'm not really cold anymore. But thanks for the offer."

"Okay, but you want to take it along, just in case?"

"No. That's okay." Cheryl smiled up sweetly. Ian gave a shrug then opened his trunk again and tossed the shirt back on top of the basket. After he slammed the trunk closed, he led Cheryl to the pathway beside his house, leading to the beach.

"Wow, you're right on the beach!" Cheryl said when they reached the sand. She stopped a moment and slipped off her sandals.

"I know. It's a great rental. Awesome location."

"I thought Marlow House was one of the first houses in Frederickport," Cheryl said as she and Ian walked along the beach. In one hand she carried her purse and in the other her sandals.

"It is."

"Then why didn't they build it where yours is? Didn't the guy who founded the town also build Marlow House?"

"Yes. Frederick Marlow, he was Walt Marlow's grandfather."

"Well, if I founded a beach town, I'd build my house right on the ocean!"

"So you're familiar with the history of Marlow House?" Ian asked.

"Just from your article. When you introduced yourself back there, I recognized your name."

"Ahh, so you read my article." Ian smiled.

"Yes. It was very interesting."

They walked in silence for a few moments before Cheryl asked, "So you and Dani's friend are…you know…are like a couple?"

"I suppose." Ian shrugged.

"How long have you been going together?"

"Going together? I can't say we're going together exactly."

"So how long have you known each other?"

"Umm…three weeks."

"Only three weeks?"

"That's almost a month." Ian grinned.

"So you just met each other." Cheryl beamed at the news. "For a minute back there I thought it was something more serious."

Ian glanced over at Cheryl and arched his brows. "Who says it isn't?"

"Oh, silly." Cheryl giggled, playfully pushing Ian's hip with hers. "You're walking on the beach with me, not Lily."

Ian stopped and looked at Cheryl. "So?"

Holding her shoes and handbag, she stopped walking, looked up into Ian's face, and smiled. "So…I could see how you were looking at me back there," Cheryl said in a breathless whisper.

"Cheryl, if I gave you the wrong impression, I apologize."

"No, that's okay." Cheryl stepped closer, her body almost touching his. "You're being loyal to Lily. I think that's sweet."

"Umm…" Uncomfortable with the turn of the conversation, Ian glanced down, his gaze landing on her cleavage. Startled by the sight, his gaze shot up into Cheryl's smiling face.

"You two have only known each other for a few days, so it isn't like you really owe her loyalty. You just met. But I understand if you're a little confused right now. I just want you to know I'm interested. Very interested." Cheryl pressed her body against his before taking a step back. Flashing a coy smile, she turned and started walking down the beach. When Ian didn't follow and just stood mute, watching her walk away, Cheryl looked over her shoulder and yelled playfully, "Are you coming or not?"

Shaking the cobwebs from his head, Ian caught up to Cheryl. They walked silently side by side for about five minutes. Finally Ian spoke. "Are you always so bold?"

"Now you've hurt my feelings," Cheryl said with a pout.

"How so?"

"You make it sound like I come on to every man I meet, which is not true. But I felt something between us, Ian. Admit it, you felt it too."

When Ian didn't respond, Cheryl said, "Did you know my parents were killed with Danielle's? And my brother."

"No. I didn't know that."

"They were killed in an airplane accident. It taught me how short life is. Now when I see something I want, I go for it. I want you."

"I'm sorry about your parents—your brother. But you don't even know me," Ian said quietly, still walking alongside Cheryl.

"I read your article about the Missing Thorndike. I looked you up. You're a very talented journalist. I had no idea you were staying across the street from my cousin."

"While I'm flattered, you still know nothing about me. I imagine if you got to know me better, you'd find me quite boring."

"Oh, I seriously doubt it," Cheryl purred. "Anyway, it's the chemistry between us. I felt it immediately. I know you did too." Cheryl reached over to take Ian's hand. Just as she clasped onto his fingertips, he pulled his hand away from her, not commenting on the gesture.

"You know, I own half of Marlow House—half of the Missing Thorndike."

"Lily mentioned something about that. But I thought your aunt left her estate to Danielle."

"Our aunt was suffering from Alzheimer's. There's no way she would have left me out of the will had she been in her right mind. Dani knows that."

"Danielle never mentioned your aunt had Alzheimer's." Ian glanced over at Cheryl.

"Of course she wouldn't mention it. Why would she? I have to thank you for writing the article about the Missing Thorndike. Until I read it, I didn't even know our dear aunt Brianna had passed."

"You didn't know?" Ian stopped walking and looked at Cheryl.

She came to a stop and looked up into his face. Shaking her head sadly, she said, "No. Dani and I haven't been close for years. I tried, mind you, but after her husband made a pass at me—"

"Made a pass at you?" Ian interrupted.

"The night before their wedding. Can you believe that? Dani didn't. She should have, because what happened? He cheated on her during their entire marriage. It all came to a very public and embarrassing end when her cheating husband was killed in a car accident with his lover. Of course, I'm sorry he was killed, but he did cheat on my cousin. And he was responsible for the rift in our relationship."

"And you think contesting your aunt's estate will mend that rift?"

"Half of the estate rightfully belongs to me. It's not my fault Dani tried to cut me out of our aunt's will."

"Are you taking Danielle to court?"

"I plan to talk to our aunt's attorney first. Hopefully we can get this settled without me resorting to legal action. But I've already talked to an attorney who believes I have a very strong case."

Cheryl dropped her shoes and purse to the sand and looked up at Ian, her eyes wide. "Let's not discuss this anymore. I'd rather talk about us."

"There is no us," Ian said, shifting his weight nervously.

Never taking her eyes from Ian, Cheryl licked her lips and whispered, "There could be."

"Cheryl, I just met you, you're Danielle's cousin…" Ian glanced around for an escape route.

"Have you slept with her yet?"

"Excuse me?"

"Lily. Have you two…you know?"

"That's really none of your business." Ian combed his fingers through his hair.

"You haven't. I can tell. I'm glad." Cheryl leaned closer. "Would you like to kiss me?"

"Excuse me?"

"Then we'll know. Don't you think it would be much kinder for Lily if we simply got this out of the way now? You kiss me, and if there's no chemistry, then you don't have to keep wondering. But if there's chemistry, you can let Lily down gently before she's too emotionally invested in the relationship. It really would be the kindest thing."

"Who said I was wondering?" Ian took a step back.

"Fine. Deny the attraction if you want." Cheryl leaned over and picked up her shoes and purse from the sand. "I just wanted you to know how I felt about you."

"I think we should get back to Marlow House. I need to get Sadie."

"Sadie? Who's Sadie?" Cheryl scowled.

"My dog. Remember, my dog Sadie."

"Oh. That's right. Okay." They turned and started walking back to Marlow House.

"It's nice they don't allow dogs on this beach," Cheryl said a few moments later.

"Why do you say that?"

"The dog poop. People with dogs always leave shit all over the beach."

"I never do that. I always pick it up."

"Eww…" Cheryl cringed. "That's gross. That's something I can't figure out, how people can just pick up their dog's poop with their hands."

"A hand typically covered with a plastic bag."

"Still, that's gross. I'm just glad they don't allow dogs down here, and I don't have to see all the poop."

"Not far from here they allow dogs on the beach. I didn't notice any. It's a clean beach."

"Well, I'll remember to use this beach and not that one."

EIGHT

Gloria Comings, Mr. Renton's assistant, was at the front desk when Danielle entered the attorney's office later that afternoon. "Ms. Boatman," Gloria greeted her without standing up.

"Hello. Mr. Renton is expecting me," Danielle said with a smile as she glanced around the front office. Its rustic walls, paneled in knotty pine, looked more suitable for a mountain cabin than a business office. Many of the framed black-and-white photographs hanging on two of the four walls depicted the Oregon coast, while others were of two men fishing.

"Yes, he is. You can go right in." Gloria pointed to a closed door on the far wall behind her desk.

Danielle gave her a nod and smile before making her way to the door. Glancing over the photographs, she noticed the fishermen in the pictures all seemed to be the same two men. One fisherman was tall and lean while the second one was short and grossly overweight. The stark contrast between the two reminded Danielle of the 1930s comedy duo Laurel and Hardy; although, she didn't think Hardy had been shorter than Laurel.

When she reached the door, Danielle paused and looked back at Gloria, who was busy sorting through papers on the front desk. "Excuse me, who are the men in the photographs?"

Gloria looked up and turned around to face Danielle. "Why, that's Mr. Renton and Mr. Carmichael, Mr. Renton's partner."

"The one who passed away?"

"Yes. Those two loved to fish."

"Oh..." Danielle gave Gloria a smile and then turned back to the door. She wondered, *Is Mr. Renton Laurel or Hardy?*

Danielle knocked on the door and was quickly greeted with, "Come in!"

As soon as Clarence Renton stood up from his desk and started walking toward Danielle to shake her hand, she had her answer—Hardy. Of course, he was much shorter than Hardy, and there was no thin mustache. In fact, he looked nothing like Oliver Hardy save for the stark difference of his physical appearance when standing side by side with his former business partner. Now that she had a closer look, she decided he looked more like a clean-shaven Santa Claus, with his round body, ruddy cheeks, bright blue eyes, and snowy hair.

"Ms. Boatman, so nice to meet you at last!" Clarence enthusiastically shook her hand and then guided her to a chair facing his desk.

"I really appreciate you seeing me today," Danielle said as she took a seat.

"Well, what is this about a cousin?" Clarence sat back down behind his desk and looked at Danielle.

"My cousin, Cheryl, showed up at Marlow House this afternoon."

"Yes, you told me that. But what I don't understand, I was under the impression you didn't have any family."

"Not that I know of, except for Cheryl, who I really have nothing to do with."

"How are you related, exactly?" Clarence leaned forward, resting his elbows on the desk.

"Her mother was my father's sister. Her parents and brother were killed with my parents in the plane accident."

"Yes, I remember you telling me about that, but I wasn't aware you had a surviving cousin. And she's related to Brianna?"

"In the same way as I am, by marriage. Brianna's husband was our grandfather's brother."

"Humm...and you say she's attempting to claim a share in the estate?"

"Do you think I'll have a problem? Does she have a case?"

"I am a little concerned that I have never heard of her before—

that your aunt never mentioned her. I was under the impression you were her only relative, albeit by marriage."

"So are you saying Cheryl might have a claim?"

"Not exactly. But considering your aunt's mental health during her last months..."

"Her mental health? I don't know what you're saying?" Danielle frowned.

"She had Alzheimer's, you know."

"No, I did not know. Why am I just now hearing about this?"

"Well, I don't think it will be a problem. Your aunt authorized her last will before her illness. At least, before it was diagnosed. I just never considered there could be a problem, since you were her only relative, or so I thought."

"But she didn't leave her entire estate to me." Danielle felt a headache coming on.

"As you know, she left a considerable amount of her estate to her favorite charities. I never worried about any of them contesting what she left you. But now that you tell me there's another great-niece..."

"So how long was my aunt sick? Why didn't you ever mention it?" Danielle rubbed her temples.

"You know she moved to Italy after her husband died. It wasn't long after that she had me write her last will. About a year before her death, she was having some difficulties living on her own. We arranged for her to be moved into an assisted-living situation where they could take care of her."

"Why didn't you ever tell me? She sent me letters that last year. She seemed fine to me."

"From what I understand, Brianna had her good days and bad." Clarence shrugged.

"And this may give Cheryl a claim to the estate?"

"I'm a little concerned she might claim Brianna's illness caused your aunt to forget your cousin. After all, she's not mentioned in the will."

"But you said Aunt Brianna got sick a few years after she wrote the will."

"It was diagnosed a few years later."

"Why didn't you ever mention any of this to me, that Brianna had been ill?"

"I saw no reason to mention it. I assumed you already knew."

"How would I have known?" Danielle asked.

"Ms. Boatman, you were already so upset over your aunt's passing, I didn't think it was necessary to add to your burden by elaborating on the harsh details of her final days."

"Well, I wish I had known," Danielle said quietly.

"I am sorry." Clarence sounded contrite. "As for your cousin's claim, let me look into a few things for you, and I'll get back to you the first of next week."

"Thank you. Will you be at the open house?"

"I plan to come. Unfortunately, Ms. Comings won't be able to make it. She's taking off this afternoon for Portland to spend the holiday with family."

"I understand. I'm glad you'll be able to make it."

"You mentioned something on the phone about your cousin having an attorney already looking into this?"

"The only thing she really said was that her attorney thought she had a good case. Not sure he's really looking into it. Knowing my cousin, it's always possible she made up the part about the attorney, or it might be some guy she went out with, and he told her off the cuff. I don't honestly know."

"Do you know if she's planning to contact me?"

"Umm…actually, I sort of gave her the impression I would arrange that," Danielle said sheepishly.

"I don't want you to worry. I'm confident Brianna was in full possession of her faculties when she wrote that will and that she didn't leave Cheryl out because she forgot about her, but because she didn't want to include her," Clarence said with far more enthusiasm than he had shown earlier. He then grew pensive and asked, "Your aunt did know Cheryl existed, didn't she?"

"Yes. Aunt Brianna and Uncle Harry came to the US a few times when I was younger. The family would get together, and that included Cheryl."

"Let me see what I can find out, and hopefully we can get this all sorted out."

"I appreciate it." *I wonder what this is going to cost me.*

"I understand you intend to sell the Missing Thorndike? Quite a find there. I would never have imagined it was in Marlow House."

"Yes, it was right there in the attic, stuffed behind a loose board."

"Amazing. Who would have ever imagined someone like Walt

Marlow was the one responsible for taking that necklace. And to think it was there all those years."

"A few people knew. George Hemming knew. Apparently, Walt Marlow told him he took it—or at least alluded to the fact."

"Did Marie Nichols tell you that?"

"Yes. Although, initially she didn't specifically mention the Missing Thorndike, just that Walt Marlow—according to her father —was involved in a jewel heist."

"Really…Perhaps that explains Adam's curiosity."

"Adam?"

"Have you met Marie's grandson?"

"Yes, yes, I have. What did you mean Adam's curiosity?"

"Gloria told me Adam quizzed her about the house a few weeks before you arrived. Asked what was still in it, what had been removed. He even wanted to have a look inside."

"Did she let him inside?"

"No. She figured he was checking it out as a possible rental. I ran into him a few days later; he asked me when the new owner was showing up. I figured Gloria was right. Of course, if you had decided to put the house in the rental market, I would have recommended Bay View Rentals, not Frederickport Vacation Properties. They have a better reputation."

"Do you think he wanted to see inside because of the Missing Thorndike?" Danielle already knew the answer to her question.

"I suppose I find the idea amusing, especially if Marie told her grandson about the necklace." Clarence chuckled again. "But no, probably not. I'm sure Marie would have told Adam that story years ago, so if he were interested, he would have already found some way to get into the house. No, I was just being overly suspicious."

"Perhaps," Danielle muttered under her breath.

"I understand you have a buyer for the necklace already."

"Yes. He's going to be here after the weekend. Which is why I need to get this thing with Cheryl cleared up."

"You'll have to put that on hold for right now."

"What do you mean?"

"Until we get this straightened out with your cousin, you really shouldn't sell the necklace."

"I need to sell it so I can pay the damn inheritance tax," Danielle said impatiently. "I really don't want to lose this buyer."

"Don't worry about that now," Clarence said as he stood up.

"Let me look into a few things and get back to you as soon as possible. You just focus on your open house."

"That is a little hard to do," Danielle grumbled. She stood up and picked up her purse off the floor.

"Now, now, it will all work out. One way or another." Clarence walked Danielle to his office door and opened it.

"Thanks for seeing me today," Danielle said as she walked out the doorway into the front office.

"It was nice to finally meet you in person," Clarence said. "I'll see you at your open house."

NINE

Much to Cheryl's annoyance, Sadie greeted her and Ian when they reached the side gate of Marlow house. Danielle typically left the gate wide open; that had made it easy for Ian to arrange his first meeting with Danielle and Lily and for the times he would walk over in the evenings and catch Lily sitting on the bench under the moonlight. But this afternoon the gate was shut. Sadie sat inside the enclosure, barking for Ian to come inside and play.

"Hello, girl," Ian greeted as he pulled the unlocked padlock from the latch and pushed open the gate. Cheryl followed Ian inside the yard, careful to avoid Sadie, who insisted on jumping on Ian.

On the far side of the yard, Lily looked up from the ground, croquet mallet in hand, preparing to hit a ball. Instead, she let the mallet rest against the grass as she waved to Cheryl and Ian. Cheryl ignored her greeting and made her way to the kitchen door. Ian waved in return. By the time he reached Lily, Cheryl had already gone into the house.

"That was a quick walk," Lily said, briefly glancing over to the door leading into the kitchen.

"If I ever offer to take that woman anywhere ever again, please hit me in the head with a croquet mallet." Ian shuddered.

"What happened?" Lily glanced back to the house and then to Ian.

"I don't think you'd believe me." Ian shook his head in disgust.

"Did she make a pass at you?" Lily asked with a grin.

"How did you know that?"

"Dani said she hit on Lucas before their wedding." Lily looked down, positioned the mallet behind the ball, and gave it a little tap, sending the ball toward its target.

"According to Cheryl, it was the other way around." Ian followed Lily as she continued to play croquet.

"She told you that?" Lily asked as she hit the ball again. It went astray, flying into a nearby bush. Before Lily could retrieve the wooden ball, Sadie flew into the bushes and snagged it, then dashed across the yard in the opposite direction. "Sadie! Bring that back!" Lily called out.

"Yes, but I have a feeling your version is more accurate." Ian watched as Sadie ran around the yard with the wooden ball in her mouth. "You know, she isn't going to bring it back." Ian laughed.

"So what happened between you two down at the beach?" Lily asked as she walked to Sadie, who was now lying on the lawn, energetically chewing on the ball.

Following Lily, his hands tucked into the back pockets of his jeans, he said, "I don't want to go into it. Let's just say she made me an offer she didn't think I could refuse."

"Were you tempted?" Lily asked when they reached Sadie. She leaned down and grabbed the ball. In a scolding voice she said, "You don't want to chew on that!"

"Tempted?" Ian glanced at the house and then back to Lily. He smiled and said, "Strangely not."

"Strangely?" Lily looked at the slobbery croquet ball in her hand. Wrinkling her nose in disgust, she wiped the ball on her apron. Sadie ran off in the opposite direction, expecting Lily to throw the ball. Instead of throwing it, Lily slipped it into her apron pocket.

"I am a man, Lily. When a beautiful woman hits on you—"

"So tell me," Lily interrupted, "you couldn't do it because she just didn't compare to me, right?"

"Partially."

"Partially?" Lily wrinkled her nose and lightly smacked the side of Ian's leg with the croquet mallet.

"Ouch!" Ian snatched the mallet from Lily.

"Oh, that didn't hurt," Lily scoffed.

"True, but I'm not going to wait around for you to take a second swing."

"So what was the other reason you didn't accept her gracious offer?"

"Honestly?" Ian looked up at Marlow House. He could see Cheryl standing in her bedroom window, looking down at them.

"Yes, why?" Lily glanced toward the house. She saw Cheryl standing in the window.

"High-maintenance women, especially those with an exceptionally high opinion of themselves—well, are rather a turnoff for me."

"Ahh, I get it, you tend to go for slobs with low self-esteem?" Lily teased.

"Well…" Ian critically eyed Lily, his eyes moving up and down her body. Smirking, he reached out and tugged her messy ponytail. "I wouldn't say you have low self-esteem."

"Oh, thanks!" Lily laughed. "Hey, give me back that mallet; I wanna smack you again."

"I don't think so. You're dangerous with that thing." He wrapped an arm around her shoulders and led her to the bench. They sat down.

"Did you know Brianna Boatman had Alzheimer's?" Ian asked.

"Alzheimer's? I didn't know that. How did you find out?"

"Cheryl told me. That's why she believes she has a claim on the estate. Because her aunt wasn't mentally competent to make her will."

"Do you think that's true?" Lily glanced up at the house. Cheryl was no longer standing at the bedroom window.

"I have no idea. But if she wasn't mentally competent when she had that will written, Cheryl might have a legitimate claim."

"Damn. That really mucks things up."

"Where is Danielle?" Ian glanced over to where Danielle normally parked her car.

"She went to see Mr. Renton, her attorney."

"Hopefully he'll have good news for her. I'd hate to see Danielle forced to share her estate with that woman."

"*That woman.*" Lily chuckled.

"I think for the first time in my life I understand how a woman feels when a man makes an unwelcome advance," Ian said in a serious tone. "Yesterday if you'd asked me if a beautiful woman coming on to me—coming on strong—would turn me off, I would have laughed."

"Do you have to keep calling her a beautiful woman?" Lily grumbled.

"Well, she is. I mean physically speaking. But I have to admit, she made me extremely uncomfortable out there."

"After Cheryl made a pass at Lucas, he told Dani about it and she confronted her cousin. Cheryl insisted it was all a mistake, that she had too much to drink."

"Cheryl's version was that Lucas made a pass at her. She says that explains her and Danielle's fractured relationship. According to Cheryl, Lucas cheated on Dani throughout their marriage, and when he was killed in the car accident, he was with his lover."

"Well, the last part of that is true enough," Lily said with a sigh.

"It is?"

"I have no idea if he cheated on her throughout their marriage. When I first met them, they seemed to have a good marriage. I never noticed him having a wandering eye or being inappropriate with other women. But during that last year, before he was killed, their business had really taken off. They started to make a lot of money, and he seemed to change. Danielle was never heavy into material stuff, but Lucas was suddenly spending money like crazy. A new car, a new house, and he spent way more money than Dani did on clothes. In fact, he'd get annoyed because she wasn't dressing up to their new station in life—as he put it."

"Sounds like a nice guy," Ian scoffed.

"He was. No, I mean really, he used to be when I first met him. But he changed a lot that last year. That's why I don't think he was cheating on Danielle earlier in their marriage."

"Were Danielle and Cheryl close before the incident at the wedding?"

"No. According to Dani, they've never been close. When they were teenagers, Cheryl used to hit on Dani's boyfriends. That's why she wasn't terribly surprised when she hit on Lucas."

"Now I'm just starting to feel cheap," Ian grumbled.

"Ahh, because you aren't special?" Lily teased.

Ian chuckled in reply.

Sadie gave up on waiting for Lily to throw the ball. She walked to the bench and sat down between Ian's and Lily's feet.

"I do have a question for you," Ian asked.

"What?" Lily reached down and gave Sadie a pat.

"Why were you playing croquet all alone?"

"Oh, that." Lily laughed. "Danielle and I thought it might be cool to put the croquet set up in the backyard for the open house—an old-fashioned touch. After I set it up, I decided to try it out."

They sat in silence for a few minutes. Finally, Lily said, "I keep thinking about Cheryl's claim. Danielle was so excited with opening the B and B. This really bugs me."

"I was thinking about that myself. I suppose, worst-case scenario—Danielle can pay off Cheryl with the proceeds from the sale of the necklace. After all, in the beginning she thought it was a fake. From what I understand, considering what the house is worth, Danielle could easily cover half of the estate's worth from the sale of the necklace and still have money left over."

"That's true, if Cheryl was willing to let Dani keep Marlow House."

"Why wouldn't she? I didn't get the impression Cheryl was thrilled with this place," Ian said.

"According to Dani, Cheryl has a habit of wanting whatever Dani has. If Cheryl thinks her cousin really wants Marlow House, she might decide she wants it too."

TEN

Walt watched as Cheryl crawled along the attic floor on her hands and knees, inspecting the baseboard. Still wearing her bathing suit and short summer shift, her bottom waddled in the air as she made her way across the floor. Walt had never seen a thong bathing suit bottom before and was quite fascinated at the sight.

It was obvious to him she was treasure hunting. He smiled when she reached the loose board where he had once hidden the Missing Thorndike. Of course, it was no longer there, but by Cheryl's gleeful squeal when the board came off in her hand and she discovered the secret cubbyhole, the woman clearly thought she had stumbled upon new treasure. Her hand was shoved into the cubbyhole when Danielle walked in the room a moment later. Danielle noticed Walt first, but he didn't see her. He couldn't take his eyes off the woman crawling around below his feet.

Glancing down, Danielle saw what was capturing Walt's attention. "Just what do you think you're doing?" Danielle asked Walt, who responded with a sheepish shrug.

Cheryl stood abruptly and pulled the hem of her dress down to cover her skimpy bathing suit bottom. "I'm just looking around," she said as she straightened her clothing and brushed her hair back.

"Looks like you're taking apart my woodwork."

"It's my house too," Cheryl insisted.

"What are you looking for? More treasure?"

"There's probably more here. The article said you found it in the attic. Was it in there?" Cheryl pointed to where her hand had just been.

"Yes. And now it's locked up in a safety deposit box at the bank, so no reason for you to take the house apart."

Cheryl's eyes darted around the room. "I'm sure there's more here."

"You are, are you? What makes you sure of that?" Danielle asked.

Walt stood by Cheryl, leaning casually against the wall while he smoked a cigar, his attention now on her cleavage. Glancing up briefly, he noticed the unfriendly glare Danielle cast in his direction. "Oh, come on, Danielle, you can't begrudge a man for looking."

"You're dead," Danielle snapped.

"Are you threatening me?" Cheryl gasped.

"No, of course not." Danielle cursed herself for responding to Walt.

"I heard what you said!"

"I meant to say you're dead wrong. There are no other hidden treasures in the house."

"How do you know that?"

"Well, for one thing, I went through the entire house already. How do you think I found the necklace?" Danielle lied.

"What made you go through the house?"

"Well…Marie Hemming told me Walt Marlow might have taken the necklace. And since it was never found, I decided to have a look."

"Who is Marie Hemming?"

"Her name is Marie Nichols now. Hemming was her maiden name. Her father used to live in the house across the street, the one Ian's renting. He was friends with Walt Marlow, and apparently, Walt once implied he took the necklace."

"Who was Walt Marlow again? I can't keep all these names straight. I remember reading something about it in the article."

"His grandfather founded Frederickport and built this house. Walt Marlow inherited Marlow House from his grandfather."

Cheryl seemed distracted. Glancing around, she sniffed the air. "There it is again. That cigar smell. Awful. You need to get rid of it if you expect people to stay here."

Danielle smiled and said, "Walt Marlow was murdered in this room. Right where you're standing."

"Well, that's not nice," Walt said with a scowl. "You don't have to sound so happy about it."

"I understand he used to smoke cigars," Danielle added, a mischievous lilt to her voice.

"You're just saying that to freak me out." Cheryl glared at Danielle.

"I thought you read Ian's article about the necklace. It mentioned Walt Marlow, how he died, where he died."

"Sure, I read the article." Cheryl shrugged. "I suppose I skimmed that part."

"But not the part about the necklace," Danielle grumbled.

"You should have contacted me, Dani. It was wrong of you."

"What are you talking about?"

"She was my aunt too. You should have told me she died."

"You didn't even know her," Danielle countered.

"I met her before."

"What, when we were kids? Did you ever write her, visit her when you were older?"

"Dani, my relationship with Aunt Brianna is really none of your business. But she was my aunt, and you should have told me when she died. You should have told me she had Alzheimer's."

"How did you know that?"

"Aha! You did know! I knew it! You knew she was impaired and you took advantage of her so she would leave you her estate!"

"I didn't know she had Alzheimer's. Not until today. Mr. Renton told me," Danielle insisted.

"Mr. Renton? Who's that?"

"Aunt Brianna's attorney."

"I thought we were going to see him together!"

"You went to the beach with Ian, and when I spoke to Mr. Renton on the phone, he said if I wanted to see him today I had to go right down to his office."

"You're trying to pull something, Dani. You could have come down to the beach and gotten me."

"Well, I didn't. And according to Mr. Renton, Aunt Brianna wrote her will years before she came down with Alzheimer's."

"You know that often goes undiagnosed."

"What is it you really want, Cheryl?"

"Just what's mine."

"We both know Aunt Brianna had no reason to leave you part of her estate. You had nothing to do with her. But you obviously want something. That's why you're here."

"No, Dani. I'm here to stake my rightful claim to half of the estate. And my attorney says I have a solid case."

"Next week I have a buyer coming to look at the necklace. The house was already appraised. How about I simply pay you from the proceeds of the necklace for whatever half of the estate is worth. In turn, you agree that settles any claims you have, and you can go back to California and leave me alone," Danielle said wearily.

"Why would you do that?" Walt stood up straight, no longer leaning against the wall. The cigar in his hand vanished.

"So your attorney agrees; I do have a case," Cheryl said smugly.

"It isn't that, Cheryl. I just want to move on with my life, and I don't need you complicating things for me. If that means I only keep a share of the funds from the necklace, so be it."

"This is ridiculous," Walt grumbled. He began pacing back and forth between Cheryl and Danielle.

"Why would I want to sell the necklace?" Cheryl asked.

"So we can divide the estate." Danielle thought the reason was obvious.

"Maybe I don't want to," Cheryl said stubbornly.

"What do you mean?"

"It's not like I need the money," Cheryl told her. "How often does someone have the opportunity to own—and wear—something so unique?"

"Maybe you don't need the money, but I can't even afford to pay the inheritance tax on the necklace. Are you saying you want to buy out my share of the necklace?"

"Don't be ridiculous," Cheryl scoffed. "Why should I pay for something that I already own?"

"For one thing, you might not be entitled to half the estate. And even if you were, you'd only own half of the necklace."

"What about this house?" Cheryl asked.

"What do you mean?"

"Half of the house is mine."

"Cheryl, I said I would buy you out of your imagined half with the proceeds from the necklace. It would be like selling off the estate—the house and necklace—and then splitting the money. And if you are so determined to keep the necklace, then you'll have to buy out half the necklace minus half of what the rest of the estate is worth."

"But I want my share of the house."

"Why in the world do you want part of this house? You have your own house in California. I can't believe you want to move to Oregon. You have your friends and life back there."

"You just want the house because of what's hidden here," Cheryl snapped.

"What do you mean, what's hidden here?"

"You know very well what I mean! I don't believe for a moment that man just stole one necklace. I bet he stole all sorts of jewelry, and it's hidden throughout this house."

"If that were true, then whatever we find wouldn't be ours to keep anyway. It would have to go back to the rightful owners."

"Please stop talking like I was a thief," Walt grumbled.

"You found that necklace and got to keep it. So don't tell me you wouldn't be able to keep whatever else you find," Cheryl insisted.

"That was different. Walt Marlow inherited the necklace and it was passed down to his heir, which was Aunt Brianna's mother."

"That's just stupid. Why would he inherit a necklace he stole? You're just making this stuff up."

"Your cousin isn't very bright," Walt said. "But considering what you've offered her, I'm beginning to think a serious lack of intelligence runs in your family."

Danielle glared at Walt before telling Cheryl, "You need to reread Ian's article. The necklace I found in this house was a fluke—a one-of-a-kind find. I'm not going to give you half of Marlow House, but that's not because I think there's more buried treasure here. Maybe we should just fight it out in court. If you win there, I've no doubt the judge will make us sell the necklace anyway to settle the estate."

"That's fine with me, Dani. But if the judge forces us to sell the necklace, then the house goes too!" Cheryl stormed from the room. The sound of her angry footsteps on the wooden stairs reverberated in the attic.

"I'm glad you decided to fight her in court," Walt said when he no longer heard Cheryl's footsteps. "I don't believe she has a legitimate claim."

"I'm not so sure about that. Mr. Renton wasn't all that reassuring."

"What do you mean?"

"Cheryl might very well be able to prove she has a viable claim in the estate. What if I'm forced to sell Marlow House?"

"You can't leave, Danielle."

"Why do you care? You practically called me stupid a minute ago."

"I didn't mean that. I was frustrated at how you seemed to just give up—were willing to give her whatever she wanted. I'm sorry; I didn't realize your attorney felt she might have a claim. But we both know your aunt intended for you to have the house, and we both know why. And while we can't prove that, I'm sure there will be some way to fight Cheryl in court."

"What you don't understand, Walt, is that I don't really have the resources to fight her. I don't imagine I'll be allowed to spend the money from Aunt Brianna's estate to pay for legal fees. Her parents left her very wealthy. She has a lot more money than I do to fight this. Hell, I imagine her estate is worth twice what I'll get for the Missing Thorndike."

"I don't understand. Then why does she care about your aunt's estate?"

"Very simple, Walt. Because I got it."

ELEVEN

Cheryl retreated to the Red Room for the rest of the afternoon. The door was shut and Danielle assumed her cousin was napping. It wasn't until later that evening, after Lily had left with Ian for dinner and the sun set, did Cheryl make another appearance. Somewhat disheveled, her mass of tangled blond curls in disarray, she stumbled into the kitchen, looking for food.

"What's for dinner?" Cheryl asked Danielle, who stood at the counter, whipping up a cream cheese concoction for the open house.

"I don't know about you, but I had a tuna sandwich, and Lily and Ian went out."

"You aren't making dinner?" Cheryl fairly whined.

Danielle glanced up. "No. Why would you think I would?"

"You aren't being a very gracious hostess." Cheryl looked around the kitchen for something to eat.

"I save my hospitality for invited guests."

"I don't know why you're being so mean to me, Dani."

"I'm busy, Cheryl. You show up right before my open house and drop all this on me. You and I will have to sort this out after the weekend. I have a million things that need to be done before Friday."

Cheryl eyed the chocolate cake sitting on the counter. "Fine, I'll just have cake for dinner."

"You touch that cake and you lose a hand!" Danielle snapped.

"Why can't I have a piece of cake? I'm hungry."

"For one thing, it's for the open house."

"It's going to be all dry by then."

"It will be if you cut into it. If you're hungry, there's some tuna left over in the fridge, and the bread's in the breadbox on the counter."

Cheryl let out a little grunt but went to make herself a sandwich.

"When you're done there, you might as well help with the open house."

"What do you mean?"

"For starters, you need to make sure the room you're staying in looks like it did when you arrived."

"I don't want anyone going into my room!"

"It isn't your room. Anyway, the point of the open house is to let people take a tour through Marlow House, even the room you're staying in."

"Fine. I'll straighten it up on Friday morning."

"There's a list by the phone. Look through it, and find something you can do."

A few minutes later, Cheryl walked over to the phone, sandwich in hand, and picked up the sheet of paper from the counter. Glancing through the list, she frowned. "I'm not doing any of this. I didn't come here to be your slave."

"I thought you wanted a share of this house?"

"It doesn't mean I want to turn it into a bed and breakfast. It's a stupid idea." Cheryl tossed the list back on the counter and went to the table with her sandwich. "Strangers in the house. It's not like I need the money. If you insist on doing it, don't expect me to help."

"Fine. Just don't make any more messes."

"I don't believe you really care about all this B and B nonsense, anyway. It's what's hidden in the house you really want. Otherwise, you wouldn't be so anxious to sell the necklace and pay me off. The only thing I can't figure out is why in the world you want strangers in the house."

"Please, not the hidden treasure again." Danielle stopped what she was doing and turned to face her cousin. "Cheryl, it was foolish of me to say you could stay. I think it would be best if you check into a motel until we work this out. Who knows, maybe you are right and the court will give you half of the estate, but for now it belongs to me, not you. At the moment, you have no legal claim on the property. So for now, I want you to leave."

Cheryl looked up from her sandwich and stared at Danielle. She said nothing but continued to eat while looking at her cousin. After she took her last bite, she stood up and smiled. "No, Dani. I've already moved into the room; and I'm not moving out."

Danielle silently watched as Cheryl sashayed from the kitchen, leaving behind on the kitchen counter a pile of crumbs, an open loaf of bread, and a dirty Tupperware container that had been used to store the now eaten tuna salad. Shaking her head in disgust, Danielle tidied her cousin's mess and cursed herself for allowing Cheryl beyond the first floor of Marlow House.

Danielle let out a weary sigh and considered all that she needed to do before the party—and what she had already accomplished. While Lily was out with Ian, she planned to finish making the food for the open house. Tomorrow, Joanne Johnson was arriving to give Marlow House a cleaning from top to bottom. Fortunately, it was already fairly clean, except for the room Cheryl was using.

In the morning, Danielle had errands to run. She would ask Lily to stick around Marlow House to make sure Cheryl didn't get into too much mischief. Danielle had to pick up the brochures from the printers. The postcards she had ordered had arrived the day before. She had wine to pick up, and her last stop was the bank, where she was meeting Joe Morelli.

Ben Smith from the museum had recommended a local upholster who was reasonably priced and qualified to work on antique furniture. To Danielle's delight, the upholsterer was able to finish the work in time for the open house and promised to deliver the pieces in the morning.

It was almost 8 p.m. when Danielle finished up in the kitchen. She was just wiping down the counter when the doorbell rang. Her first thought was that Lily had forgotten her key. Tossing the rag on the counter, she went to answer the door, wiping her hands on the sides of her denims as she walked down the entry hall.

When she opened the front door, it was not Lily but Sergeant Joe Morelli.

"I know it's a little late, but I saw the light on," Joe said with a grin.

Looking up into his warm brown eyes, she smiled and opened

the door wider to let him in. "Well, this is a pleasant surprise, Sergeant Morelli."

He stepped inside the entry and looked around. "Have you had any break-ins lately?"

"If I can count my cousin," Danielle said as she shut the door.

"Your cousin? Oh, you have company. I'm sorry…"

"No, not company, exactly. My cousin just surprised me with an unwelcomed visit. She's upstairs now. I'm glad you stopped by."

"I wanted to make sure we're on for tomorrow. Do you still want me to go with you to pick up the necklace?"

"If you don't mind."

"No problem. Are you sure you don't want me to spend the night too?"

Danielle's eyes widened.

"I meant while you have the necklace here. I could sleep downstairs."

"Oh, I knew what you meant," Danielle lied. "But like I told you, once I get it back to Marlow House, it will be fine. They installed the safe last week, and that's where I'm keeping it when I'm not wearing it for the party. Then back it goes to the bank until the buyer arrives next week."

"So you're still selling it?" Joe followed Danielle into the parlor.

"That was my plan…at least, until my cousin arrived." Danielle glanced up to the ceiling. "Can I get you anything to drink, something to eat?"

"No, I'm fine." Joe took a seat. "What do you mean, until your cousin arrived?"

"Looks like my cousin, Cheryl, is going to contest my aunt's will."

"Isn't it a little late for that? Hasn't it been through probate?"

"I'm not sure how all that works. I talked to the attorney today, and he's looking into it." Danielle sat on a chair facing Joe.

"So she believes the estate should have gone to her?"

"I didn't know we had company," Walt said when he appeared in the parlor the next moment.

"Half of it, anyway." Danielle tried to ignore Walt, who eyed Joe with intense curiosity. "The attorney doesn't think it would be advisable to sell it until we work this out with my cousin. But I don't know if the buyer will be willing to wait. And if he isn't, will I be able to find another one who can match his offer?"

"Who is this man? Why is he here?" Walt asked. "And why do you keep looking at him like that?"

"Unfortunately, when it comes to sorting out inheritances, things can get brutal even in the closest families," Joe said.

"Well, Cheryl and I aren't that close. Never have been. I considered just knocking her off and burying her in the backyard, but your brother-in-law did such a nice job out there, I really would feel bad messing it up."

"Great, now gallows humor?" Walt said.

Joe laughed and said, "Glad to hear you resisted the temptation. I'd hate to have to arrest you."

"Yeah, it would probably mess up the open house too."

"So he's a policeman. But why is he here?" Walt circled the room, watching Danielle and Joe. "I can't believe it; you're flirting with him. I'll be damned; you look about to swoon."

Danielle took a deep breath, resisting the temptation to shoot Walt a dirty look. Focusing her attention on Joe, she said, "I want to thank you again for finding that old police report on Walt Marlow's death. It really helped to convince the readers it wasn't a suicide. If Walt Marlow was here, I imagine he would be very grateful. Or at least, he should be."

"Ahhha, so that's who he is." Walt sat on the couch's arm and looked down at Joe. "So he's the one who's going with you to the bank to pick up the necklace. I suppose that's a good idea. Once you get it back here, I can keep an eye on it."

"It was an interesting case. I'm looking forward to the open house, by the way. And my offer still stands. I'd be more than happy to spend the night here."

Walt jumped to his feet, scowling at Joe.

"I appreciate your offer—to guard the necklace." Danielle flashed Walt a warning to back off. The last thing she needed was for him to start moving the furniture or toss about Lily's stack of magazines.

Walt kept quiet until after Joe left thirty minutes later.

"What exactly is going on between you two?" Walt asked when Danielle returned to the parlor after showing Joe to the door.

"I don't know what you mean—or how that is any of your business. You should just be grateful for his help."

"I already said I was grateful."

"Did you?" Danielle flopped down on the couch and grabbed a magazine off the side table. She began thumbing through it.

"I didn't realize you two had become so—friendly."

"We've just gone out to lunch a few times."

"You never told me that."

"I didn't realize I needed to keep you informed of my social calendar," Danielle said primly.

"I didn't realize you had a social calendar."

Danielle tossed the magazine on the table and glared up at Walt. "Well, that's rude."

Walt shrugged. "I suppose I'm a little surprised he's the kind of man you would go after."

"I'm not going after anyone. Joe is a nice guy, and we have gone out a couple times—very casually on lunch dates. Sheesh, I don't need you drilling me like my father."

"I am hardly your father."

"Okay, considering your age, then like a grandfather! No, make that great-grandfather."

Walt vanished.

TWELVE

Cheryl stood outside the jewelry store window, looking in at the display. There didn't appear to be anyone in the store except for the man behind the counter, who gave her a little wave when he noticed her standing outside the shop. She stood there for a few more minutes before making the decision to go inside.

"Good morning," the man cheerfully greeted her. He flashed a smile, showing off straight white teeth. "Beautiful day, isn't it?"

Cheryl thought he was pleasant-looking enough, with a clean-shaven face and curly brown hair trimmed neatly above his ears. She found his dark blue polyester slacks and crisply pressed powder blue dress shirt dreadfully out of style. If she were to guess his age, she would say he was in his mid-forties.

"Too cold for me. Is it always so miserable in the summers here?" Cheryl walked to the counter and looked down, browsing the selection of diamond rings locked in the glass case.

"I suppose it is a little cooler than normal for this time of the year," the man said with a shrug. "Are you looking for anything in particular?"

"I was wondering, was this the jewelry store where they brought the Missing Thorndike?"

"Oh, you read the article!" The man beamed. "Yes. For some reason they thought the diamonds and emeralds were fake, but I recognized the piece immediately."

"So you were the one who looked at it?"

"Yes, I was. Quite a thrill, I tell you. My name is Samuel Hayman, by the way. This is my store. When I was just a kid, my grandfather told me about the necklace. We always wondered who had taken it. A real shock to find out Walt Marlow, of all people, stole the necklace."

"So tell me, were there many jewel heists in Frederickport back then?"

"What do you mean?"

"Did your grandfather ever mention other jewelry that went missing when Walt Marlow was alive? I've heard some jewel thieves are often members of the social circle they rob—like that Marlow guy. They go to all the parties and social gatherings, and no one suspects anything while they're being ripped off."

"Umm…no…not that I've ever heard of. Why?"

"Oh, I was just curious." Cheryl shrugged and continued to look down at the display case.

"So are you visiting family or friends here?"

"You can tell I'm not a local?"

"Rather got that impression, plus I don't remember seeing you around before. And I would definitely remember such a pretty woman."

Cheryl grinned at the compliment and then said, "Actually, I'm staying at Marlow House."

"I didn't know they were open for business yet. I'm going to their open house tomorrow."

"Well, I'm not a guest per se. I'm one of the owners," Cheryl said proudly.

"Owners? I don't understand. I thought Danielle Boatman owned Marlow House."

"Dani is my cousin. Actually, I'm the only relative she has. You see, Brianna Boatman, the former owner of Marlow House, was my great-aunt too. She was very ill during her last years, Alzheimer's."

"Oh, I'm sorry to hear that. I didn't know."

"I don't wish to speak ill of my cousin, but I'm afraid she was a tad eager when she learned Aunt Brianna had left her Marlow House. Obviously, Aunt Brianna intended to leave it to both of us, but with that horrid disease…" Cheryl sighed dramatically then said, "Which is why I'm here to straighten out the estate."

"How does your cousin…umm, feel about all this? I know that necklace is part of the estate, and it's worth over a million dollars."

"Well, I admit she wasn't thrilled when I showed up. But she'll get used to the idea. I was wondering, do you know which bank my cousin keeps the necklace at? I noticed there are several banks in town."

"The one just next door," Samuel told her.

Fifteen minutes later, Cheryl entered the bank next door to the jewelry store and walked up to one of the bank tellers.

"How can I help you?" the teller asked.

"I need to speak to the bank manager."

"I can help you with deposits and withdrawals, but if you need to speak to someone about another banking matter, you can sign in over there." The teller pointed to a sign-up sheet on the far counter.

"I need to speak to the bank manager. If I sign up there, will I be able to see her?"

"Actually, it's a him. Can you tell me what this is about? Maybe I can direct you to the right person."

"It's about the Missing Thorndike."

"You mean the necklace?"

"Yes. I want to see it."

"Excuse me? You want to see it? I don't understand." The teller looked around nervously.

"Oh, don't get all jumpy," Cheryl said with a laugh when she noticed the change in the teller's demeanor. "I didn't come here to steal the necklace. After all, I don't need to steal it, since I own half of it."

"I don't know what you're talking about." The teller glanced around nervously. When she spied the bank manager, she waved him over.

"What can I help you with?" the bank manager asked when he walked up to the teller's window. He smiled at Cheryl.

"Are you the bank manager?" Cheryl asked before the teller could make introductions.

"Yes. I'm Steve Klein. Was there something I can help you with?"

"I was hoping to have a look at my necklace. I don't want to take it out of the bank or anything, but I've never seen it in person and I really would love to."

"I don't understand…" The manager frowned.

"This woman claims to own the Missing Thorndike," the teller explained.

"I'm afraid that's not possible." The manager sounded far less friendly than he had a moment before.

Cheryl put out her hand and said, "I'm Danielle Boatman's cousin, Cheryl Hartford."

"I still don't understand," the manager mumbled as he shook Cheryl's hand.

"Dani and I are the only remaining members of our great-aunt's family. Aunt Brianna meant to leave the estate to both of us, but I'm afraid she had Alzheimer's during her last years, and sadly…well, she forgot about me. I know Aunt Brianna would never have intentionally left me out of her will. She was such a dear."

"I really don't see how any of that is the bank's business," Steve said.

"Well, you have our necklace here. So naturally I want to see it, since it belongs to me too."

"Ms. Hartford, unless your name is on the safety deposit box," Steve began.

"It's not here anyway," the teller interrupted.

"What do you mean?" Cheryl asked.

"Why, Ms. Boatman left not forty-five minutes ago with the necklace."

"The necklace isn't here?" Cheryl asked angrily.

"I'm afraid not," the teller said.

Without saying another word, Cheryl turned and stormed to the exit.

"Susan, I really wish you hadn't told her that," Steve said after Cheryl left the bank.

"But it isn't here."

"I understand that. But it's not in our customers' best interest for us to be informing strangers when they leave the bank carrying something of such value. What one of our customers takes out of their safety deposit box is no one else's business."

"I'm sorry, Mr. Klein. I didn't think. But she said she was Ms. Boatman's cousin. Anyway, everyone knows she intends to wear the necklace during tomorrow's open house. So it's not really a secret the necklace is going to be out of the bank."

"Damn foolish if you ask me. Wearing something like that. Just asking for trouble. I wonder if that woman really is who she says she is," Steve mumbled.

Steve was about to go to his office and call Marlow House to verify the fact the woman who identified herself as Cheryl Hartford was indeed Danielle's cousin when Clarence Renton walked into the bank. Steve quickly excused himself from the teller and went to Renton.

"Clarence, I was hoping you could answer a quick question for me."

"If I can. What's the problem?"

"Did you see that woman who just left the bank a few minutes ago?"

"The blonde with the generous rack?" Clarence whispered.

"Damn, Clarence, no way for you to talk." Steve stifled a chuckle.

"I may be old, but I'm not dead. Good-looking woman, what about her?"

"Do you know if she's Danielle Boatman's cousin?"

"You mean Cheryl Hartford?" Clarence glanced at the doorway he had just entered.

"So she is the cousin?" Steve asked.

"I don't know if she's the cousin. I've never met her before. But I know Ms. Boatman's cousin is here in Frederickport, staying at Marlow House."

"She says she owns half of the Marlow estate."

"Well, she is making that claim. Off the record, mind you. Just between you and me, Steve."

"Is it valid?"

"Enough that it's upset Ms. Boatman. Don't repeat me. But you know how it is, someone dies and all the distant relatives crawl out of the woodwork."

"She wanted to see the necklace."

"Did you explain to her you can't simply open someone's safety deposit box just because they want a peek inside?" Clarence laughed at the idea.

"I started to, but then Mrs. Mitchell blurted out that the necklace isn't here."

"So she's really going to wear it at the open house?" Clarence asked.

"I guess so. She calls it publicity. I call it foolishness."

THIRTEEN

"I think I've just died and gone to heaven," Adam Nichols mumbled under his breath as he watched the buxom blonde breeze through the doorway of Lucy's Diner. Alone at his booth, he sipped his water and watched as she glanced around the diner, looking for a free table. Even the lunch counter was full.

Cheryl stood at the entrance of the diner, a few feet from Adam's booth. The sign at the entrance said *seat yourself*, yet she didn't see any openings. The kitchen and lunch counter were to her left, with a line of booths to her right and tables directly ahead. From the kitchen area, a waitress rushed in her direction, carrying a tray with four lunch plates. Cheryl attempted to flag her down.

"I'm afraid it will be a thirty-minute wait," the harried waitress told Cheryl as she rushed by.

"Thirty minutes?" Cheryl groaned, again looking around for someplace to sit.

"It's the beginning of a holiday weekend," Adam called out. "Always gets crazy around here this time of year."

"It isn't the weekend yet, and I'm starved!" Cheryl stomped a foot in frustration.

"You're welcome to join me. The waitress hasn't taken my order yet. In fact, I'd be honored to buy you lunch."

She turned to his booth and smiled. "Really?" Pausing a moment, she asked, "How do I know you aren't a serial killer?"

"I grew up in this town, just ask the waitress. We haven't had a mad killing spree in Frederickport since—well, since ever. So if I am a serial killer, I obviously go out of town to find my victims, so you're safe."

Walking closer to Adam's booth, Cheryl giggled then asked, "But why would you want to buy me lunch?"

"I hate eating alone. But mostly, you're a very beautiful woman—which I'm sure you already know. What man wouldn't willingly buy you lunch just to have the pleasure of your company for a few hours?"

"A few hours? That is a rather long lunch, isn't it?" Cheryl said as she sat down in the booth.

"What can I say, I'm an optimist." Adam reached across the table and offered his hand in greeting. "I'm Adam Nichols. I promise I am a respectable local businessman; I own Frederickport Vacation Properties."

Cheryl accepted his hand and gave it a brief shake. "I'm Cheryl Hartford. I'm staying at Marlow House. Do you know it?" She picked up a menu from the end of the table and opened it.

"Marlow House? Why sure. Who doesn't? Big party there tomorrow. I was under the impression they weren't taking guests yet."

"Oh, I'm not a guest. I'm Danielle Boatman's cousin." Cheryl looked through the menu.

"Ahh, well, maybe you shouldn't be sitting with me. Danielle Boatman isn't particularly fond of me."

"She isn't?" Cheryl set the menu down and looked at Adam.

"Well…has she mentioned anything about me?"

"No. Why would she?"

"Let's just say she got the wrong impression. Since then, well, I don't think she's thrilled with me."

Cheryl quietly considered the possibilities for a few moments before saying, "Ahh, I understand."

"You do?"

"I can only think of one reason my cousin would have a problem with such a handsome and charming man—the scorned woman."

"Scorned woman?"

"She thought you liked her more than you did—and when she found out you didn't share her feelings, she got all…well…you know. That's just Dani. She could never take rejection well. I guess this means you won't be at the party tomorrow."

"No. I'm going to be there. She's friends with my grandmother, and I've promised Grandma I'd take her."

"That's sweet of you, taking your grandma."

A moment later the waitress came to the table and took their order, then left to get their beverages.

"I hope you won't be angry at me, but I'm afraid it's going to be impossible for me to sit here without staring at you. You've got to be one of the most beautiful—no, possibly the most beautiful woman I've ever seen. Are you a model or something?"

"Oh…" Cheryl blushed. "Actually, I have done a little modeling. Of course, they want stick figures, and I just have too many curves."

"Yes. I can see that. All in the right places, if you don't mind me saying."

"Oh, you are very naughty, Adam Nichols!" Cheryl giggled.

"I guess you just bring out the naughty in me."

"It isn't easy looking like me." Cheryl sighed dramatically.

"It isn't? I would think the world would fall at your feet."

"No." Cheryl shook her head. "Take my cousin, Dani, for instance. She has always been so jealous of me. It really isn't my fault I look like this!"

"That's a shame. Danielle shouldn't be jealous of you."

"She shouldn't?" Cheryl frowned.

"Why no, I mean Danielle is also an attractive woman."

"Do you think she's as pretty as me?" Cheryl sounded offended.

"Oh no…" Adam said quickly, realizing his blunder. "I just meant she is an attractive woman, not as beautiful as you, of course. But she should be able to appreciate her beautiful cousin without being jealous."

"Yes," Cheryl said, pleased with Adam's explanation. "I agree."

"Is this your first time in Frederickport?"

"Yes. I just learned recently about Aunt Brianna's death."

"Brianna? You mean the one who left Danielle Boatman Marlow House?"

"Yes. But that is a mistake. It was supposed to go to both of us."

"I hadn't heard that."

"My great-aunt had Alzheimer's and became forgetful in her later years. Dani and I were her only remaining relatives, and it was the horrid disease that made her forget to mention me in the will."

"If she wasn't in her right mind, how could she execute a will?"

"Exactly! That's what my lawyer back home told me too. You know, no one even told me my aunt had died. Dani certainly never contacted me. But why would she? She obviously wanted to keep me in the dark, hoping I would never find out. But after that article came out about the necklace, well, I hired a private detective. I was shocked to hear Aunt Brianna had Alzheimer's."

"I assume you're going to contest the will?"

"Of course!"

"Is she still selling the necklace next week?"

"How did you know about that?" Cheryl asked.

"Like I said, she and my grandmother are friends. But it's pretty common knowledge around here."

"Well, not if I have anything to say about it!"

"You don't want to sell it? I heard it's worth over a million bucks."

"I'm not sure. I'd like to look at it first. Try it on. How thrilling to wear something that exquisite!"

"I'd love to see it on you. The Missing Thorndike needs to be worn by someone like you to do it justice."

"You do know how to flatter a girl." Cheryl reached over and patted Adam's hand. "Why is it again they call it the Missing Thorndike?"

"Because it belonged to the silent screen star Eva Thorndike."

"You mean silent movies?"

"Yes. I guess she was pretty famous back in her day. The Thorndikes had money. They used to spend summers here, starting back before Eva became famous. The necklace was a family heirloom. When Eva died, the necklace went missing. It became known as the Missing Thorndike."

"And Walt Marlow stole it?"

"It appears so. Your cousin found it in the attic."

"Well, maybe when all this is resolved, the estate that is, I'll simply keep the necklace."

"You can afford to do that?"

"Of course." Cheryl laughed. "I don't need the money from my aunt's estate. It's simply a matter of principle. And…well, I do love diamonds and emeralds."

"It's really too bad your cousin doesn't like me. I think you and I could have a lot of fun together."

The next moment the server brought their beverages.

"What does Dani have to do with it?" Cheryl asked after the waitress left their table.

"For one thing, about now I'd love to ask you if I could call you while you're here, maybe I could take you out to dinner, show you around the area. But with you staying with your cousin and with what she now thinks of me, well, I wouldn't want to do anything to make you uncomfortable."

"Don't be silly. Dani and I rarely agree on anything. In fact, I would love for you to be my date at the party tomorrow. Oh, I know you have to bring your grandma and everything, but after you get there. I imagine she already knows most of those people. You don't have to stay by her side, do you?"

"I certainly don't. Grandma will be perfectly fine once we get to the party. I'd be honored to be your date. But are you sure?"

"Yes, I am. And if you think about it, it will be our second date."

"It will?" Adam smiled.

"Why certainly. After all, you're buying my lunch today." Cheryl smiled sweetly.

"So tell me, Cheryl, do you ever kiss on the first date?" Adam teased.

"Well…sometimes." Cheryl's eyes flashed to the table and then back up to Adam. The corners of her mouth turned into a smile.

"Really?" Adam grinned.

Before Cheryl could respond, the waitress brought their lunch.

"You know, it really isn't your fault Dani wasn't your type. It's wrong of her to be mad at you," Cheryl said after the waitress left the table.

Cheryl was just about to pick up her fork when Adam reached across the table and placed his hand over hers. "You are definitely my type."

"I am?" Cheryl whispered.

"Oh yeah." He squeezed her hand.

"You think I'm sexier than my cousin?"

"There is no comparison." Adam gave Cheryl's hand another squeeze and then let it go. He picked up his burger and took a bite.

"Oh, you must think I'm terribly forward!" Cheryl folded and unfolded her napkin.

"I can tell you're an honest woman. One who doesn't play games."

"That's so sweet of you to notice," Cheryl said. "So…tell me about your business. Do you just manage other people's properties, or do you have your own rentals?"

"Both. My great-grandfather was one of the original Frederickport pioneers. He and my grandparents acquired quite a bit of property over the years, and of course, I've picked up a few along the way."

"I'm impressed. Do you have anything right on the beach?"

"Are you looking for something?" Adam asked.

"I'll admit I was a little disappointed Marlow House isn't right on the ocean. If the man who built the house really founded this town, why didn't he build the house closer?"

"Some people don't want to be that close to the water. Not sure why Frederick Marlow built his house where he did. As for your question, yes, I have several beachfront properties. Of course, those are typically booked up several years in advance."

"I suppose I can understand that. And that's great for you, to keep them rented."

"Actually, I do have a beachfront house that's vacant right now."

"I thought you said they're normally booked up several years in advance?"

"Normally, that's true. The family that rents this property has been coming every summer for six—no, seven years now. Just weeks after they arrived this season, there was a death in their family. Packed up and went back home. They won't be coming back this summer."

"So it's empty?"

"Yes."

"I'd love to see it."

"You would?"

"I don't know if staying at Marlow House while we settle my aunt's estate is going to work out for me. Dani doesn't want me. She's made that clear enough. I may need someplace to stay for a while, and I would love a place right on the ocean."

"If you want, I'd be happy to take you over there after we finish lunch."

"I'd love that!"

FOURTEEN

The front door to Marlow House was unlocked when Cheryl returned later that afternoon. She found Danielle in the parlor with Lily, Ian, and a man she had never seen before. The four stood in the middle of the room, laughing at something one of them had just said but stopped when she barged into the room.

"Where is it?" Cheryl demanded, her eyes darting about the room.

"Well, hello to you too," Lily muttered under her breath.

Walt suddenly appeared, standing next to Cheryl. "Has the party already started?" he asked.

"Where is what?" Danielle asked, trying to ignore Walt, who had just walked over to the sofa and sat down.

Cheryl turned to the man she didn't know and asked, "Who are you?"

"I bet you're the cousin," he answered with a grin.

"This is Joe Morelli," Danielle introduced. "Joe, this is Cheryl, the cousin I was telling you about."

Joe started to put out his hand in greeting and say hello, but Cheryl abruptly turned from him without acknowledging the introduction and asked Danielle, "Where is the necklace? I want to see it."

"It's already locked up in the safe," Danielle explained.

"What safe?"

"When did you leave this morning?" Lily asked. "We never heard you leave."

Cheryl looked over to Lily and snapped, "I didn't know I was supposed to inform you of my comings and goings." She turned back to Danielle and said, "I stopped at the bank. I wanted to see our necklace, but they told me you took it out of the vault."

"Not a vault exactly, more like a safety deposit box. And what were they doing, telling you about my business?"

"It's my business too."

"I'm going to have a little talk with that bank manager," Danielle grumbled.

Cheryl stomped her foot impatiently and said, "So where is it? Go get it. I want to see it!"

"Is your cousin always so demanding?" Walt asked.

"I told you, I already put it in the safe. You can see it tomorrow when I wear it to the open house."

Ian and Joe watched silently from the sidelines, occasionally exchanging glances.

"You're wearing it to the open house, here? Are you crazy? I forbid it!" Cheryl stomped her foot again.

"Your cousin reminds me of a horse when she does that," Walt noted. "Pawing the ground with her hoof." Danielle glanced over to Walt, trying her best to suppress her giggles.

"You forbid it?" Lily asked.

"This is none of your business, Lily. It is between me and my cousin," Cheryl said, again bringing the heel of her shoe down hard against the wood floor.

"I swear, if you stomp your foot one more time, I will start stomping mine—on top of yours!" Danielle warned. "You're going to scratch the wood floor with your damn heels, if you haven't already."

"You do know the front door was unlocked. Anyone could just walk in here," Cheryl said.

"Yes, I know that," Danielle said dryly. "You just did."

"I assume the safe you're talking about is somewhere in this house?" Cheryl glanced around. "It isn't in this room, is it? I don't think it would be wise to have a safe in the front of the house."

"That's none of your business," Danielle said.

"This house is half mine!" Cheryl started to stomp her foot again, but Danielle flashed a threatening look and picked up her own foot, daring Cheryl to proceed. Reluctantly, Cheryl set her foot back on the floor and forced her feet to stay still.

"I rather wish she would have attempted it," Walt said with a chuckle. "Curious to see if you'd carry through with the threat."

Ignoring Walt, Danielle said, "That is still to be determined. But one thing I do know, I paid for the safe with my own money, so keep your hands off it."

Cheryl turned to Joe again and asked angrily, "Who are you again?"

"I'm Sergeant Morelli, a friend of Danielle's. I escorted her home from the bank—you know, to keep her and the necklace safe."

"Really?" Cheryl's expression softened. "Does that mean you're staying here to guard it?"

"Joe isn't an armed guard. He works at the local police station. He was just doing me a favor," Danielle explained.

Joanne Johnson walked into the parlor and announced, "I finished upstairs, all except the—"

"Who are you?" Cheryl interrupted.

"Cheryl, please stop blurting out *who are you* every time you run into someone you don't know. Tomorrow this house is going to be filled with people you don't know, and if you greet everyone with the same snotty question, you're not going to make my guests feel very welcome."

"You know how I feel about turning this house into a bed and breakfast! I don't want strangers constantly coming and going."

"In all fairness to your cousin," Walt said, "I did feel the same way at first."

Joanne stood silently at the doorway, studying Cheryl. She knew Danielle's cousin was visiting; in fact, she had come downstairs to ask about the room Cheryl was staying in. It was the only room on the second floor she hadn't touched.

"We can talk about that later, Cheryl." Danielle turned her attention to Joanne and asked, "What were you saying?"

Cheryl flashed her cousin a dirty look and then went to the sofa. She flopped down, not realizing the seat was already taken. Walt let out a little shout and stood up abruptly, his body moving through Cheryl's. Grumbling, he scooted over and sat next to her on the couch.

Silently, Ian took a seat on one of the leather chairs, pulling Lily with him. She sat on his lap.

"I finished the second floor, but I haven't done anything with the Red Room yet. Do you want me to put the clothes in the closet? There's also the stuff on the dresser," Joanne began.

"That's my room!" Cheryl jumped up. "What are you doing in my room?"

"Joanne is cleaning the house for the party," Danielle explained. "You promised to straighten the room."

"I told you I'd do that in the morning before the party," Cheryl said.

"I'm sorry, but I really can't vacuum in there or dust with everything all over the floor," Joanne explained.

"I said I'll take care of it!" Cheryl snapped.

"There is no reason to be rude to Joanne. She's just here to do her job," Danielle said.

Cheryl looked from Danielle to Joanne. She guessed Joanne was in her fifties. Dressed in denim jeans and a button-down, short-sleeved cotton blouse, the cleaning woman fidgeted nervously with a rag.

"I'm sorry. We have not been introduced; you're the cleaning woman? Joanne, is it?" Cheryl asked sweetly.

"Yes, Joanne Johnson. I've been cleaning Marlow House for years. I worked for Ms. Boatman's aunt."

Tired of standing, Joe sat in the chair next to Ian and Lily. The three exchanged glances, yet withheld comment.

"She was my aunt too. I'm Cheryl Hartford; I was also Brianna's great-niece. I'm one of the owners of Marlow House," Cheryl explained.

"Cheryl, please stop saying that!" Danielle said impatiently.

"Well, it's true!"

"She is a bit of a bulldog, isn't she?" Walt observed. "Gets ahold of something and won't let go."

"You don't know that," Danielle told Cheryl.

"Excuse me, but what do you want me to do with the room?" Joanne interrupted.

Danielle looked from Joanne to Cheryl and then back to Joanne. "I guess leave it. Cheryl can clean it up in the morning."

"Okay. That's all I wanted to know. I'm going to go up now and see what I need to do in the attic." Joanne made a hasty exit.

"I think you two scared poor Joanne," Ian said with a chuckle.

"I just wish she'd stop saying she owns Marlow House!" Danielle said impatiently.

"Now you know how I felt when you first arrived," Walt told her.

"I'm sorry, Dani, but it is the truth, you know it," Cheryl said.

"I think Danielle has a point, Cheryl," Ian interrupted. "At least until this gets straightened out in court. For now, the house legally belongs to your cousin, and she's been working very hard on this open house. It's really not fair of you to barge in and disrupt everything, maybe even ruin the open house."

"I don't intend to ruin anything," Cheryl said defensively.

"Causing a scene—stirring up controversy—you don't think that could potentially ruin Danielle's promotion for the bed and breakfast?"

"It's not my intent to ruin anything, but I don't think she should turn this place into a bed and breakfast."

"Let me ask you this, Cheryl," Ian said in a serious voice. "Let's say the court decides you have no claim on the estate, that Danielle is the rightful heir. She is an adult and has the right to decide what she wants to do with her life—the same as all of us. But if you, in your false belief that half of the estate is yours, disrupt the opening for her business, even damage her reputation by implying she's trying to cheat you—you return to California to your own life while Danielle stays here and is left to clean up the mess you've created. Do you honestly think that's fair?"

"What I think is unfair," Cheryl said angrily, "is being cheated out of my inheritance!" She turned to the doorway and marched from the parlor.

Those left in the room stared mutely at the doorway and listened as Cheryl noisily made her way up the stairs to the second floor of Marlow House.

"Wow, Ian," Danielle said at last, turning from the open doorway to where Ian sat in the chair with Lily. "Thanks. I really appreciate your support."

"I meant it," Ian told her.

Lily turned in Ian's lap. Wrapping her arms around his neck, she pulled him close, kissing his cheek. "Well said, Ian."

"All I can say," Joe said as he stood up to leave, "I haven't seen that much drama since Millie Samson accused Joyce Pruitt of stealing her strawberry preserve recipe after Joyce won first place at the county fair."

UPSTAIRS, Cheryl found Joanne in the attic, preparing to clean the windows.

"I wanted to apologize for being so abrupt with you down there," Cheryl said after she walked into the attic.

Joanne turned and faced her. "I got the impression you were angry at your cousin, not at me. I think I stepped into the crossfire."

"It's just that Dani so infuriates me! She knows Aunt Brianna left this house to both of us."

Joanne didn't know how to respond, so she said nothing.

"Did you know my aunt?" Cheryl asked.

"I worked for her for years, but we never met in person. We did speak on the phone."

"Did she ever mention me?" Cheryl asked.

"She mentioned a niece. I always assumed she was talking about Danielle."

"Did she say Danielle?" Cheryl asked. "When she was talking about her niece, did she say her name was Danielle?"

"Honestly, I don't remember."

"Do you know where the safe is?" Cheryl asked.

"The safe?"

"Danielle had a safe installed for the Missing Thorndike. I want to make sure it's in a secure place; after all, it belongs to me too."

"You'll have to ask your cousin about that. If you'll excuse me, I really need to finish up in here." Joanne turned to the window, her back now facing Cheryl.

Cheryl sighed impatiently and then turned back to the doorway and headed downstairs to search for the safe.

FIFTEEN

Early Friday morning, Ian helped Lily drape red, white, and blue fabric bunting along the top of the fencing surrounding Marlow House. Clusters of white stars filled the navy blue top portion of the bunting's half circles, while red and white stripes trimmed the bunting's lower edge. Before Ian arrived to help, Lily had inserted the flagpole Danielle had purchased at the local hardware store into its holder on the porch wall, next to the front door.

The grounds surrounding Marlow House no longer resembled an unruly jungle. The gardener had transformed the yards into an impressive parklike setting, with freshly mowed green lawns and manicured flowering shrubbery. None of the shade trees had been removed, yet those too had been meticulously groomed. Lily planned to unlock and open the wrought-iron double gate leading to the side and backyards of Marlow House to provide easier access for the guests to come and go.

Inside, Danielle organized food for the festivities. Cheryl was still in bed. Lily and Danielle had decided to let her sleep as long as possible to keep her out of their way. The delivery van with the rental lawn furniture Danielle had ordered was arriving at 10 a.m. It would be Lily's job to arrange the white plastic lawn furniture in the back and side yards to provide outdoor seating for the guests.

Overhead the sun was shining with only a smattering of white puffy clouds in the blue sky. According to the weather report, it was going to be a sunny day with temperatures in the low eighties. That was a little warmer than recent weather, which suited Danielle. The slight morning breeze gently rustled the patriotic bunting and brought life to the new American flag hanging by the front porch.

Before attending to her kitchen duties, Danielle had opened all the windows on the lower floor, filling Marlow House with fresh beach air. Walt stood silently at the open parlor window, drinking in the bracing scent. Why he was unable to smell the fresh air prior to Danielle's arrival, he was unsure. But the why and how did not concern him. He was simply appreciative that he could now enjoy the gift.

Walt could hear the sounds of Ian and Lily's laughter and playful banter drifting in from outside as they decorated the grounds. At one time, he had been suspicious of Ian, but he had come to accept his presence and no longer believed he held some dark secret. Walt reminded himself that perhaps he should have listened to Sadie. After all, Sadie trusted the man in spite of the fact Ian had lied to Danielle and Lily about what he did for a living.

Glancing down, Walt looked at Sadie, who slept soundly in the space occupied by his feet, which wore—as they did every day—polished dress shoes. These days the dog seemed to spend more time at Marlow House than at the rental across the street, where she lived with Ian. Walt would miss Sadie when she left at the end of the summer to return to California with Ian. He wondered if he should convince Danielle to get a dog.

Hearing whom he thought was Danielle walking down the entry hall to the parlor, Walt moved from the window to the open doorway. It wasn't Danielle but her cousin, and by the way she carried her shoes and kept looking back to the door leading to the kitchen, it was obvious to him she did not want her cousin to know she was up.

Unaware of Walt's presence, Cheryl walked through his body and into the parlor and then gently closed the door behind her, leaving half of Walt's body still in the room. Annoyed, he let out a grunt and stepped back into the parlor.

Cheryl let out a cry of surprise when she saw Sadie. "What are you doing in here?"

Instead of greeting the new arrival, Sadie lifted her head briefly and looked at Cheryl then glanced over at Walt before laying her chin back down on her front paws.

"Yes, Sadie, she is annoying," Walt agreed.

"I suppose I can't stick you out in the hallway. I really don't need to get Danielle's attention. Damn dogs."

Walt watched as Cheryl stepped over Sadie, walked to the window, and looked outside, eavesdropping for a moment on Ian and Lily.

"I don't understand what he sees in her," Cheryl muttered under her breath. "But I sure as hell am not going outside and getting roped into some silly job or letting my cousin put me to work in the kitchen."

Moving from the window, Cheryl grabbed a magazine, sat down on the sofa, and began flipping through its pages. Walt walked to the sofa and looked down at the unaware young woman, who now had her bare feet propped up on the far arm of the small sofa as she leaned against the opposing arm. She had tossed her pink high-heel shoes on the side table, and he assumed she intended to slip them on when the guests started arriving. The careless manner in which she dumped her hard spiky shoes on the cherry wood tabletop annoyed him. She obviously was not concerned about scratching the furniture.

She reminded him of a flapper, the way the pink fabric of her short summer dress revealed a generous portion of thigh. If her hem hiked up another inch, he would have a clear view of her underpants.

FIDGETING with the radio in the kitchen, Danielle searched for a music station. Preoccupied with the task, she didn't notice Joanne coming through the kitchen door.

"Good morning," Joanne greeted her as she entered the kitchen, closing the door behind her.

Danielle looked up from the radio and turned to Joanne. "Morning."

Joanne set her purse on the kitchen counter and said, "Lily and Ian are doing a wonderful job decorating. It looks very patriotic out there."

"One thing you can say about second grade teachers, they know how to decorate for the holidays." Danielle laughed.

"What would you like me to do first?" Joanne asked.

Danielle considered the question for a moment then said guiltily, "This morning I was moving one of the plants in the library and I tripped and got potting soil everywhere. I salvaged the plant, but I'm afraid I didn't finish cleaning the mess; I got sidetracked. Sorry about that. Think you can finish cleaning it up?"

"Certainly." Joanne smiled.

"Also, go up in my room and get the brochures, I left them on my dresser. They go on the table in the library, where I have the business cards. After that, I guess just help Lily and Ian. I'm going to head upstairs in a few minutes and take my shower."

"Okay, I'm on it."

"Thanks, Joanne."

"No problem."

En route to Danielle's bedroom to pick up the brochures, Joanne passed the door to Cheryl's room. It was closed with a note attached. Taking a closer look, Joanne read the note: *Private Residence, do not enter.*

Remembering how the room had looked yesterday and Cheryl's promise to clean it, Joanne hesitantly knocked on the door. There was no answer. Ignoring the note, Joanne opened the door and peeked inside the room. Articles of clothing and towels littered the unmade bed and floor. Strewn atop the dresser were makeup and toiletry items. Propped against the far wall was Cheryl's open suitcase, half filled with clothing.

There was no sign of Cheryl. Joanne walked into the room and looked around. Reaching down, she picked up one of the towels. It was still wet. Shaking her head, Joanne tossed the towel onto the bed.

"I better ask Danielle if she wants me to clean this up," Joanne said aloud.

She left Cheryl's room, shutting the door behind her. After picking up the brochures from Danielle's room and a broom from the storage closet in the hallway, Joanne headed to the library.

SILENTLY WATCHING CHERYL, Walt wondered if she had done the one thing Danielle had requested—clean the bedroom she was using. That morning when Walt had peeked in the room while Cheryl slept it actually looked worse than it had the day before. He couldn't imagine it was possible for her to have straightened it since that time. It was obvious she had spent a good portion of the morning applying her makeup and fixing her hair.

Leaving Cheryl on the sofa, Walt moved from the parlor to the entry hall. En route to the stairs, he looked into the kitchen and saw Danielle, who was cheerfully plating food for the open house while moving to the beat of the music playing from the radio.

Continuing down the hall, he paused a moment at the open door of the library. There he saw Joanne, who was busy arranging something on a table.

When Walt finally arrived at the Red Room, the door was closed. He took a moment to read the attached note before walking through the wall into the room. Walt looked around and shook his head in disgust.

He glanced at the nightstand clock. Guests would start arriving in a couple hours. That was assuming there would be no early bird arrivals, those who liked to show up unfashionably early for a party. Danielle, Lily, and Joanne had their hands full with the final touches for the open house, and it didn't look like Cheryl intended to clean the room. Apparently, her solution to the mess was to shut the door.

Walt focused his energy on the items strewn across the bed and floor. Clothing and towels lifted into the air and effortlessly made their way to the open suitcase. He then focused on the dresser, sending Cheryl's personal toiletry items—some of the jars still open—floating across the room to land in the pile of clothing and damp towels inside the suitcase. A clean, unworn blouse spilled from the luggage, not quite covered by the items added by Walt. Giving the blouse a nod, he watched it rise and wipe down the dresser, removing any evidence of spilled makeup and lotion. Before returning the crumpled and now stained garment to the suitcase, he used it as a dust rag to wipe down the rest of the furniture in the room, careful to use its clean side.

Directing his energy to the closet, he willed the doors to fly open. Looking back to the suitcase, he watched as the lid closed and the zipper secured the items inside. With minimal effort, the suitcase lifted from its place on the floor and drifted to the closet, then set itself on the top shelf before the closet doors closed.

All he had left to do was make the bed, which he did quickly. Satisfied with the results, he opened the bedroom door and removed the note and masking tape, making them into a tight wad before sending the litter sailing across the hallway, through the opened bathroom door, and into the trash bin.

He was about to go downstairs but paused when he heard someone coming up the staircase. If it was Cheryl, he decided it would be amusing to stick around and see her reaction to her room.

"There you are," Danielle greeted him in a whisper when she reached the top of the landing. "Is Cheryl still sleeping?"

"No, she's downstairs in the parlor with Sadie."

"I didn't know Sadie was inside. But I did see the parlor door shut. I'm glad to hear Cheryl's up. I need to take a quick shower, and I wanted to see if she ever cleaned up her room like she promised. If I have to do it, I'd rather do it before I take my shower."

"Are you done in the kitchen?"

"Yes. Oh, do you think you can keep an eye on Sadie in case Cheryl lets her out of the parlor? She's never been a food thief before, but I'd rather her not jump up on one of the counters and help herself. Plus, chocolate is bad for dogs, and I think I overdid the chocolate goodies," Danielle said as she made her way to the Red Room.

"I'll have a little talk with Sadie," Walt said as he watched Danielle look in Cheryl's room.

"Wow, she did it." Danielle couldn't believe what she was seeing.

"Not exactly." Walt stepped to the doorway with Danielle and looked inside the room.

"What do you mean?" Danielle glanced up at Walt.

"Your cousin is a slob. I knew you and Lily had your hands full, so I just wanted to help."

"You cleaned Cheryl's mess?"

"It wasn't hard. I simply put everything in her suitcase, wiped down the furniture, and made her bed."

"When you say you put everything back in her suitcase, what does that mean exactly?"

"Just that. All of her personal belongings she left lying around. Although, the wet towels were probably yours. You'll want to get those out of her suitcase later."

"Umm…when I glanced in here last night, I noticed her makeup on the dresser. You didn't by any chance put the lids back on her…well, lipstick, lotion…whatever…before putting her stuff in the suitcase?"

"No. Why should I? I just gathered everything that wasn't supposed to be here and put it in the suitcase."

"And where is the suitcase?"

"In the closet."

"Oh my…" Danielle didn't know if she should laugh or cry. "Well…thanks…but do you think you could do me another favor?"

"Certainly, what?"

"After your little talk with Sadie, could you try to convince Cheryl—without throwing a croquet set at her—to stay downstairs. I would prefer she not see how her room was cleaned up until after the guests leave tonight."

SIXTEEN

Lawn furniture dotted the side and backyards of Marlow House, suitable for groupings of four or six. Should a larger group wish to converge, it would be easy enough to rearrange the light-weight chairs and tables.

Small floral arrangements of red, white, and blue carnations—each adorned with a miniature American flag—decorated most of the tables. Inside there were additional flower arrangements, some more varied in their blossoms and larger than what was outside. Those had been sent over as congratulatory gifts from local merchants and friends Danielle had met since moving to Frederickport.

Earlier in the week, Danielle had discovered a treasure trove of antique platters and serving dishes stacked neatly in the bottom of the dining room hutch. Those she used to serve her culinary party treats. Keeping with the patriotic theme, she used fresh blueberries, strawberries, and raspberries to decorate many of the desserts.

An assortment of crackers, gourmet cheeses, rolled deli meats, and finger sandwiches filled platters. Candy bowls brimmed with confectioneries purchased from the local candy store. Bottles of beer and soda chilled in tubs filled with ice, and pitchers of brewed iced tea, garnished with freshly sliced lemons, waited to be poured.

Ian went home to get ready for the party, taking Sadie with him. After a quick shower and changing his clothes, he returned without the dog. When he entered the front door, Cheryl greeted him. She had what appeared to be chocolate frosting smeared across her bottom lip. He didn't say anything.

She seemed taller than the last time he had seen her. Glancing down, he immediately recognized her shoes—the same pair he had found under the parlor couch, which explained her new height.

"You're the first one to arrive!" Cheryl cheerfully announced.

"Actually, I've been here all morning." Ian walked inside and looked around. "Where are Lily and Danielle?"

"Getting dressed, I suppose. I figured someone had to be down here to welcome the guests."

Ian glanced at his watch. "They shouldn't be arriving for another half hour at least."

"You're here."

"Umm…yes, I am." Ian started to walk down the hall toward the kitchen.

"Where are you going?" Cheryl followed after him.

"To the kitchen."

"Don't you think you should wait in the parlor?"

"Why? I'm hungry, and I imagine with all this cooking Danielle's been doing, I'll find something."

"You can't take any food yet! Danielle told me I wasn't to eat anything until the guests arrived."

Ian paused a moment and looked at Cheryl. "Chocolate lipstick?"

Cheryl frowned a moment then realized what he was saying. Licking her lips, she removed the evidence of her snack. "I live here. I can eat whatever I want."

The sound of footsteps coming down the stairs interrupted their exchange.

"You clean up nice," Lily greeted him when she reached the landing and spied Ian standing outside the door of the kitchen.

"So do you," Ian said, stepping closer to Lily, leaving Cheryl standing alone by the kitchen doorway.

He reached out, touched the end of her braided hair, and said, "Red…" His hand dropped from the braid to the hem of her white shorts. Lightly touching the hem, he said, "White…" From the hem of the shorts, his hand moved upward and touched the navy blue collar of her crisp blue and white blouse and said, "And blue. Very patriotic."

Lily laughed and asked, "How do you like the braid? Dani did it."

"Very nice, but I rather like your hair wild and free."

"Like me?" Lily grinned.

Cheryl let out a snort. "*Oh, brother.*"

"You should see Dani; she looks amazing," Lily said, ignoring Cheryl's comment. "Of course, she couldn't dress casual like this and wear the necklace; that would look silly. She found a fabulous vintage dress at a little shop in town, and it fits her like a dream. She fixed her hair in a fishtail braid, looks so feminine. I wish I could braid hair like that. When I try to braid my own hair, I end up looking like Raggedy Ann."

"You don't look like Raggedy Ann now," Ian said with a chuckle.

"That's because Dani braided my hair, not me. I only know how to do a traditional braid."

"Well, I don't even know how to do that. But I don't think I'd look terrific in braids, so it has never been an issue." Ian laughed.

"Oh, funny." Lily gave Ian's arm a playful swat.

Disgusted with the conversation, Cheryl was about to go into the kitchen when she heard another set of footsteps coming down the staircase. Curious about her cousin's new dress and anxious to see the necklace, she stepped away from the kitchen door and walked toward Ian and Lily.

Walt was already standing unseen next to Lily and Ian. Looking to the staircase, he watched as Danielle appeared, wearing her new pale green dress and antique diamond and emerald necklace.

"You look beautiful," Walt whispered.

Danielle flashed him a smile.

"You look gorgeous," Ian said, letting out a whistle.

"Doesn't she?" Lily agreed.

"Let me see the necklace!" Cheryl rushed toward her cousin, groping her neck.

"Careful, Cheryl. You're going to break it." Danielle stepped back.

"Then take it off. Let me try it on!" Cheryl said excitedly.

"Not now. After everyone leaves, you can try it on. But not now." Danielle pushed Cheryl back. The doorbell rang.

"Behave yourself, Cheryl," Danielle hissed as she straightened her dress and watched to see who was at the door as Ian went to answer it. She suspected it was Joe Morelli, who had promised to arrive early.

"Security is here," Ian said with a laugh as he let Joe into the house.

"Wow, you even came in uniform," Danielle said with a grin.

"Hi, Joe," Lily greeted him.

"You really didn't need him," Walt scoffed. "I am here, after all."

"Ladies, you look lovely." He glanced over at Ian as if checking out his appearance and said with a shrug, "Ian, meh." Turning back to the women, he patted the gun in his holster and said, "According to the chief, I'm here on semiofficial business."

"Well, I sure as hell feel safer," Ian said dryly as he slammed the front door shut.

"You guys want a sandwich? I have a ton of food in the kitchen, and we have a while before guests start arriving," Danielle offered.

"Yes! I'm starving. Lily was a slave driver this morning!" Ian moaned.

"I try," Lily said with a grin.

"If the guests aren't arriving, then take off the necklace and let me try it on!" Cheryl stomped her right foot angrily.

"Knock it off, Cheryl, or I'll have Joe arrest you."

"Please, no domestic squabbles," Joe teased.

Determined to have a closer look, Cheryl reached out and grabbed hold of the necklace. Everyone but Walt had their backs to the cousins. Seeing what Cheryl was doing, Walt raised his hand and gave her a powerful shove, sending her stumbling backwards away from Danielle before falling onto the floor, landing on her bottom with a thud. The sound caught the attention of the others. They turned around quickly, surprised to find Cheryl sprawled on the floor.

"She hit me!" Cheryl screeched.

Joanne, who had been in the kitchen, heard the commotion and stepped out into the hall.

"I didn't touch you!" Danielle held the necklace protectively. To her surprise, it came off her neck. "But you apparently broke the necklace!"

"She assaulted me!" Cheryl wailed, grabbing her cheek, which was already starting to show evidence of bruising.

Joe walked over to Cheryl and put out his hand. She took it and stumbled to her feet, still holding onto her injured cheek.

"It's your own fault. You shouldn't have been grabbing at the necklace. If it had been me, I would have smacked you too." Lily walked to Danielle and inspected the damage.

"I didn't hit her," Danielle said weakly as Lily looked at the necklace.

"Looks like one of the little loops broke by the latch," Lily said.

Joe reached out and touched the side of Cheryl's face.

"Ouch!" Cheryl winced.

"Maybe you should put some ice on that," Joe suggested.

"I should have you arrest her!" Cheryl cried.

"I didn't see what happened," Joe said. "But if I did arrest her and she told the court you grabbed the necklace off her neck, I think you might end up in a bit of trouble yourself, considering what that necklace is worth."

"But it's half mine!"

"For the time being, legally the necklace belongs to Danielle. You have no rights to it. Maybe you can get the courts to overturn the terms of your aunt's will. But for now, keep your hands off the necklace. Do you understand?" Joe said.

Cheryl glared at Joe and then looked over at Lily, Ian, and Joanne, who silently stared in her direction. Stomping her foot again, she turned her back to them and marched to the parlor and threw open its door. Angrily she entered the room and slammed the door behind her.

"What am I going to do?" Danielle asked, looking at the necklace in her hands.

"There's some of that wire in the kitchen," Joanne suggested, "that Lily was using for some of the decorations. It's pretty thin but strong."

"That would work," Lily agreed. "For now, just resecure the latch with the wire. No one has to see it."

"Wonderful," Danielle scoffed. "A million-dollar necklace held together with craft wire."

"Just be happy it happened now and not at the party," Lily said as she led the way into the kitchen.

Once in the kitchen, Danielle handed the necklace to Joe, who offered to make the repair. Sitting at the kitchen table, she watched as he secured the latch to the chain using the wire. After the makeshift repair was complete, Joe handed the necklace back to Danielle.

"I really didn't hit her," Danielle said as she fastened the necklace back around her neck.

"I didn't see what happened," Joe said. "But it was probably just a reflex."

"Reflex?" Danielle asked with a frown.

"She was obviously hit on the face," Joe said. "You probably didn't even realize you'd done it."

"I'm sorry, Danielle," Walt said. "They think you hit your cousin. I didn't mean to hit her. I just wanted to push her away."

"Dani, Joe is right. The way she was grabbing at you, I don't blame you for knocking her on her butt," Lily said.

"But I didn't," Danielle said tersely.

SEVENTEEN

Danielle was in her room, touching up her makeup, when there was a knock at the bedroom door.

"Dani?" came Lily's voice from the hallway.

"Come in."

Lily opened the door and asked, "You okay?"

"I really didn't hit her. Where is everyone?"

"Downstairs in the kitchen, why?"

"It was Walt."

"Walt hit her? Is he here?" Lily glanced around the room. She sniffed the air but didn't notice any tobacco scent.

"No."

"Why did he hit her?"

"He didn't mean to. She was grabbing for the necklace, and he pushed her away. I'm afraid he pushed a little too hard and his aim wasn't terrific. Smacked her in the face."

"And knocked her on her butt. Serves her right."

"But everyone thinks I hit her."

"I know. We were talking about it in the kitchen. They don't really blame you. They sort of figure it was a knee-jerk reaction on your part. At least Ian and Joe think that."

"What does Joanne think?"

"She didn't say. Actually, she didn't say much."

"I don't go around hitting people!"

"I know that."

"But you thought I did."

"I'm sorry, Dani. I just figured if it was me, I would have knocked her on her butt already. To be honest, I was kinda proud of you, considering the crap she's been getting away with. Although, I noticed she cleaned her room. That surprised me."

"She didn't. It was Walt."

"What do you mean?"

"Walt. He was trying to help, so he dumped everything in her suitcase and made her bed. Put the suitcase in the closet."

"Well, good for him! Gotta love a ghost that cleans house!"

"I don't know about that. When I say he dumped everything in her suitcase, I mean that quite literally. She had makeup and crap all over the dresser, and he just dumped it with her clothes in the suitcase. I imagine when she opens it, everything is going to be stained with makeup and who knows what."

Lily started to laugh. "I really do like Walt!"

"Easy for you to say. There's going to be hell to pay when Cheryl opens her suitcase tonight."

"Let's worry about that later. We have a party to go to, and you look terrific. Come on, let's grab something to eat and try to forget about your annoying cousin."

Danielle went downstairs to the kitchen with Lily. She had just enough time to finish half a sandwich when the doorbell rang.

Ian glanced at his watch then said to Danielle, "You're on, kid."

"Let's get this party rolling!" Danielle said cheerfully.

By the time Danielle, Lily, Ian, and Joe reached the front door, Cheryl had already answered it. Standing in the entry was Marie Nichols and her grandson, Adam. Danielle greeted the elderly woman with a quick hug and was taken aback when she noticed Cheryl clinging to Adam's arm.

The group noisily exchanged greetings, and when Marie noticed Danielle eying her grandson and Cheryl, she reached over, patted her hand and whispered, "Oh, I am sorry, dear. I know we hoped something would work out between you and my grandson, but it seems your lovely cousin has snatched him up." Marie's whisper was loud enough for Cheryl to overhear. Cheryl glanced up and looked Danielle in the eyes, smiling. Taken aback by Marie's comment, Danielle wasn't sure how to respond.

"You've done a great job decorating Marlow House, Danielle.

Quite patriotic," Adam said. Danielle wasn't sure if he was ignoring his grandmother's comment or hadn't heard it. Since he and Joe had been talking at the time, it was possible he hadn't, even though Cheryl, who stood close by his side, had obviously heard it.

"Thank you, but Lily and Ian did most of it. And thanks for bringing your grandmother today," Danielle said politely.

"I wouldn't have missed it for the world." Adam grinned at Cheryl, who giggled and squeezed his arm.

"Am I missing something? Have you two met already?" Danielle asked.

"Seems they met yesterday," Marie explained.

"They met yesterday?" Danielle asked under her breath.

"So that's the necklace," Adam said, taking a step closer, pulling away from Cheryl. Diamonds and emerald sparkled, brightly illuminated by a ray of sunshine streaming in one of the windows. Adam let out a low whistle of appreciation.

"Just don't try to touch it, or she'll hit you," Cheryl said as she reached up to touch her bruised cheek.

"Oh, dear, what happened?" Marie took a closer look at the fresh bruise.

"Dani hit me."

"I did not hit you!" Danielle insisted.

The doorbell rang again.

"I can't believe Danielle would hit you on purpose. I'm sure it was an accident," Adam said, giving Danielle a kind smile. He took Cheryl by the arm and whispered, "Why don't you take me on a tour?"

"Your cousin has a peculiar sense of humor," Marie murmured. She watched her grandson and Cheryl walk toward the library.

Ian opened the front door and greeted the six people standing on the front porch. Danielle didn't have time to think about Cheryl. Guest after guest flooded into the house.

Joe stuck by Danielle's side as Ian and Lily played tour guides and led groups of visitors through Marlow House and then took them outside for refreshments. Joanne took charge of the food, intermittently taking fresh platters outside, refilling dishes, offering beverages, and cleaning up after the guests.

Danielle knew some of her guests but not all. Ben Smith and Millie Samson from the museum showed up, as did Samuel Hayman from the jewelry store. Danielle's attorney, Clarence

Renton, arrived about an hour after Marie and Adam. Steve Klein, the bank manager, showed up with his wife and several bank employees. They claimed they could only stay for a short time, yet ended up in the backyard, enjoying the refreshments and each other's company, and didn't seem in a hurry to leave. Danielle resisted the temptation to scold them for discussing her bank business with Cheryl. But the last thing she wanted was for Cheryl to overhear the conversation and start telling more people she'd hit her.

She was delightfully surprised when Astoria resident Emma Jackson showed up, accompanied by a young couple from Emma's church. Emma, the centenarian who had been an eyewitness many decades ago, had placed Walt Marlow's killer at the scene of the crime. On Lily's suggestion, Ian had arranged a meeting with Emma and had since decided to do an article and possibly a book on the woman's life.

Danielle spent most of her time mingling and modeling the Missing Thorndike while answering questions about Marlow House and what the bed and breakfast would offer to its guests. Yet it was the necklace that seemed to capture the most attention. Some people wanted to reach out and touch the brilliant stones, but Joe gently discouraged guests from handling the piece, reminding them the necklace was an antique.

It wasn't until after 2:00 p.m. that Danielle was able to tear herself away from her guests and grab something to eat. Joe excused himself to visit the restroom, believing Danielle and the necklace would be reasonably safe while he stepped away for a moment.

A number of the people who had stopped by had already left, but a group of twenty or more gathered in the backyard, taking advantage of the rented lawn furniture and enjoying the food Danielle had prepared, while a few more played croquet. New guests continued to arrive but at a trickle.

"I think your open house is a success," Lily said when she entered the kitchen a few minutes after Danielle. They were alone in the room.

"Seems like a good turnout. I'm trying to remember everyone's name. I should have had them wear name tags."

"What's with your cousin and Adam? Did you have any idea they knew each other?"

"Not a clue. According to Marie, they met yesterday. I guess

Cheryl asked him to be her date for today. Marie was rather tickled. I think she wants to get her grandson married off." Danielle shuddered at the idea.

"What in the world was Marie talking about? You and Adam?"

"Don't ask me. I don't know what that was about. If she only knew how I really felt."

"I about died when she said it. But you better be prepared for Ian after the party."

"Ian? What do you mean?"

"He thought it was pretty hilarious—you and Adam. Expect some teasing."

"Just tell him to be prepared. I might have to knock him on his butt. You know I can do it."

"Humm, right. With Walt's help. Speaking of Walt, is he here?" Lily glanced around the room.

"He was a minute ago. I think he's in the library."

"I thought he was going to stick by you and help watch over the necklace."

"I don't know. Maybe after knocking Cheryl on her butt, he decided he'd just leave the job to Joe." Danielle shrugged and looked out the kitchen window into the backyard.

Lily glanced outside and spotted Joanne talking to one of the guests. "That Joanne has sure been a big help today."

"You've all been so helpful. Couldn't have done this without you."

"No problem, it has been lots of fun. I've met some really nice people today."

Danielle pointed out the window and asked, "Who is that woman Joanne is talking to?"

"The one in the green straw hat?"

"Yes. I don't remember being introduced to her."

"I can't remember her name; her granddaughter keeps calling her Gran."

"She's here with her granddaughter?"

"Actually, with her grandchildren and daughter. See the five people hovering around her chair?"

Squinting her eyes to get a clearer view, Danielle studied the people standing around the elderly woman, who looked up from her chair, talking to Joanne. There were two women and three men.

"The shorter woman is the daughter. I remember her name,

Joyce. The others are Joyce's kids. I swear, the way those four hover around that woman you would think she was Queen Elizabeth."

"Doting family?"

"According to Marie," Lily explained, "the woman is loaded. Her husband invented something—what exactly I have no clue—and she is super rich but tighter than a tick. Marie's words. I guess she lives with Joyce, but the grandkids dote on her, just to make sure they're in grandma's will when the old broad kicks the bucket. Also Marie's words."

"Maybe they simply love their grandma? But I wonder, do you think Marie worries Adam is only nice to her so he stays in her will?"

"I don't think so. The way she looks at her grandson, I doubt she even considers that possibility. Is that what you think?"

"Actually, I sort of get the feeling the thief really does love his grandma." Danielle sighed.

"I was kind of surprised he stuck up for you this morning."

"What do you mean…oh, you mean about how it was probably an accident about me hitting Cheryl."

"Yes. Did you see the dirty look Cheryl gave him?" Lily asked.

"I missed that. But this whole Adam and Cheryl thing rather freaks me out."

"I know what you mean." Turning from the window to Danielle, Lily asked, "Are you and Joe going with us to the fireworks show later?"

"I considered it. But I really feel funny leaving the necklace here alone, even though it'll be in the safe."

"Walt will be here," Lily reminded her.

"I know. I'll think about it. Although, by the time everyone gets out of here and I put whatever food we have left away, I'll probably be ready to just put my feet up and crash."

"Ian and I will help you put the food away, and we can worry about cleaning up in the morning. Walt will take care of the necklace. I think you and Joe need to come with us. A fireworks show will be a fitting ending to your open house."

"Let me think about it."

EIGHTEEN

Clarence Renton stood alone under the shade of a maple tree along the outer perimeter of the side yard. He watched the Kleins playing croquet with several of the tellers from the bank. They kept laughing and seemed to be enjoying themselves.

Beyond the players and to their right were the tables and chairs set up for the day's event. Most of the chairs were occupied, and everyone seemed to be either eating or drinking while happily chatting away to those around them. Beyond the people and chairs was Marlow House.

Samuel Hayman, a can of beer in each hand, walked up to Clarence. "You looked thirsty." Samuel handed Clarence a beer.

"Thanks, Samuel. You must have read my mind." Clarence accepted the can and promptly opened it, taking a sip.

"Nice turnout," Samuel said, nodding toward the group of party guests. Standing under the tree, they watched the croquet players.

"I'd say it was a success," Clarence said.

"I'm sure most of them showed up to get a look at the Missing Thorndike."

"You're probably right." Clarence took another sip.

"I was wondering, do you think Brianna O'Malley knew that necklace was hidden in the house?" Samuel asked.

"If she did, she never said anything to me about it. But I don't see how she would have known."

"I think she might have. I was talking to Adam Nichols about it the other day, and according to Adam, his grandma knew about Walt Marlow stealing that necklace."

Clarence turned to Samuel. "It doesn't mean Brianna knew the necklace was in the house."

"Marie and Brianna O'Malley were friends," Samuel said.

"They were? I didn't know that."

"Yes, Adam claimed they were good friends." Samuel looked over the crowd and spied Cheryl with Adam. The two stood by the wine table. Before grabbing the beer, Samuel had considered pouring himself a glass of wine at the table. The bottles had already been opened, but each was loosely re-corked, waiting to be poured. He watched as Cheryl picked one up and pushed the cork into the bottle.

"That cousin is sure a good-looking woman." Samuel nodded toward Cheryl.

"Yes, she is." Clarence looked over at Cheryl and sipped his beer.

"Is it true she owns half this place and the necklace?"

"I really can't discuss that," Clarence said.

"Well, I guess Danielle Boatman isn't thrilled her cousin showed up. I heard she hit her."

"Good lord, Samuel, please don't be spreading rumors like that," Clarence said impatiently.

"It's not a rumor. Joanne told me she saw the bruise." Samuel continued to watch Cheryl, who tucked the bottle under one arm and ran toward the back gate. "What is she doing?"

"Looks like she's taking off with a bottle of wine." Clarence chuckled. The two men watched as Cheryl tucked the bottle into the bushes by the gate, looked around to see if anyone was watching, and then ran back to Adam.

"That's odd." Samuel frowned.

"Not really. I remember doing that. Of course, I was sixteen at the time, not an adult."

"What do you mean?"

"Come on, Samuel, when you were a teenager you never stole some of your parents' booze and stashed it in the bushes so you could get it when you went out later?"

"I never drank when I was a teenager," Samuel said seriously.

"Of course not. What was I thinking?" Clarence muttered.

"YOU WANT to play when they're done? It actually looks like fun," Cheryl asked Adam. She stood with him by the wine table, her arm looped around his. They watched the small group playing croquet.

"It sure looks like the set from the attic," Adam mumbled.

"You mean the attic here?" Cheryl glanced up to the attic window.

"Yeah. There was an old set up there. Looks just like this one… but it can't be the same one."

"I saw Lily bring it down from the attic. Why do you say it can't be the same one?"

"Because the other one…never mind." Adam shook his head. While Cheryl might claim to have issues with her cousin, he didn't want her to say anything that might get back to Danielle. Such as confirming the fact he knew about the special croquet set in the attic, the one that had been fitted with some sort of remote control device. That was the only explanation he could find for how the balls and mallets had hurled across the attic. He knew they hadn't flown across the room on their own. He couldn't believe Danielle would use that set today.

"Nice to see you again," Samuel Hayman greeted Cheryl as he walked up to the pair, carrying his now empty can of beer. "Adam, how are you doing?"

"Sam." Adam gave him a nod. "So you two already met?"

"Yes, we met yesterday when I stopped in his store," Cheryl explained.

"I expected Bill to be here. I understood he fixed the window after the break-in." Samuel tossed his empty can in the nearby trash bin.

"Who told you that?" Adam asked.

"What break-in?" Cheryl asked.

"Your grandmother mentioned it." Samuel looked from Adam to Cheryl. "Marlow House was broken into about a week after your cousin arrived. Someone broke the library window. But apparently, they didn't take anything."

"Was that before the necklace was found?" Cheryl asked.

"Yes," Samuel said.

"They must have been looking for the necklace! Who is this Bill?"

"He does some handyman work for me," Adam explained. "He had some other plans for today, and he's already seen the house, no reason to stop by again."

"I guess." Samuel shrugged. "Never considered whoever broke in was looking for the necklace."

"I doubt they were," Adam said. "Just some kids screwing around."

"Are you staying long?" Samuel asked Cheryl.

"I'm not sure. I need to get this inheritance thing straightened out with my cousin. I'm afraid this open house was a little too much for her. She's never been quite right since her husband was killed."

"I thought you told me you hadn't seen her for years?" Adam asked.

"Well, no, but I do try to keep an eye on her. After all, I am the only one she has left." Cheryl smiled sweetly.

"Have you tried the necklace on yet?" Samuel asked.

"No. I'm afraid Dani has been very selfish with it." Cheryl leaned toward Sam, pointed to her bruised cheek and whispered, "She even hit me over it!"

"I'm sure it was an accident," Adam said.

"You weren't here!" Cheryl flashed Adam an angry scowl and released hold of his arm.

"So she really did hit you," Samuel said.

"Yes. I just wanted to take a closer look, and she knocked me to the floor! Just like that!"

"Oh, Cheryl, I don't think—"

"You keep saying that, Adam! I'm beginning to think you do have feelings for my cousin. You weren't there! But they all saw it—Ian, that housekeeper, and the cop guy who is supposedly here to guard the necklace."

"Joe saw her hit you? What did he do?" Samuel asked.

"He didn't do anything. Claimed he didn't see exactly what happened. But he saw me on the floor. Saw my bruised face."

"I'm really sorry." Samuel shook his head. "She seemed so nice."

"You want to see where she found the necklace?" Cheryl asked.

"I heard it was in the attic, but I haven't been up there yet," Samuel said.

"Come, I'll show you." Cheryl started to walk toward the house with Samuel but paused when she realized Adam hadn't moved. She looked back at him. "You coming?" she asked impatiently.

Adam let out a sigh and reluctantly followed the pair. They entered the house through the kitchen door and found Lily and Danielle inside, talking to Joanne. The moment Cheryl spied Danielle, she immediately latched onto Adam's arm again, holding it possessively.

Polite hellos were exchanged as Cheryl and the two men made their way to the door leading to the hallway. Just as they reached the door, Cheryl glanced back toward Danielle, who was watching her and Adam. Impulsively, Cheryl leaned toward Adam and kissed his cheek.

"What was that for?" Adam asked when they stepped into the hall.

"I just wanted you to know how much I'm looking forward to tonight—just you and me—alone," Cheryl whispered.

When they reached the second floor, Samuel paused and said, "I haven't been up here yet."

"Not much to see, just a bunch of bedrooms." Cheryl shrugged. When she noticed the door to her room open, she frowned. "What the heck?" She marched to the doorway and looked inside.

"What's wrong?" Adam asked as he and Samuel walked to the doorway of the Red Room and looked inside.

"This is my room. I had the door closed with a note expressly stating for no one to go inside. How dare they! Is a little privacy too much to ask?" Cheryl looked at the back of the door and saw the note had been removed.

"This is a nice room," Samuel said, looking inside. "I understood all the rooms were going to be open for viewing."

"I wonder what she did with my stuff. Darn Dani. She makes me so mad!" Cheryl stomped her foot and then took a deep breath and calmed down. "Go ahead and look at the other rooms on this floor. I'm going to the bathroom, then we can go to the attic, and I'll show you where she found the necklace." Cheryl headed to the bathroom.

"She and her cousin certainly don't seem to get along," Samuel commented after Cheryl shut the bathroom door.

"That's an understatement," Adam said with a chuckle.

"So what's the deal, Adam, you dating her?"

"We just met yesterday, but yeah, I suppose we're dating."

Hasty footsteps were heard coming up the wood stairs. Both men looked toward the landing. It was Clarence Renton.

"Samuel, Adam," Clarence greeted them. Then he chuckled and said, "Damn, you two together make a beer."

Both men laughed and then Adam said, "I would have thought you'd already been through the house."

"Yes. I was coming up here to use one of the bathrooms. The ones downstairs are occupied. You two touring the house?" Clarence asked.

"We're waiting for Cheryl," Samuel explained, nodding toward the closed door of the nearby bathroom. "She's going to show us where Danielle found the necklace in the attic."

"I noticed you two seemed pretty chummy already," Clarence told Adam.

"What can I say, I'm irresistible." Adam laughed.

"Are you two going down to the fireworks later?" Samuel asked.

"Nah. I'm thinking something a little more private." Adam grinned. "Wine, nice little bungalow overlooking the ocean."

"Your house is a couple blocks from the beach," Samuel said.

"Who says I'm taking her to my house?" Adam grinned.

"If you go down by the beach, you'll see the fireworks anyway," Clarence reminded him.

"Can't see much from the south side," Adam said.

"I was thinking about going when I leave here. What about you, Samuel?" Clarence asked.

"I don't think so. I'm not really one for fireworks," Samuel said.

NINETEEN

Guests continued to come and go, and according to the clock in the library it was a few minutes past 5 p.m. Danielle suspected that by nightfall she could safely say a majority of Frederickport residents had toured Marlow House. At least, it seemed that way.

According to the invitations she had sent out, the open house ended at dusk. She suspected that by that time most people would be gone anyway, off to watch the firework show or to get together with their own families for a Fourth of July barbecue.

Many of the guests only stopped by for a short time, to get a look at the Missing Thorndike, have a quick tour of the house, and grab something to eat. But a few lingered, reluctant to leave.

In the library, Marie Nichols and Emma Jackson sat across from each other in the leather chairs, reminiscing about the early days of Frederickport as other guests leisurely moved in and out of the room while touring the house. Ian and Joe stood together at the library doorway, chatting, while Ian watched the front door for new arrivals, and Joe kept an eye on Danielle, who stood on the far side of the library with Lily.

"So that is little Marie," Walt said as he appeared, standing next to Danielle.

"Where have you been for the last hour?" Danielle asked.

Lily frowned and sniffed the air, then announced in a whisper, "Walt's here. Hello, Walt."

"I've been around. I can't tell if she looks like her mother or father." Walt eyed Marie. "The last time I saw them they were both much younger than she is now."

Samuel Hayman entered the library and after exchanging a few words with Ian and Joe, walked directly over to Marie. He placed a hand on her shoulder and then leaned down and whispered something into her ear. Marie laughed gaily. She reached up, patted his hand, and then said something to Emma. From where Danielle, Lily, and Walt stood, they couldn't hear what the three were discussing, but it looked as if Marie had just introduced Samuel to Emma.

"I thought Samuel had left," Lily murmured.

"Why did you think that?" Danielle asked.

"When I took some trash out a while ago, I saw him drive off in his car. Guess he decided to come back."

"That has to be Jacob Hayman's grandson. Looks just like him," Walt said.

"If that's the person who started the local jewelry store, yes."

"What are you guys talking about?" Lily asked in a whisper.

"The man who owns the jewelry store." Danielle nodded toward Samuel. "The one who appraised the necklace for us."

"Wait a minute," Walt said, looking curiously from Danielle to Samuel. "Are you telling me the jeweler who appraised the necklace for you is Jacob Hayman's grandson?"

"I don't know about that." Danielle shrugged. "You just said that has to be Jacob Hayman's grandson. I know that Samuel's grandfather founded the jewelry store he owns. So if your Jacob Hayman was the one who started the jewelry store, then yeah, that's his grandson."

"I hate this," Lily grumbled, annoyed that she could only hear Danielle's side of the conversation.

"I remember when Jacob opened the store. It was a couple of years before…well, before my untimely death. I always thought it was a strange coincidence he decided to open a store here."

"What do you mean?" Danielle asked.

"Jacob owned a jewelry store in Portland before opening one in Frederickport. From what I recall, he closed it down a few years before he opened one here. As for the coincidence I'm referring to, his Portland shop is where Eva had the necklace appraised. He's the one who told her the diamonds and emeralds were fake."

"Seriously?" Danielle looked over to Samuel, who chatted with Marie, unaware he was the subject of their conversation. "Was Jacob the one who did the appraisal?"

"His signature was on the document," Walt said.

"What? Come on, you have to tell me what he said!" Lily whined.

"The jeweler who told Eva Thorndike the diamonds and emeralds were fake was Samuel's grandfather," Danielle whispered to Lily. "Samuel's grandfather used to own a store in Portland. That's where Eva took the necklace when she suspected the stones had been switched."

"But why, why did he lie?" Lily asked.

"Tell Lily I wonder about that too. It really makes no sense. What did he have to gain by telling her they were fake?"

"Maybe he hoped she'd leave the necklace with him, and then he could take out the real diamonds and emeralds and put fake ones in," Danielle suggested.

"I always knew Jacob to be an honest man. I can't see him doing something like that. Eva never mentioned anything about him wanting her to leave the necklace with him."

"He wonders about that too. Says he thought Jacob was an honest man," Danielle said.

"Didn't Samuel mention that his grandfather opened up his shop in Frederickport after the Thorndike went missing?" Lily asked.

"Tell Lily he did. From what I remember, it was at least five years after Eva's death. I had no idea his store was still open—or that his grandson owned it now."

"Walt said he didn't open the store here until after Eva's death," Danielle said.

"How funny is that? The grandfather says the stones are fake—and the grandson insists they're real. Damn, what happens if the grandfather was right and the grandson is wrong?"

"It might get Cheryl out of my hair." Danielle smiled at the thought. "Although, I wouldn't hold my breath. If you'll recall, the insurance company insisted on having their own appraiser look at the necklace before they'd insure it. These damn stones are real."

"Where is your cousin, by the way? I've barely seen her?" Lily asked.

"I haven't seen her or Adam for a couple hours. I'm actually surprised she hasn't started bugging me again about trying on the necklace."

"Are you going to let her?" Lily asked.

"Yes. I really don't care if she tries it on. But knowing her, I was afraid she'd refuse to take it off, and I didn't want to wrestle her to the ground in front of my guests to get it back."

"If you ladies will excuse me," Walt said as he moved toward Marie, Emma, and Samuel.

"Walt just left us," Danielle explained. "I think he's eavesdropping on Marie's little group. I guess I better get back to mingling."

"Me too. I'll go check on Joanne," Lily said.

DANIELLE FOUND Mr. Renton chatting with a small group in the parlor. She hadn't had an opportunity to have a real discussion with the attorney beyond the initial greeting when he had first arrived for the open house.

Stepping away from the small group, Mr. Renton walked to Danielle. "I'd say your party is a success."

"I'm delighted with the turnout." Danielle stood alone with Clarence in one corner of the room while the other people continued their discussion.

"And that necklace looks beautiful on you; everyone is talking about it."

By reflex, Danielle's right hand lifted to her throat and lightly touched the necklace. "I keep checking to make sure it hasn't fallen off."

"I met your cousin. Actually, she was playing tour guide. Showed several of us where you found the Missing Thorndike."

"She's convinced there are more hidden treasures in the house. What did you tell her about the estate?"

"Just that now was not the time to discuss it. She's going to stop in my office on Monday, after the holiday weekend."

"Have you found out anything? I mean, does she have a legitimate claim?"

"Like I told your cousin, we should discuss this later. But I still think you should contact your buyer and delay the sale of the necklace. At least until this is resolved."

"I was really hoping I wouldn't have to do that." Danielle groaned.

"I think it would be for the best. Your cousin also said something that I found disturbing."

"What was that?"

"She claims you hit her. Even showed me a bruise."

"I did not hit her."

"I couldn't imagine you would. Exactly how did she get that bruise?"

"She grabbed for the necklace and tripped. I did not touch her. But she fell backwards and swears I hit her."

"I don't understand. If she fell backwards, how did she get a bruise on her face?"

"I…I suppose she hit herself when she fell."

"Humm…"

"Honestly, Mr. Renton. I did not hit my cousin."

"There you are!" Cheryl said to Danielle as she walked into the parlor. "The party is almost over. Can I please try on our necklace now?"

Danielle looked from Mr. Renton to Cheryl. Glancing past Cheryl, she spied Joe, who was standing in the entry, talking to several of her guests. He had stayed faithfully by her side for most of the day, only leaving to use the bathroom or standing guard at doorways, as he was now, visiting with other guests.

"Where's Adam?" Danielle asked. It was the first time she had seen Cheryl that day without Adam close at hand.

"I think he's talking with his grandmother in the library. So can I, please?"

"Sure," Danielle said with a sigh. Reaching back, she unlatched the necklace as Cheryl anxiously waited to try it on. The other guests in the room gathered around them, watching the valuable piece being passed from one cousin to the other.

"It looks beautiful on you," Samuel Hayman said as he entered the parlor. "I knew it would."

"Oh, does it? Does it?" Cheryl glanced down at her chest, trying to get a better look.

"It is absolutely exquisite," Mr. Renton said.

"I wish I'd find something like that behind my floorboards," one of the guests said.

"You really should go look at yourself in the mirror," Mr. Renton suggested. "It's quite spectacular."

"Oh yes! I will." Cheryl turned from Danielle.

"Cheryl, where are you going?" Danielle asked.

"Just to the bathroom, I'll be right back!"

Before Danielle could respond, Cheryl rushed from the room.

"She'll be fine," Mr. Renton said. "It's just down the hall, and Joe's out there."

Danielle smiled at her attorney in spite of the fact she wanted to smack him. Turning back to the doorway to let Joe know Cheryl had the necklace, the front door opened and a new group of guests walked into the entry.

Before she could get to Joe, Mr. Renton pushed passed her and walked toward the library. The guests from the parlor spilled into the entry to greet the new arrivals.

It took Danielle a few minutes to finally reach Joe, and when she did, he grabbed her arm and informed her the necklace was missing.

"Yes, I know." Danielle touched her throat. "I let Cheryl try it on. She went to the bathroom to look in the mirror."

"Let's get over there and get it back," Joe said. He and Danielle pushed through the small group.

When they reached the bathroom door, Danielle gave it a little knock. "Cheryl?"

"Just a minute, I'll be right out," a voice that was not Cheryl's called back. A few moments later, the door opened and a woman Danielle didn't recognize stepped out.

"It's all yours," the woman said cheerfully as she walked away.

Danielle pushed in the powder room and quickly discovered it was empty. "Darn her, where did she go?"

"She probably went to one of the other bathrooms since this one was occupied."

"Or another mirror," Danielle suggested.

"Maybe."

Danielle quickly raced through the first floor, then ran up to the second floor, Joe at her heels.

"She isn't up here," Danielle said after she looked through all the rooms.

Lily jogged up the stairs and, when she reached the second-floor landing, asked, "What's going on? I saw you two running up here."

"We're looking for Cheryl. She has the necklace," Joe explained.

"She took it?" Lily asked.

"I let her try it on," Danielle said.

"I hate to be the one to tell you guys this, but Cheryl just left with Adam. I saw them drive off just a minute ago."

"What?" Danielle gasped.

"Stupid stunt," Joe grumbled.

"I don't think this is a stunt. I think they just stole the necklace!" Danielle said.

"I seriously doubt it. I've known Adam a long time, and I don't think he's going to walk off with a million-dollar necklace in front of all these witnesses. Not so sure about your cousin."

"Maybe you don't know him as well as you think," Danielle grumbled.

"Let's keep this between us," Joe suggested. "The fewer people that know those two knuckleheads are joyriding with the Missing Thorndike, the less chance someone will try to take it from them."

"You're wrong, Joe. This is not a simple joyride," Danielle said as she and Joe followed Lily down the stairs.

"What car did they take?" Joe asked.

"I don't know. I just saw Adam come into the library and whisper something to his grandmother. When I looked outside a few minutes later, I saw him and Cheryl holding hands in the backyard, running toward the street. They got into some car and drove off. I think it was white or tan. Didn't get a good look at it."

TWENTY

Not everyone in Frederickport was sleeping on Saturday morning when the sun began to rise in the east. It cast a yellow orange glow over the quiet beach community, burning off the morning fog. Joe had just returned home to catch a few hours of sleep when he got the call that Adam Nichols's car was spotted parked next to a beach bungalow on the south end of town. According to the deputy on the phone, it was one of Adam's rentals.

Cheryl still hadn't returned, but her car remained parked on the street in front of Marlow House, where it had been when she ran off. Adam hadn't shown up at his place, and until Joe received the phone call from the deputy, he was beginning to suspect Adam and Cheryl had slipped out of town, though no one had seen Adam's car along that stretch of highway.

Instead of going to bed to grab a little sleep, Joe got back into his car and headed to the south side of town. He was tempted to give Danielle a call and let her know what was going on, but he didn't want to wake her up if she had managed to fall asleep. She was annoyed with her cousin but was hesitant to treat the situation as a robbery. But if the necklace didn't resurface, she would be forced to do that in order to collect on the insurance.

When Joe pulled up to the rental bungalow, Adam's car was still in the driveway, partially hidden by the shrubs along the property line. Everything was quiet on the street, and by all appearances, most nearby residents were still sound asleep.

After parking his car, Joe got out of his vehicle and began walking up the driveway to the front door. The house's front windows were wide open, and he didn't hear any sounds coming from inside, no voices, television, or radio playing.

Irritated that Adam and Cheryl's prank had caused him a sleepless night, he pounded on the door. It took a few minutes of intermittent knocking before Joe heard sounds coming from inside the house.

"Hold on, I'm coming. Don't break the damn door down," came Adam's voice from inside the house.

The door flew open. Wearing just boxers and socks, his uncombed hair damp from perspiration, Adam stood in the doorway, staring at Joe. He frowned and glanced around the front porch. "I thought you were Cheryl."

"Where is she, Adam?" Joe asked, pushing his way into the bungalow and looking around. An opened bottle of wine sat on the coffee table with two glasses. One glass was empty, while the second one was full.

"Hell if I know. I thought you were her." Adam scratched his head and stumbled into the tiny kitchen off the living room. He grabbed the coffeepot and then cursed when he realized there was no coffee in the house.

Joe followed Adam into the kitchen. "Would you stand still for a moment and talk to me!"

"Hey, do you have to shout?" Adam rubbed his right temple. "My head is killing me. What are you doing here anyway?"

"I'm looking for Cheryl."

"Why?"

"For one reason, she didn't come home last night."

Adam laughed and asked, "Did Danielle Boatman send you looking for her cousin because she doesn't approve of my company? I'm pretty sure she's reached the legal age of consent. Don't you think you're overstepping your legal authority by tracking down grown women who simply want to stay out all night?"

"Not if she's staying out all night with a million-dollar necklace that doesn't belong to her."

"What are you talking about?" Adam frowned.

"That's pretty obvious."

"Are you trying to say she had the Missing Thorndike with her?"

"Don't play dumb, Adam. She was wearing it when you two took off."

"She was not. I think I would've noticed that!"

"Are you seriously standing there and telling me she didn't have the necklace with her when you two left Marlow House?"

"If she did, I sure as hell didn't see it. She wasn't wearing it."

"I need to talk to her. Where is she?"

"Isn't it obvious I don't know? I thought you were her."

"Let's sit down. I want you to start at the beginning and tell me everything you remember, beginning when you first met Cheryl up until this morning when I started knocking on your door."

Adam combed his fingers through his hair and gave a little nod before walking back into the living room and sitting on the couch. Joe sat on a chair facing him.

"Let's see," Adam began. "I was downtown at Lucy's on Thursday for lunch. I had just sat down at a booth. The place was swamped. Cheryl comes walking in. There's no place for her to sit, so I ask her to join me; after all, she's pretty hot. I buy her lunch. We talk. She invites me to be her date at the open house. She tells me she might be looking for someplace to rent because she doesn't get along with her cousin. I bring her down here; show her this place. We spend the afternoon together. That was pretty much it."

"Did you have sex with her?" Joe asked.

"You asking because you're being nosy, or is this a legitimate question?"

"I'd say it's legitimate enough."

"No, we just spent the afternoon together. Anyway, yesterday I take my grandmother to the open house. When I get there, Grandma pretty much does her own thing, and I spend the day with Cheryl. We ate some food, drank some beer, talked to people. You saw us. About twenty minutes or so before we left, Cheryl told me she was getting bored, asked me if I was about ready to leave. I said sure. She went to go use the bathroom, and I went to tell my grandmother we were taking off. I wanted to make sure she had a ride home. I met Cheryl outside a few minutes later; we got in my car and came down here."

"And then what?"

"We came down here. Had a glass of wine. Went to bed. Next thing I remember is you knocking on the door. When I woke up and didn't find Cheryl in bed with me, I assumed it was her knocking on the door. Figured she'd gone outside for some reason and locked herself out."

"So you're telling me when you went to bed with Cheryl—when she undressed—you never saw the necklace?"

"Well, actually…" Adam rubbed his head again. "All that is a little fuzzy."

"What do you mean?"

"After I finished my wine, things started to spin. I remember Cheryl laughing, calling me a lightweight. She sorta helped me into the bedroom. Helped me tug my pants and shirt off. I remember her pulling down the sheets and asking me if they were fresh or from the people who had just checked out. I don't think I answered her, just pretty much fell into bed. That's the last thing I remember until you started knocking."

Joe looked at the opened bottle of wine sitting on the table. Calculating the amount of wine still in the bottle, he didn't think more than two glasses had been poured. Of those two glasses, one was still full. It appeared that only one glass had been consumed.

"Do you always get so light-headed after just one glass of wine?" Joe asked.

Adam shook his head. "No. But I didn't have much to eat yesterday, and I had taken an allergy pill right before we left Marlow House. Plus, I had a few beers at the open house. Sort of figured that's why it hit me so hard. I don't know. It was weird."

"Where did you get the wine?" Joe asked.

"Cheryl took it from the party."

"We need to find Cheryl, Adam. Last night she put on the necklace in front of a room full of witnesses and then ran off to look at herself in the bathroom mirror. She didn't return, and the last time anyone saw her was a few minutes after she put on the necklace—with you leaving the party."

"Hey, wait a minute, if she took that damn necklace, I didn't have anything to do with it. And the last time I heard, it wasn't a crime to spend the night with a pretty woman."

"So why bring her down here? Why not take her to your own house?"

"Seriously, Joe? It's a no-brainer. Take her to my house or to a little romantic bungalow right on the beach."

"Maybe you wanted to bring her down here so no one would find you."

"I'll admit, Cheryl liked the idea of coming down here where no one would look. She asked me not to tell my grandmother where we were going. But that was because she didn't want her cousin interfering. It had nothing to do with the necklace. Like I said, she didn't have the necklace."

"Why didn't you answer your cellphone? We called a number of times," Joe asked.

"I turned if off when I left Marlow House."

"Do you have any idea when Cheryl left?"

"No. I really don't."

Two officers from the local police department showed up at the door. Joe stood up and asked, "Can we look through the house?"

"No problem, look away." Adam remained on the couch while Joe stood up and opened the door for the two officers. After a brief exchange, one accompanied Joe in searching the bungalow while the other officer walked the perimeter of the property and walked down to the nearby beach to see if Cheryl was anywhere in sight.

An hour later, Joe called Danielle to tell her he hadn't found Cheryl or the necklace. He hated to do it, but he didn't have any other choice. He needed to let her know what was going on and wanted to see if perhaps Cheryl had showed up at Marlow House.

"Did you find her?" Danielle asked when he got her on the phone.

"I found Adam but not Cheryl. I assume she didn't return to Marlow House?"

"No, she didn't. But what do you mean you found Adam but not Cheryl? They left together; Lily saw them."

"Adam admits he left with her. According to him, she didn't have the necklace. And if she did, he swears he didn't see it."

"Then why did he leave with her?"

"I guess the same reason any heterosexual man might leave with a pretty woman."

"Why isn't she with him now? Her car is still here. Did he drop her off somewhere?"

"Adam said he brought her down to one of the bungalows in his rental program. It's vacant, right on the beach. According to him, he had a glass of wine and all he remembers after that is getting dizzy, Cheryl helping him into bed, and then him blacking out. The next thing he remembers is me knocking on the door to the bungalow this morning. When he woke up, Cheryl wasn't with him. He thought that's who was knocking on the door. Seemed genuinely surprised that I wasn't Cheryl and has no idea where she went. I believe him."

"Well, I don't!" Danielle snapped. "We all saw her take off with that necklace. He did something to her; I know it! You need to search that house and see if he has the necklace stashed somewhere."

"We already looked through it. If he has it, it isn't in that house. I've known Adam a long time; I don't think he's capable of doing something sinister to your cousin."

"Why not? He already broke into Marlow House!"

"What do you mean?"

"The break-in. When Craig called you over. It was Adam and Bill. They knew the necklace might be hidden in the house and they broke in trying to find it. Bill is the one who broke the library window."

"I don't understand; how do you know that? Why didn't you say something before?"

"I…I figured after I found the necklace they were no longer a threat. I didn't want to upset Marie by having her grandson arrested."

"But how do you know he and Bill broke into the house?"

"I can't say."

"Why can't you say?"

"Please, Joe, that doesn't matter right now. Frankly, I don't really care about the necklace. I never did. I know my cousin has driven me crazy most of my life, but I don't want anything bad to happen to her. I have this gut feeling something has."

TWENTY-ONE

Danielle sat at the kitchen table, reading the *Frederickport Press*'s Saturday morning headline: *Missing Thorndike Goes Missing Again.*

"I really wish they hadn't run this story." Danielle groaned.

Coffee pot in hand, Lily walked to the table and refilled Danielle's mug. "You really can't blame them, Dani. That reporter was here when Cheryl took off. And you said you wanted publicity."

"I suppose you're right. This will certainly bring the bed and breakfast more publicity than I imagined." Danielle set the paper on the table. After adding cream to her coffee, she took a sip.

"I wonder where she went." Lily sat down at the table and picked up the paper.

"I could slap her. Such a stupid stunt. She's just put herself in danger by running around with something that valuable. And now that the newspaper ran that article with her picture, what happens if the wrong person finds her?"

"I'm surprised you're so worried about her safety. After all, it may not be a stunt. Have you considered she might have actually stolen the necklace and has no intention of returning? She might be out of the country by now."

"Absolutely not, Lily. Why would Cheryl so publicly steal something like that?"

"Umm…for the money?"

"Maybe I'd agree with you if Cheryl didn't already have money. Her parents' estate was worth over five million dollars. No way would she so publicly become a fugitive over something of less value than what she already has. That doesn't make sense. No, Cheryl is simply pulling one of her stunts."

"Maybe she's spent all her parents' money. That happens, you know," Lily suggested.

"I don't know. I suppose that's possible," Danielle said with a weary sigh.

"I'm sorry, Danielle. I should have stopped her," Walt said when he appeared by the table.

"Good morning, Walt. It wasn't your fault."

"Walt is here?" Lily looked around and sniffed the air. "I don't smell cigar."

"Please tell Lily I don't have a cigar in my hand every minute."

Lily's eyes widened as she watched the chair seemingly move by itself as Walt sat down at the table.

"He's not smoking right now. He's trying to cut down. Not good for his health," Danielle told Lily.

"Glad to see you still have your sense of humor," Walt said.

"Really?" Lily asked.

"I'm teasing, Lily. He doesn't have a body to worry about."

"Well, that's what I thought," Lily mumbled.

"So where were you, Walt, when she tried on the necklace?" Danielle asked.

"I'm afraid I got distracted in the attic. A couple of your guests were up there discussing my murder and speculating where exactly it happened."

"And you couldn't tear yourself away?" Danielle asked.

"What is he saying?" Lily asked.

"I would've thought you'd wait until I was in the room to let her try on the necklace so I could keep her from taking it."

"I certainly didn't think she would just run out of the house with the necklace. Especially not in front of a room full of people."

Walt shook his head and said, "Well, your friend Joe was certainly no help. None at all."

"It's not Joe's fault," Danielle said. "It all happened too fast. If I want to blame anyone, it's Mr. Renton."

"Your lawyer? Why is it his fault?" Lily asked.

"It was his bright idea for Cheryl to go look at herself in a mirror."

Lily's cellphone began to buzz with an incoming text message. Picking up the phone, she read the message and then sent a return text. "That was Ian; he wanted to know if we were awake and if Cheryl ever showed up. I told him she was still missing and invited him over for coffee."

INSTEAD OF COMING up the front walk, Ian and Sadie entered the grounds by the side gate and came to the kitchen door. Lily got up from the table and let them in. Sadie immediately rushed to Walt and jumped up, her front paws landing first on his lap and then the chair.

"Get down, Sadie, you know better than to jump up on the table," Ian scolded.

"That's okay, girl, but you better get down," Walt said gently. Sadie let out a little whimper and put her front paws back on the wood floor. She sat next to Walt's chair.

"Good morning, Ian," Danielle greeted him after Lily gave her hello.

"Morning, Danielle. Still no word from your cousin?"

"I'm afraid not."

Lily handed Ian a cup of coffee. When he started to take Walt's chair, she gently guided him to an empty seat. "No, sit here. I spilled something on that one and just wiped it down. It's still damp," Lily lied.

"So what's going on?" Ian asked as he sat down.

"Joe called a little while ago. He tracked down Adam."

"I thought Lily said Cheryl is still missing?" Ian asked.

"She is. Ian found Adam, but Cheryl wasn't with him. Apparently, they spent the night together at some beach house in his rental program. Adam insists she didn't have the necklace with her. He says she left sometime during the night, but he doesn't know when."

"When he says she left during the night—did she take his car? I see hers is still parked on the street."

"No. If Adam is to be believed, then she walked somewhere."

"I take it you don't believe him," Ian asked.

"Think about it, I know he and Bill were willing to break in here to find the necklace before we did." The night before, Danielle had told Ian about Adam and Bill breaking into Marlow House.

"You suspect they broke in. I'm still not convinced they actually did," Ian corrected.

"I told you, Bill fixed the window and didn't balk when I refused to pay him."

"There could be several explanations for that," Ian said.

"Why are you being so contrary?" Lily asked.

"I'm not being contrary, Lily. I'm trying to be objective and look at the situation from all angles."

"I'm worried about my cousin, Ian."

"I thought she drove you nuts? Something I can understand."

"That doesn't mean I want something bad to happen to her."

"Who says anything bad is going to happen to her?" Ian asked.

"How safe can it be, her running around town with that necklace?"

"I'm just not convinced she's in any danger. Every day people walk around wearing expensive jewelry and nothing happens to them," Ian said.

"Right, and you also hear of someone getting killed over a pair of expensive tennis shoes," Lily quipped.

"True, Lily. But this is quiet Frederickport, not exactly a hot spot of criminal activity. It's just that I've met Cheryl and spent a very awkward afternoon with her. I can see her sitting in some little beach cottage, posing in front of a mirror as she models the necklace, while all along laughing her butt off over the fact she's driving her cousin crazy."

"But she took off with Adam, and now she's missing, and he claims she never had the necklace," Danielle reminded him.

"I'm not saying Adam is telling the truth. I'd be surprised if he didn't know she had the necklace with her. But I imagine when he woke up this morning and found her and the necklace gone, reality sank in. Who knows, she could have had him convinced she was one of the rightful owners of the necklace and had as much right as Danielle to be wearing it. But by this morning, it probably dawned on him that he might very well be seen as an accomplice to a very public jewel heist and that the only way to protect himself was simply to lie."

"So you don't think he has the necklace and…well…did something to Cheryl to make her disappear?" Danielle asked.

"I suppose anything is possible. But publicly leaving with her like that makes me doubt it." Ian shrugged.

"Joanne's here," Walt announced. A moment later, there was a knock at the kitchen door.

"It's Joanne," Danielle said from the table, waving for her to come in.

Joanne opened the door, walked into the kitchen, and set her purse on the counter. "Good morning. If I can believe the morning paper, your cousin and the necklace are still missing."

"I'm afraid so." Danielle went on to tell Joanne about Joe finding Adam, while Joanne poured herself a cup of coffee.

"I wonder when I should call the insurance company," Danielle asked a few minutes later. "I really didn't want to go public with this yet. But since Joe and the local police department are looking for Cheryl and the necklace, it's a moot point."

"I was wondering," Lily began. "Since Cheryl claims to rightfully own half of the Marlow estate, couldn't the insurance company argue the necklace isn't stolen—it's with one of the owners. Therefore, they aren't required to pay?"

"According to Mr. Renton, the necklace legally belongs to me. I don't see why the insurance company wouldn't pay the claim."

Lily went on. "Yes, but if they prove she had a legal claim to the estate—"

"Wouldn't Cheryl have to be here to do that?" Joanne interrupted.

"Oh…I suppose so." Lily shrugged.

"If the necklace isn't found, it would be in Danielle's best interest if Cheryl wasn't found either. With her gone, there's no one to contest the will, and Danielle can claim the insurance money," Joanne suggested.

"Goodness, Joanne, you make it sound like I had a motive to make my cousin disappear!"

"Oh, I'm sorry. I was just thinking out loud. I didn't mean to imply you had anything to do with her disappearance."

"Obviously not," Lily said. "After all, we all saw her take off with the necklace."

TWENTY-TWO

Shortly before noon on Saturday, Joe Morelli arrived at Marlow House. Accompanying him was his partner, Brian Henderson, another officer from the Frederickport Police Department. Lily showed them both to the library, where Danielle was waiting.

Danielle stood up when the two officers, both dressed in uniform, entered the room. "Any news?" She immediately recognized the officer with Joe. They had met briefly the previous week when Joe had taken her out to lunch. Officer Henderson was much older than Joe, old enough to be his father, she guessed.

"Nothing yet," Joe said. "We wondered if we could have a look at the room Cheryl was using."

"What for?" Danielle asked.

"Maybe there's something up there that might give us a clue as to where she went," Joe said.

"Umm…okay…but there really isn't anything up there. The room was straightened up for the party. It looks pretty much the same way it did before she arrived."

"She didn't take her things with her, did she?" Brian asked.

"No. As far as we can tell, she just took her purse. We found her cellphone in the kitchen after she left with Adam," Danielle explained.

"What about her other things? I assume she arrived with a suitcase, clothes," Brian asked.

"Yes, she did, but I don't see how that's going to help you," Danielle said.

"Is there some reason you don't want us to look at her things?" Brian asked.

"Of course not!" Danielle said quickly. "It's upstairs, come with me." She reluctantly led them upstairs while dreading what they would find in the suitcase. *Damn Walt for trying to help*, she silently cursed.

When they got to the Red Room, Joanne had just removed the bed sheets. The mattress was bare save for the quilted mattress pad. "Afternoon, Joe, Brian," Joanne greeted them. She looked at Danielle and asked, "Do you want me to put fresh sheets on the bed or just the bedspread?"

"Probably just the bedspread for now. But I'm going to use the bed for a minute so if there's something else you need to do." Danielle walked to the closet and opened the door. She pulled Cheryl's suitcase from the closet shelf and tossed it on the bed.

"This is it," Danielle said.

Instead of leaving the room, Joanne stood and watched as Brian opened the suitcase.

"Oh my god," Brian said, wrinkling his nose. An unpleasant odor emitted from the suitcase, a result of the damp towels in conjunction with the assortment of spilled lotions and toiletries. Gingerly, Brian lifted one item after another from the suitcase. "This is a mess. Why in the world would she cram everything in there like this?"

"She obviously didn't intend to come back. Looks like she's stained everything in her suitcase with that makeup," Joe said, looking down at the jumble of fabric, now damp, stained, and smelly.

Joanne took several steps toward the bed, looked down at the open suitcase, and said, "She didn't do that."

"How do you know she didn't?" Joe asked.

"You were here, Joe, when I asked her about cleaning the room —the day before the party."

"Yes. And I seem to remember Danielle telling you not to worry about it, that Cheryl would clean the room in the morning."

"She also apologized to me later," Joanne said.

"What do you mean?" Joe asked.

"I was up in the attic, cleaning the windows, when she came up not long after her little scene about the room. She apologized for being rude and admitted she was upset with her cousin. I think she really believes half of this place is hers."

"Did she mention the necklace?" Joe asked.

"The only thing I recall, she asked me where the safe was."

"The safe?" Brian asked. "What safe?"

"I imagine she's talking about the safe I installed to keep the necklace in until I could return it to the bank," Danielle said.

Joanne nodded. "Yes."

"What did you tell her?" Joe asked.

"I told her she needed to talk to her cousin about that. I really did not want to get involved. Oh, I didn't tell her I didn't want to get involved. I just told her she'd have to ask her cousin about the safe."

"I still don't understand why you're certain she didn't pack the suitcase," Brian said.

"Because on Friday morning I came upstairs to get the brochures out of Danielle's room to put in the library. I noticed the door to Cheryl's room was shut and there was a note on it. Curious, I read the note. It said something like private resident or private quarter. Something like that and to stay out. From what I understood, Danielle wanted all the rooms open for people to see, plus Cheryl had agreed to clean the room. I knocked; when there was no answer, I peeked inside. The room was a mess, clothes everywhere. Wet towels on the floor. I decided to ask Danielle what she wanted me to do about it."

"And what did she say?" Brian asked.

"She never asked me," Danielle answered.

"That's true, I didn't," Joanne said. "I went to the library first, to put the brochures on the table and clean up some potting soil that had spilled on the floor. While I was cleaning up, I noticed Danielle going upstairs. I figured she'd see the mess for herself. When I was done in the library, I went upstairs to see if I could help Danielle, but she was in the bathroom, taking a shower, and by that time, the room was already straightened up. I just assumed Danielle cleaned the room. But if she didn't, I suppose someone else in the house must have."

"Did you see Cheryl go up the stairs? There's a clear view from the library door to whoever is going up and down those stairs," Brian said.

"I only saw Danielle going upstairs—but that doesn't mean

someone else didn't. I wasn't watching the door. Yet I'm fairly certain it wasn't Cheryl."

"Why do you say that?" Joe asked.

"When I came back downstairs, I found Cheryl in the parlor. I didn't want her to snap at me again, so I didn't say anything about the room. Yet I did ask her how long she'd been in the parlor. She said all morning. But I suppose it's possible she went upstairs, and I didn't see her, and she didn't mention it."

"Was the room cleaned up when you came up to take a shower?" Brian asked Danielle.

"I honestly didn't notice," Danielle lied. "There was just so much to do."

"Did you pack your cousin's suitcase?" Brian asked.

"Of course not," Danielle said.

"Did Lily?" Joe asked.

"No, Lily wouldn't do something like that."

"Then who did?" Brian asked.

"I have no idea, but does it really matter?" Danielle asked.

"I'm sorry," Joanne blurted out. "I didn't mean to imply Danielle or Lily were responsible for the suitcase. People were coming and going that morning. Excuse me; I need to get back to work." Joanne turned and quickly left the room, shutting the door behind her.

"In answer to your question, Ms. Boatman, everything matters," Brian said seriously. "Did you have some idea that Cheryl was planning to leave Marlow House without her suitcase?"

"Of course not. Why would you ask that?"

"That would mean you intended for her to find her suitcase like this."

"I told you, I wasn't the one who put all that stuff in there. Anyway, what does any of that matter? Even if I had done it, which I didn't, what does that have to do with the fact that she ran out of here—with a room full of witnesses, including Joe—with the necklace?"

"I'm just trying to get a better idea of your relationship with your cousin."

"I will admit I've never been fond of my cousin," Danielle said. "I would be perfectly happy to never see her again. But that doesn't mean I would ever hurt her."

"No one has suggested you hurt her," Brian said.

"What I mean, I don't want anyone to hurt her. I'm frightened for Cheryl. She's missing, and having that necklace makes her vulnerable."

"So you believe she's in danger? Who do you know who'd want to hurt her?" Brian asked.

"I don't know anyone in particular, aside from maybe Adam. After all, he was the last one seen with her. And I know he was interested in that necklace long before I found it."

"What are you talking about?" Brian asked.

"Danielle seems to believe Adam and Bill Jones were the ones who broke into Marlow House. Remember, Craig called me when he found the library window broken and the front door wide open," Joe explained.

"I don't remember anything about Adam and Bill being questioned," Brian said, looking from Danielle to Joe.

"I didn't want to upset Marie," Danielle explained. "And I didn't have any real proof. But I knew both men heard Marie tell Ian about Walt Marlow possibly taking the necklace."

"And because of that you think they're the ones who broke in?" Brian asked incredulously.

"Well..." Danielle took a deep breath. "I decided to test my hunch. I called Bill to fix the window—the window I believed they broke. When he was done, I told him I wouldn't be paying him for the repair because I knew he and Adam were the ones responsible."

"What did he say?" Brian asked.

"He asked me why I wasn't calling the police if I was so convinced he and Adam had broken into the house. I told him I didn't want to upset Marie and since he fixed the window I'd consider us even."

"What did he do?" Brian asked.

"He just looked at me, sort of dazed, and left. That was the last time I saw him. I found the necklace after that and didn't feel they were really a threat anymore. After all, everyone knew I kept the necklace at the bank."

"Was Bill at the party?" Brian asked.

"No. I didn't invite him," Danielle said.

"But you invited Adam?" Brian asked.

"I invited Marie. I consider her a friend. I understood Adam would probably be bringing her, but I didn't think there would be a problem."

"Even with the necklace here?" Brian asked.

"I figured stealing something that everyone knows exists is much riskier than taking a treasure that everyone assumed went missing years before. I didn't think Adam was that type of jewel thief."

"But you think he's responsible for your cousin's disappearance?" Brian asked.

"I'm beginning to think he isn't as harmless as I originally thought. She left with him. Where did she go that night? She obviously didn't walk back here, and no one has come forward to say they saw her."

"I'd like to take this down to the station so we can look through it down there." Brian dropped the few items he had touched back into the suitcase and zipped it up.

"I guess that's okay," Danielle said, looking to Joe for some sign of support.

BRIAN TOSSED Cheryl's suitcase into the trunk of the police car. When he got in the vehicle with Joe, he asked, "Do you think this is just some publicity stunt?"

"Absolutely not. I was there, remember? Danielle would have to be one hell of an actress to pull something like that off."

"She's a good-looking woman. You wouldn't be the first cop to be sucked into some conniving woman's web."

Joe laughed and turned on the ignition. "You've become jaded. And I think you're totally off base, Brian."

"Have you talked to Bill and Adam about the Marlow House break-in?"

"No. Danielle just told me about it this morning."

"I remember when Jones was a teenager. Arrested him a few times for drinking. He was a wiseass back then but never got into any real trouble. Can't recall Adam Nichols ever being a problem. Aside from a few of the local dads wanting us to arrest him for seducing their daughters."

"How old were the daughters?" Joe asked.

"Fourteen, fifteen. As I recall, he had just turned eighteen. Had to have a good talk with him about jail bait."

"But you didn't arrest him?" Joe asked.

"Nah. He was just doing what teenage boys do. Maybe I should have a chat with Bill."

Joe glanced over at Brian, who sat in the passenger side of the car. "What about?"

"See what he says about Boatman's break-in story. If Adam really did have his eye on that necklace, then maybe he isn't as innocent as he professes."

"I seriously doubt Bill will have anything to say. As far as I can tell, Danielle's sudden belief those two broke in is nothing more than her imagination working overtime. She's grasping at straws because Cheryl and that necklace have gone missing."

"What about her story that she refused to pay Bill for the repair?"

"Honestly, I'm not sure how to take that," Joe confessed.

TWENTY-THREE

Danielle didn't have to call the prospective buyer of the Missing Thorndike and tell him to postpone his visit to Frederickport until after the necklace was recovered. By Sunday, state, national, and Internet news sources carried the story. Danielle suspected Ian's initial article on Eva Thorndike helped boost interest in the necklace. Had Ian's article never run, she doubted many would be interested in what appeared to be nothing but a family squabble over an inheritance. Danielle had intended to call the buyer Sunday night and tell him there was no reason for him to come, yet he called first, asking if the stories were true.

Wearing the necklace to the open house proved to be a far more successful marketing tool than Danielle ever anticipated. Of course, she doubted it would have garnered such notice had Cheryl not taken off with it. Despite the attention Marlow House Bed and Breakfast received in the press—and the calls she was getting from prospective guests wanting to make a reservation—she was not taking advantage of the successful marketing stunt. A stunt, in Danielle's opinion, that had gone horribly wrong.

By the time Wednesday afternoon rolled by, Cheryl was still missing. The police had received numerous Cheryl sightings, yet none had panned out. It was as if she had simply disappeared into thin air. There was no activity on any of her credit cards or bank accounts. According to Cheryl's friends back in California, whom the police had contacted, none had seen or heard from Cheryl since she had left California for Oregon.

Danielle kept thinking of Ian's theory—Cheryl was holed up in some beach bungalow, enjoying the attention she had created while wearing the necklace—like some princess, preening in front of the mirror. She could actually imagine Cheryl doing something like that, and she preferred thinking that was the case, because the alternative was too dark. She couldn't believe Cheryl had actually stolen the necklace and made herself a fugitive; that made no sense at all. If she wasn't playing some reckless game, it meant Cheryl was in real trouble.

"I just turned down another reservation," Lily said after hanging up the telephone in the parlor. She glanced over at Danielle, who stared off into space, an open book in her hands. When Danielle didn't respond, Lily said, "How's your book?" Still no response. Raising her voice, Lily asked, "Dani, enjoying your book?"

Danielle jerked her head slightly, coming out of her fog, and looked over at Lily. A vacant expression on her face, she blinked her eyes and glanced down at her hands. Closing the book, she tossed it on the floor and said, "Not really."

"Dani, are you sure you don't want to start taking reservations? It might be good for you, help occupy your time."

Danielle sighed. "I just can't focus on running a business. Not with Cheryl missing."

"It's been five days. Where do you think she went?"

"I wish she hadn't left her cellphone here. We might have been able to use it to track her."

"Maybe." Lily studied Danielle. "So you still think something bad happened to her?"

"I keep hoping she's just kicking back somewhere, punking us. But then…I don't know…I don't see her staying away this long for some silly prank. Cheryl gets bored easily."

"What's going on with Adam?" Lily asked.

"When I talked to Joe this morning, he said Adam is sticking with his story. And they really don't have anything to charge him with. From what I hear, the publicity this thing has been receiving has given his rental business a boost. Seems everyone wants to rent that bungalow where Cheryl supposedly spent Friday night."

"Rather ironic, if you think about it," Lily murmured.

"How so?"

"Well, one of your great fears about Ian's article, before you found the necklace, was that your guests would be nothing but treasure hunters and come here for a chance to search the rooms and rip off paneling."

"I see what you mean. Some think Cheryl stashed the necklace in the beach bungalow. While I seriously doubt that's the case, I have a feeling Adam doesn't really care if his guests are treasure hunters or not, as long as they pay the rent on time."

The desk phone began to ring. Lily sighed. "Another reservation to turn away?" Picking up the receiver, she said, "Hello, Marlow House Bed and Breakfast."

"Danielle Boatman?" a male voice asked.

"Who can I say is calling?" Lily asked.

"Her attorney, Clarence Renton."

Lily placed her hand over the receiver and looked at Danielle. "It's your attorney, Mr. Renton."

Danielle got up from the sofa, walked to the desk, and took the phone's receiver from Lily. "Hello, Mr. Renton."

"Hello, Ms. Boatman. Can I assume your cousin is still missing?"

"Unfortunately, yes. So far, no trace of her."

"I'm afraid we have a little problem," Mr. Renton began.

"I have a big problem all right. Although I have a feeling you're talking about something else. What's wrong?"

"A Marvin Burrows just left my office. He's Cheryl's attorney from California."

"Does this mean she's been in contact with him? Is she okay?"

"No. According to Burrows, he hasn't heard from her. Apparently, he wants to move ahead with her claim against the estate."

"I don't understand. How can he do that without Cheryl?"

"If he legally can is still to be determined, but I'm fairly confident of his motive."

"Which is?" Danielle asked.

"His client is missing with a very valuable piece of jewelry, which legally belongs to you. I have a feeling he's attempting to protect his client by establishing she has a legal right to the piece."

"If she and the necklace are missing, why does he care?"

"I suspect he assumes she's going to resurface, and when she does, he wants to avoid her getting arrested and charged with theft. I think he's just trying to protect her."

"Do you think she's already contacted him?"

"It's possible. But he claimed he hasn't heard from her since she left California."

"What do you want me to do?"

"For the moment, nothing. Let me look into a few things."

"I was wondering—last week when I spoke to you about Cheryl's claim, you told me you were going to check into it and get back to me the first of the week. With Cheryl and the necklace going missing, I haven't really followed up with you. What did you find out?"

"I'm still waiting to hear back on a few of my inquiries. When I find out something, you'll be the first to know. I just wanted you to be aware that Mr. Burrows is in town and what his intentions are."

"Thank you, Mr. Renton. I really appreciate all your help."

"That's why I'm here, Ms. Boatman."

"What was that all about?" Lily asked when Danielle got off the phone.

"Apparently, Cheryl's attorney is in town. I assume it's the same one who says she has a rightful claim to the estate. He intends to pursue her claim in her absence."

"Can he do that? And why would he?"

"I don't know. Mr. Renton thinks the attorney is trying to protect Cheryl. I guess he figures she's going to show up, and when she does, he doesn't want her charged with theft. As part owner of the necklace, I doubt the DA would press charges, especially if she returns the necklace to the estate."

"What if she returns without the necklace?"

"I didn't ask Mr. Renton about that. I would imagine a judge would probably order her to return it, but who really knows? I have no idea how this stuff works. Life was sure a heck of a lot easier when I thought my inheritance was just a house and a few bucks."

"Ian and Sadie are here," Walt announced when he appeared in the room.

"Here where?" Danielle asked.

"Are you talking to me?" Lily asked.

"No. Walt just came in. He said Ian and Sadie are here."

"I was looking out the window. They're coming up the front walk," Walt explained right before the doorbell rang.

Lily jumped up to answer the door. A few moments later, she led Sadie and Ian into the parlor.

"I just returned from downtown, and Marlow House is all anyone is talking about," Ian told them.

"I guess in some perverse way your publicity stunt worked—too well. Of course, I always knew you had a knack for marketing," Lily said.

"Sure, all I have to do is arrange for people and valuable objects to go missing," Danielle snorted.

"Unfortunately, the problem with situations like this is how people start spinning the stories. They can get out of control," Ian said.

"What do you mean?" Lily asked.

"When I stopped at the market, I overheard two women discussing the Missing Thorndike. One woman was telling the other one that according to Samuel Hayman at the jewelry store, the entire thing was nothing but a publicity stunt."

"You're kidding me! Why would he say that?" Danielle asked.

"Was Sam still here when Cheryl took off?" Lily asked.

"Yes. Actually, he came into the parlor when Cheryl put the necklace on," Danielle said.

"Unfortunately, that tends to lend credibility to Sam's story, since he was here when Cheryl took off."

"Oh, let them talk. At this point, I don't care. The entire thing is making me ill." Danielle groaned. "It doesn't matter what they think."

"Unfortunately, it does matter," Ian corrected. "A few other patrons from the store joined the conversation, and they started discussing how it was wrong for you to misuse the services of the local police department like this."

"What do you mean misuse the police department?"

"They're convinced Hayman's story is true, which means to them you're fraudulently spending taxpayers' money. Someone even suggested you should be fined to compensate for whatever the police department spent on its investigation."

"Why in the world would Samuel Hayman spread such a vicious story?" Lily asked.

"I get the impression Hayman likes attention. Remember how he couldn't wait to call the local paper and the police after we took him the necklace?" Ian reminded them.

"Marlow House is definitely getting way more attention than I ever hoped for—I just never imagined the attention might destroy my reputation."

"No one is going to run you out of town. But there will always be people like those women gossiping at the market. I just thought you should know the rumors Hayman has been spreading. Joe knows this wasn't some publicity stunt," Ian said.

"What do I do about it?" Danielle asked.

"Maybe talk with your attorney. He might have a little chat with Hayman and remind him people can be sued over spreading false rumors—especially rumors that can damage your business."

"At the moment I have no business."

"I'm sorry, Danielle," Walt said. "This is all my fault. I never should have suggested you wear the necklace to the open house. And I never should have taken my eyes off you and the necklace while it was in this house."

"No one has called for reservations?" Ian asked.

"Are you kidding?" Lily said. "The phone has been ringing nonstop all week with people wanting to stay here."

"That's what I thought you told me the other day," Ian said with a frown. "So why do you say you don't have a business?"

"Because Danielle refuses to take any reservations until Cheryl and the necklace resurface."

"What happens if they never do?" Ian asked.

"Please don't say that." Danielle groaned.

TWENTY-FOUR

While driving down Main Street, Brian Henderson spied Bill Jones's truck parked in front of Lucy's Diner. On impulse, he made a quick U-turn and parked behind the vehicle. He didn't get out of his car immediately. Instead, he sat there for a few minutes with his engine idling.

Everything about this case irritated him. Initially, he thought it was either a publicity stunt created by the cousins or a family dispute. In either case, he didn't appreciate wasting department resources on the antics of two obviously spoiled women.

Cheryl had been missing almost a week now; she had simply vanished. Her car remained parked in front of Marlow House, there had been no activity on any of her credit cards, and no one had seen her—at least, there had been no credible sighting. Cheryl's attorney had shown up in town and was kicking up quite a ruckus down at the station—one minute demanding the arrest of Adam Nichols, and in the next, insisting Danielle Boatman was responsible for his client's disappearance.

Adam was the last one seen with Cheryl, yet they hadn't been able to come up with any discrepancies in his story. Even the wine supported Adam's version. That piece of information had not been released to the public. Not even Danielle Boatman knew.

Brian had to admit that had he been the one to show up on Adam's doorstep on Saturday morning, looking for Cheryl, he wouldn't have considered having the wine analyzed. Perhaps he had simply been a cop for too long, and having the wine tested would have seemed more in line with TV cop than reality. Yet Joe was much younger than him—and more naive, considering he seemed unable to consider the possibility that this was some publicity stunt orchestrated by the cousins to garner more attention for Marlow House.

After Adam claimed to have passed out after drinking just one glass of wine, Joe had taken the wine in to be analyzed. According to the test results, the wine was laced with the date-rape drug Rohypnol. Judging by the amount of wine remaining in the bottle and second glass, only one glass of wine had been consumed. Those results forced Brian to take a fresh look at the case.

He wondered who had been drugged—Cheryl or Adam? Had Adam drugged Cheryl, taken the necklace and then disposed of the body, perhaps tossing her in the ocean? Or had Cheryl drugged Adam, using him to throw off the police while she took off with an accomplice and disappeared?

Brian chewed on both versions and kept coming back to Adam drugging Cheryl. That would explain why the tainted wine hadn't already been disposed of. Adam would want evidence of it to support his story, whereas he would assume Cheryl would get rid of the tainted wine before taking off.

Of course, if Adam's story had been false, his lie could be exposed with a blood test to show Rohypnol wasn't in his system—if one had been taken. The chief reluctantly agreed to have the wine tested, even though Brian thought it was a waste of time. However, they didn't feel it necessary to have Adam's blood tested. It was argued that if Adam had drugged the wine and then left it there to implicate Cheryl, he would have probably ingested some of the drug after disposing of Cheryl's body.

The only problem with Adam's version was what Cheryl's attorney had to say. According to him, Cheryl was a wealthy woman—worth far more than the Missing Thorndike. Therefore, why would she do something as stupid as publicly stealing a necklace?

And yet…if the attorney truly believed that, why was he so insistent on pursuing Cheryl's claim against Boatman's estate? According to Mr. Renton, the only reason the attorney was going in that direction was to protect his client when she resurfaced.

Brian shook his head in confusion and turned off the ignition.

He was weary from flipping back and forth—Cheryl did it—no, Adam did it—it was a publicity stunt—no, Cheryl…

Since Danielle had shared her belief that Adam and Bill had been interested in the necklace before it resurfaced—so interested that they risked going to jail and ruining their reputations by breaking into Marlow House—Brian decided it was time to have a little chat with Bill. If he and Adam were in cahoots before, perhaps Bill had helped Adam dispose of Cheryl's body. He toyed with the idea of bringing Bill into the station to be questioned but decided Bill might be more candid if he didn't realize he was being interrogated.

Brian turned off his ignition, got out of the car and headed to the diner.

"Morning, Bill," Brian greeted as he sat down at the lunch counter next to him.

Bill glanced up. "Hey, Brian, how's it going? Any luck finding that woman who ran off with the Missing Thorndike?"

Ahh, good. He brought up the subject, Brian thought before saying, "The woman and the necklace seem to have vanished into thin air."

The waitress behind the counter brought Brian a cup of coffee and took his order. Bill was just finishing his breakfast of bacon and eggs.

"That necklace seems to have a habit of not sticking around." Bill chuckled. "I think this has taught Adam he needs to be more careful about the women he picks up."

"You've seen him since this all went down? How's he doing?"

"I see him about every day because of work." Bill shrugged. "Saw him Saturday afternoon a few hours after Joe rousted him up at the rental. At the time, I think he thought the whole thing was kinda funny. A lark. Figured she went back to Marlow House. But when I saw him a few days later, he wasn't laughing anymore."

"What do you mean?" Brian sipped his coffee and studied Bill's facial expressions.

"He's kinda freaked, to say the least. Figures she used him to rip off the necklace. He's not very happy about that." Bill chuckled and pushed his now empty plate to the far side of the counter.

"Danielle Boatman is convinced Adam had something to do with her cousin's disappearance."

"Well, that's to be expected, I suppose." Bill motioned for the waitress to refill his cup.

"It seems Danielle Boatman is convinced of a lot of things. From what I've seen, she has a bit of an imagination."

"What do you mean?" Bill picked up his now full cup of coffee and took a sip.

"For some reason, she's convinced Adam and you broke into Marlow House after she moved in. Before she found the necklace."

Bill stopped drinking his coffee and looked at Brian. "She said that?"

"Yeah. Of course, she didn't have any proof, just a hunch."

"So what did we get away with?" Bill set his coffee cup back on the counter.

"She thinks you were looking for the Missing Thorndike."

"And exactly how did we know the necklace was there? Are we clairvoyant?"

"Probably from Adam's grandmother." Brian shrugged.

"I see at least two problems with her hunch. First, that house had been vacant since before I was born, and if I was going to break in to look for the necklace, why would I wait until someone moved in?"

"And the second problem?"

"Danielle Boatman found the necklace in the house, we didn't. That woman is nuts. Did you know she doesn't like people to say anything that might upset Walt Marlow?"

"Walt Marlow? You mean the guy who took the necklace?"

"Yeah."

"But he's been dead for almost a hundred years."

"Exactly, see my point?" Bill smirked.

"I heard you were the one who fixed the window in the library after the break-in."

"Yeah, I'd met her when we took some photos over from Adam's grandma. Realized she was a fruit loop when I met her. When she gave us a tour of the house, her neighbor's dog was in her bedroom up on the bed. She insisted we leave the TV on in the room to keep the dog company."

"Was she pet sitting?"

"Nah, the guy who owned the dog was downstairs."

"Maybe she's an animal lover."

"Yeah, right," Bill snorted. "Anyway, I gave her some business cards. Told her if she needed any repair work done to give me a call. Figured she was in the middle of fixing up that old house, might as well try to pick up some work."

"One reason Danielle is convinced you broke that window was because you fixed it for free."

"What are you talking about?"

"According to her, after you fixed the window, she said she wasn't paying you because you broke it in the first place."

"Hell," Bill scoffed. "I'd be calling you up if she had refused to pay me."

"Do you happen to have any proof she paid you?" Brian asked.

Bill looked over to Brian and frowned. "What the hell is going on, Brian? Don't tell me you're buying her bullshit?"

"Well, it can't be that hard to show she paid you." Brian flashed Bill what he hoped would be interpreted as a nonthreatening smile.

"The truth is, Brian," Bill said after a few moments of silence. "When she called me up to fix the window—on a Sunday—I wasn't too thrilled about going over there on my day off. I told her if she could pay me in cash, I'd be happy to fix it on Sunday. Otherwise, she'd have to wait until Monday. So you gunna turn me into the IRS?"

Before Brian could respond, the waitress returned with his breakfast. After she left, he said, "Nahh, I'm not calling the IRS on you. I believe you. Have to admit, I've seen that Boatman woman doing some strange things myself." Brian thought about the suitcase and wondered why she had lied about throwing all her cousin's things into it. The stunt had probably ruined Cheryl's clothes. Of course, if Cheryl never returned, it really wouldn't matter. *Was it possible Danielle knew all along her cousin was not returning?* he wondered.

"So why didn't you go to the open house?" Brian asked.

"I thought you said you believed me?"

"I do. I was just curious. I was under the impression everyone who'd done any work on the house was included in the guest list."

"I don't know about that. We didn't get all that cozy. I fixed her window, she paid me cash, and that was pretty much the last time I saw her. If you want to know why I wasn't on her guest list, you'll have to ask her."

"You said she was crazy. What other crazy things did you see her do?" Brian asked.

"Just her general hippy-dippy attitude, I guess. Explaining things to her neighbor's dog, like it was a person who understood what she was talking about. Telling us not to discuss Walt Marlow and how he died, because it would disrupt the house's feng shui. Crap like that."

"I see…" Brian popped a piece of toast in his mouth. He considered Bill's version of the events.

"Doesn't seem to me she was that convinced Adam and I broke into her house."

"What do you mean?" Brian asked.

"Adam obviously went to the open house. He must have been invited."

"I think his grandmother was invited, and she took him."

"I don't know about that." Bill stood up. "But I got to go. Hope you find that woman and return her to Boatman. Sounds like those two deserve each other."

TWENTY-FIVE

"Danielle, if you keep turning down reservations, one of these days people are going to stop calling," Lily insisted. "And before you know it, the summer season will be over."

"I just can't open the B and B yet. Not with Cheryl missing," Danielle said as she emptied the dishwasher.

"You need something to occupy your time. You can't just sit around here and wait."

"Who's sitting around? I'm putting the dishes away."

"You know what I mean. And at the end of the month, I'll be returning to California. I can't leave you here like this. What if Cheryl never comes back? For all you know she's sitting on some tropical beach somewhere, laughing her butt off."

"It isn't just about Cheryl being missing. There are so many unresolved issues. If her attorney convinces the court she's an equal partner in the estate, does that mean I'll have to set aside half the profits for her if I open the B and B? Everything is just too damn complicated right now."

"This is crazy." Lily sat down at the kitchen table.

Danielle closed the now empty dishwasher and turned to face Lily. "You want to go down to the beach? Looks like a nice day today, and I wouldn't mind getting out of the house."

"Sure. It would probably do us both some good. How about I make some sandwiches for us to take?"

"Sounds great. I'll go upstairs and change."

"I need to change too. But I'll make the sandwiches first." Lily stood up from the table.

Danielle gave Lily a quick smile and then left the kitchen. When she reached the second-floor landing, she heard what she thought sounded like a woman's voice coming from the Red Room.

Cheryl? Danielle asked herself. *Has Cheryl come back?* Hurriedly she walked to the closed bedroom door and flung it open. Sure enough, Cheryl was standing in the middle of the room, cursing angrily.

Turning to the open door, Cheryl looked at her cousin and asked, "Where is it?"

"Cheryl! My god, where have you been?" Danielle blurted.

"What did you do with my things? Everything is gone. Where is my suitcase?"

"The police took it," Danielle said as she stepped into the room. Her first impulse was to hug Cheryl, but by Cheryl's angry expression that didn't look like a terrific idea. Danielle was surprised at the sense of relief she felt seeing her cousin safe and sound, and not in danger.

"What do you mean they took it? Why would they take my suitcase?" Cheryl shrieked.

"For one thing, you ran out of here with the necklace and disappeared for a week." The joy Danielle initially experienced quickly faded into annoyance.

"You had no right to give them my things! Call them and have them bring my stuff back."

"What is all this ruckus?" Walt asked when he appeared the next moment.

"Who are you?" Cheryl demanded of Walt.

"Can you see him?" Danielle asked.

"What kind of question is that? Of course I can see him. Who is he? Have you already turned this place into a stupid inn?"

"Madam, if you can really see me, what am I doing right now?" Walt asked.

"Good lord, stop jumping up and down on your foot. You look ridiculous," Cheryl snapped.

"Well, I'll be. She can see me too. Your cousin must share your gift," Walt said.

"I don't know what you're talking about, but please leave my room," Cheryl demanded.

"This is my house. I will not leave this room," Walt countered.

"Your house? What have you done, Dani? Did you get married again while I was gone?"

"Of course I didn't get married again." Danielle's head began to spin.

"What's with all the shouting?" Lily asked from the doorway. "Are you arguing with Walt?" Lily glanced around the room.

"Cheryl's back," Danielle explained.

"She is? Where is she? Did Joe call?"

"What do you mean where am I?" Cheryl frowned at Lily.

"Well?" Lily asked, looking curiously at Danielle. "You said Cheryl's back; where is she? Do they have her at the police station?"

"Lily…" Danielle looked from Cheryl to Lily. "Can't you see her?"

"What do you mean?" Lily glanced around the room again.

"She's standing right there." Danielle pointed toward the end of the bed.

"I'm getting a bad feeling about this," Walt murmured as he wandered toward the bed and sat down on the edge of the mattress.

"Get off my bed!" Cheryl shrieked.

Ignoring Cheryl's tantrum, Walt scooted back on the mattress, pulled his feet up on the bed, leaned against the headboard, and summoned a cigar.

"Are you okay, Danielle?" Lily asked in a quiet voice. Danielle stood mute, looking frantically from the bed to Lily. Lily took a deep breath and said, "Walt's here, I can smell the cigar. Is something going on between you two?"

"Yes, Walt is here," Danielle said quietly. "So is Cheryl."

"Well, duhh," Cheryl snapped. "Is Lily playing some sort of stupid game? Pretending she can't see me because she doesn't like me?"

"We'll be right back," Danielle said as she grabbed Lily's wrist and dragged her into the hallway, shutting the door behind her.

"Cheryl's dead," Danielle said once they were alone in the hallway.

"What are you talking about?" Lily looked back at the closed door.

"Cheryl is in the bedroom. She can see Walt. But you can't see her."

"Are you sure, Dani? You've been under a lot of stress lately."

"Yes, I'm sure. She's dead, but she doesn't realize it yet. I can't just blurt it out to her. I'm not sure what she'll do."

Inside the bedroom, Cheryl looked at Walt and said, "What in the hell is going on around here? What's up with Lily and Dani? Did my cousin rent you my room? Is that why you're still here?"

"You don't have any idea, do you?"

"You look sort of familiar." Cheryl narrowed her eyes and studied Walt.

"Who do I look like?" Walt took a puff off the cigar.

"Your clothes…are you an actor? Did Dani hire you?"

"An actor? Why would she hire me?" Walt wondered how she had jumped to that conclusion.

"You look a lot like the guy in the portrait. The one who took the necklace." After mentioning the necklace, Cheryl gasped and grabbed at her throat. "It's gone. The necklace, it's gone."

"Why do you think I'm an actor?"

"She's obviously hired you to play as if you're that guy who was murdered here. Another one of her publicity stunts. But I can't think about that now. I need to remember where I put that damn necklace."

"Why did you take it?" Walt asked.

"That really is none of your business. And I want you to get out of my room. Dani will simply have to put you somewhere else."

"I'm not an actor," Walt said as he got up from the bed and stood before Cheryl. "My name is Walt Marlow."

"Walt Marlow? That's not funny. Walt Marlow was the guy who was murdered here. You aren't him. You're just someone Dani hired that looks like him."

"Want me to prove it?" Walt asked with a grin.

"Sure, go ahead. And when you're done proving it, you can get out of my room!"

Walt suddenly disappeared. Startled by his unexpected departure, she jumped back and frantically looked around the room.

"Where did you go?" Cheryl squeaked.

"Right here!" Walt gleefully shouted as he reappeared in front of her.

Wide-eyed and speechless, Cheryl stared at Walt.

He leaned toward Cheryl and whispered, "I'm a ghost…BOO!"

Cheryl let out a blood-chilling scream. Danielle rushed back into the room and found Cheryl huddled in the far corner. Walt sat on the side of the bed, attempting to contain his laughter.

"I'm sorry." Walt started laughing again and then managed to stop. "Really I am…" He began laughing again. "It was just so easy," he choked out before breaking into another fit of laughter.

"What's going on?" Lily asked Danielle in a whisper as she glanced around the room, unable to see any ghostly activity.

"What did you say to her?" Danielle glared at Walt then looked back to Cheryl. "Cheryl, what happened?"

"Damn him," Cheryl said angrily, no longer frightened. "What is he, some sort of magician or something? Tried to make me think he was a ghost. Even pulled some silly disappearing trick. This isn't funny, Dani!"

"No…no, it isn't…" Danielle murmured, glancing over at Walt, who hadn't quite controlled his fit of laughter.

"Hey, I'm sorry, but you would've had to have been here," Walt said guiltily.

"Cheryl, I don't know how else to do this without just coming out and saying it. This is Walt Marlow. He is…well…our resident ghost."

"Ha-ha, Dani. You're just punishing me because I took off with that necklace. By the way, why haven't you asked me about the necklace yet?"

"I guess I feel there are some things more important than million-dollar necklaces."

"Like what?"

"Like explaining to my cousin that the reason she can see Walt Marlow is because she is just like him."

"What are you talking about?" Cheryl frowned.

"I'm sorry to have to tell you this, but you're a ghost, just like Walt. You're dead."

Cheryl stood there a moment staring at Dani. Finally, she broke into laughter.

"Right, Dani Boo. Seeing ghosts again." Cheryl continued to laugh.

"I can prove it," Danielle said.

"Oh yeah? What are you going to do, have your actor do his disappearing act again? Nice trick but I've seen it before in Vegas."

"Pick up that vase," Danielle said, pointing to an empty flower vase sitting on the dresser.

"What will that prove?" Cheryl asked.

"Just go ahead and do it. Pick up the vase and you'll see."

Cheryl let out a sigh and walked to the dresser, a bored expression on her face. With a disinterested shrug, she reached for the vase. Instead of picking it up, her fingers moved through it as if it were air. Startled, Cheryl jumped back and stared at the vase. She reached for it again with the same result.

"This is some trick," Cheryl muttered.

"Try something else," Danielle suggested.

"What do you mean?"

"Try picking up something else."

Flashing Danielle a dirty look, she reached for the handle of the dresser. Once again, her hand moved through the piece. A look of confusion on her face, she snatched at the lamp—the doorknob—the light switch—a pillow from the bed. After numerous unsuccessful tries, she let out a high-pitched scream and crumpled into a ball on the floor, sobbing inconsolably.

TWENTY-SIX

Danielle sat on the third step leading from the first to the second floor of Marlow House. She seriously considered running down to the drugstore and purchasing a pair of earplugs to block out Cheryl's insistent wailing. Leaning to one side, she reached back, tugged her cellphone from the back pocket of her shorts, and looked at the time. It had been over three hours since she had given her cousin the bad news. Cheryl hadn't stopped carrying on since that time.

The front door opened. Danielle looked up as she tucked her cellphone back into her pocket. Lily was back from Ian's.

"How was dinner?" Danielle asked.

"Good. Wish you would have come with us. Did you get something to eat?"

"I ate one of the sandwiches you made."

"Oh yeah, we didn't quite make it to the beach, did we?" Lily sat on the step next to Danielle.

"So where's Ian?" Danielle asked.

"I told him I was getting a headache."

"Are you?"

"Nah, but I wanted to see how you and Cheryl were doing, and I didn't think I could do it with Ian hanging around. Anyway, I couldn't stop thinking of Cheryl—wondering what happened to her. So how's it going?"

"I think I got your headache." Danielle rubbed her temples and cringed. "She hasn't stopped crying and carrying on since I told her."

Lily cocked her head and listened for any unusual sounds. "I don't hear anything."

"Be grateful. Grateful you don't have this damn gift."

Walt suddenly appeared before Lily and Danielle. Standing on the first-floor landing, he faced the two women. "You have to make her stop!"

"Maybe I could have handled the situation differently if you hadn't decided to play haunt the ghost," Danielle snapped.

"Ah, Walt is here. Hi, Walt," Lily said cheerfully.

"I'm sorry, but she's the first one I've seen—apart from you—who could actually see or hear me."

"I've gone up there a half a dozen times already. I can only take her howling for a few minutes before I have to leave. She's so damn loud," Danielle said.

"Hi, Walt," Lily said again.

"Tell Lily I say hello."

"Walt says hello. Seems my cousin's racket is getting on his nerves too."

"Walt, would you do me a favor?" Lily asked.

Upstairs, Cheryl's sobs and screams continued, yet they didn't seem as loud as they had moments before. Danielle wondered if she was finally winding down.

"Ask her what she wants," Walt said.

"He wants to know what you want."

"This whole thing…well…it is a little overwhelming. Especially now with Cheryl. I need to be reminded this is all for real, that I'm not just being sucked into someone's delusion." Lily looked to Danielle and said apologetically, "I'm sorry, Dani. I hope you understand."

"Believe me, I do. Trust me. I wouldn't blame you if you decided to call in the men in white coats," Danielle said.

"Walt, the other day you picked the croquet ball up off the kitchen floor and put it back in the bag for me. I need to know that I didn't imagine that. That you are real. Is there anything you can do to convince me I haven't been making things up in my mind?"

Danielle looked at Walt. "How about it?"

Lily turned to Danielle, hoping she really did understand.

Danielle wasn't looking at Lily. Instead, she was looking down the entry hall toward the front door. The corners of her mouth curled into a slow smile.

"Nice touch, Walt," Danielle said.

Lily looked to where Danielle was staring. She appeared to be looking at the floral arrangement Marie had sent over before the open house. Lily had faithfully watered the arrangement since its arrival. Most of the roses had since wilted and been discarded, yet a few remained.

Something caught Lily's eye—something floating between the table and where they sat on the steps. Her eyes widened at the sight. A single rose floated slowly in her direction.

Danielle couldn't help but grin as she watched Walt carry the red rose from the arrangement to where they sat. When he reached the steps, he knelt down on one knee and offered the flower to Lily.

Lily couldn't see Walt, only the red rose floating several inches from her. Grinning, she reached out and accepted the flower. "Thanks, Walt. This is really sweet."

From upstairs, Cheryl began wailing again in earnest.

Walt's smile faded. He looked up the staircase and said, "Now can we please do something about that?"

"Damn," Danielle cursed, glancing behind her up the stairs.

"What is it?" Lily twirled the rose in her hand. Bringing the blossom to her nose, she took a sniff.

"It's Cheryl again. I thought she was winding down, but apparently, she got a fresh burst. I need to talk to her, but it kills my ears being in the same room with her," Danielle explained.

"Let me do it." Lily stood up.

"You? You can't see her," Danielle said.

"I know. I can't hear her either. But she can hear me, right?"

"Lily has a point. Cheryl will be able to hear her, so Lily can say whatever she wants without having to listen to her racket," Walt said.

"I guess it's worth a try," Danielle said, cringing again from the caterwauling.

"There is one problem," Walt said with hesitation.

"What?" Danielle asked.

"Cheryl is unstable; I don't want her to throw something at Lily and hurt her. Maybe I should just go in."

"I suppose that is a possibility," Danielle murmured.

"Sure it's possible. I can talk to her!" Lily declared.

"Although I'm pretty sure she hasn't figured it out yet. Remember, I told her to pick up the vase in the bedroom, and she wasn't able to harness any of her energy."

"Umm…what are you talking about?" Lily asked.

"I don't think Cheryl could do anything to hurt you—at least not yet," Danielle explained.

"Hurt me? Oh, you mean like when Walt threw the croquet set at Bill and Adam?"

"Yes. She hasn't figured any of that out yet. Heck, she just learned she's dead."

"Dead…yeah…" Lily shuddered. "Just where is her body? What happened to her? Did someone kill her or what?"

"I've been wondering all those things myself," Danielle said. "But Cheryl won't calm down long enough for me to talk to her so we can figure all this out. I'm sure she's here because she needs to come to terms with what happened to her, and I certainly want to know where…where…"

"Where her body is?" Lily asked.

"Yes. You know, it's one thing to see her up there but quite another for me to come to the realization that she's really gone—I mean gone from this world. I don't think I've quite wrapped my head around that."

"Let me talk to her. Okay?" Lily said.

"Tell Lily if Cheryl starts throwing things, to get out of that room, and call for me immediately."

Danielle looked at Lily. "Try to talk to her, get her to understand we need to figure out what happened. She needs to come to terms with all this. But if she figures out how to start throwing furniture, get out of the room and call for Walt immediately. Deal?"

"Deal." Lily took a deep breath. "Will you make me one promise?"

"Sure, anything," Danielle said.

"If Cheryl leaves the room, please tell me. I don't want to be in there talking to an empty room. As it is, I'm going to feel silly enough."

"Deal."

Lily took another deep breath. She handed Danielle the rose and then clutched the handrail and made her way upstairs to the second floor. It seemed so quiet she found it hard to believe Cheryl was in the Red Room, screaming her head off.

"Is she still howling?" Lily called down to Dani when she reached the second-floor landing.

"Yes!" Danielle said.

"Umm…where was she the last time you were in the room? I don't want to sit on her or anything."

"She was sitting in the corner next to the nightstand."

"Okay, I'm doing this!" Lily sounded more confident than she felt.

She walked to the Red Room's door and clutched its doorknob. "Cheryl, this is Lily. I'm coming in!" Lily threw the door open and peeked inside. It didn't look like anyone was there. It was so quiet she could hear the antique clock in the hall ticking.

"Hello, Cheryl, I'm really sorry about all this. Honest." Lily walked into the room and looked in the corner where she believed Cheryl was huddled.

Cheryl stood on the other side of the room, looking into the mirror. There was no reflection. That was what had started her recent crying bout. She stopped sobbing and looked at Lily. "I thought you couldn't see or hear me?"

"I really wish you would stop crying so we can help you. Danielle and Walt want to help you." Lily continued to look into the corner, away from where Cheryl stood by the mirror.

"I am over here!" Cheryl stomped her foot in frustration. For a brief moment, when Lily had entered the room and started talking, Cheryl thought perhaps it had all been some joke. If Lily could see her, then maybe she really wasn't dead.

"Walt wasn't thrilled to find out he was dead either. But it eventually happens to all of us," Lily said, still looking into the empty corner.

Cheryl glared at Lily and screamed at the top of her lungs—that was, had she actually had lungs. Downstairs, Walt and Danielle cringed and looked up the stairs.

The scream did not faze Lily, who, oblivious to the high-pitched howl, prattled on endlessly. Initially, Lily had been a little worried that she would feel ridiculous talking to a seemingly empty room, yet once she got rolling, she couldn't stop.

Cheryl continued to wail about the injustice of it all, but after almost ten minutes of howling while watching Lily calmly babble away, Cheryl grew quiet.

"...after all, eternity is going to be a very long time, and you really don't want to spend it throwing a tantrum, do you? Don't you want to know what happened to you? I mean, you obviously don't know because if you knew, you would know you were dead, and if you knew you were dead, you would not have been so surprised when Dani told you, and then you wouldn't be screaming and throwing a fit, and if you would just calm down and talk to Dani, she could help you. Did you know she has been really worried about you, and did you notice she never asked you about the necklace because she doesn't care about the necklace, she cares about you and..."

Cheryl walked to the doorway and into the hall, leaving Lily alone in the room, still prattling on, yet now there was no one to hear her. She walked to the top of the stairs and looked down. Walt and Danielle sat on the steps below her.

"Can you make her stop?" Cheryl asked.

Danielle and Walt both turned around and looked up the stairs. Cheryl was standing on the second-floor landing, looking down at them. She seemed much calmer than before and was no longer crying.

"Make who stop?" Danielle asked as she stood up and started walking up the stairs.

"Lily, of course. Lord, that girl can talk!"

"Yes, she can," Walt said with a chuckle as he followed Danielle up the stairs.

"Can we talk now?" Danielle asked.

"Yes, I'd like that. But first, please tell Lily to stop. Or I swear, I just may start screaming again."

TWENTY-SEVEN

Cheryl stood before the massive paintings in the library and studied Walt's portrait. Tilting her head from side to side, she said, "It really is you, isn't it?"

"Did you doubt it?" Walt asked.

"What is going on?" Lily asked in a whisper. She sat with Danielle on the small couch, wishing she could hear everything that was going on. In response, Danielle reached over and gave her hand a squeeze. Lily took the gesture to mean *not now, Lily, I will tell you later*. Letting out a sigh, Lily leaned back and resigned herself to the fact she would have to wait until later to get Danielle's account of whatever was said.

"Cheryl, why don't you come over here and sit down in the chair next to Walt so we can talk," Danielle suggested.

Cheryl turned from the portrait and walked toward Walt. "I hadn't really noticed, but you are rather good looking." She sat on the chair next to him. "I suppose if I'm destined to be trapped for eternity with someone, I'd rather it be a handsome man rather than someone I can't bear looking at."

Danielle glanced from Cheryl to Walt and noticed his expression of horror at Cheryl's misguided conclusion. She wouldn't have been surprised had he taken this moment to pull one of his disappearing acts.

"You are not trapped for eternity with Walt," Danielle explained.

"Really?" Cheryl looked from Walt to Danielle. "Is there something between you two?"

"Excuse me?" Danielle asked with a frown.

"You do seem rather fond of each other. I just wondered if..."

"Cheryl, it's not really possible for the type of relationship you suggest. Can we please get back to your situation?"

"But it is possible for one between let's say...Walt and me?" Cheryl smiled at Walt.

"No," Walt snapped.

Dejected, Cheryl slumped down in her chair and looked over at Danielle. "I don't want to be dead."

"Do you have any idea what happened?" Danielle asked. "Do you know where...where your body is?"

"My body?" Cheryl began to tear up again.

"Please, Cheryl, try to stay calm. We need to sort this all out," Danielle urged.

"Is she screaming again?" Lily whispered. Danielle shook her head no.

"It's all sort of...well, foggy feeling," Cheryl said after reining in her emotions.

"It's like that at first," Walt explained. "But once you understand why things are so different, why the world as you know it is off kilter, everything will eventually come into focus. You won't remember all of it at once. But just try—what can you remember?"

"I remember wanting to go home," Cheryl said.

"Home here or California?" Danielle asked.

"My home in California. This isn't my home. It wasn't fun anymore here. Something...something scared me. I can't remember how I got back to my room here. I just wanted to get my things and leave, but everything was gone—my clothes, my suitcase—everything."

"Try to remember where you were before you returned to Marlow House," Danielle urged.

Cheryl closed her eyes, her expression somber. She let out a little gasp and said, "I was in a dark shed. I could hear the waves breaking on the beach. I was close to the ocean. But I couldn't see anything." She opened her eyes and looked at her cousin. "I remember now. I was afraid; I didn't know where I was. I could see a little bit of light coming in through the wallboards, so I ran toward the light, hoping to find a door, but then…then…"

"Then what?" Danielle asked.

"Then I was outside the shed, standing on the beach. How did I do that? I don't remember finding a door."

"You walked through the wall," Walt explained.

"I did?" Cheryl's eyes widened at the thought.

"So it was daytime?" Danielle asked.

"No, it was nighttime," Cheryl said.

"But you said you saw light coming through the wallboards," Danielle reminded her.

"It was night, but there was a little bit of light from the moon and the nearby houses."

"I bet your body is in that shed," Danielle said.

"Her body is in a shed?" Lily gasped.

"That really creeps me out when you talk about my body." Cheryl shuddered.

"I understand," Walt agreed. "Danielle just doesn't get that."

"Hey! How else am I supposed to say it?"

"Not suggesting you can phrase it differently. But I do think you are sometimes a bit insensitive," Walt said.

"I agree, she can be." Cheryl nodded.

"Oh, brother," Danielle muttered under her breath.

"What's going on?" Lily asked in a whisper.

"Ghost divas," Danielle quipped.

"Can you describe where the shed was?" Walt asked, ignoring Danielle's comment. "You say it was on the beach?"

"Yes. There was a row of sheds, about six of them, I think. Not on the beach exactly but under a rocky cliff overhang. It wasn't all sand underfoot—wild grass—about five feet from the beach. Each shed had a large number painted on its door. The one I came out of had the number three."

"Does that place sound familiar?" Danielle asked Walt.

"No. But I doubt the sheds were around back then."

"What place?" Lily asked.

"Cheryl remembers being at a beach shack. She said there was a row of six of them, with numbers painted on their doors."

"Red numbers?" Lily asked.

Cheryl jumped up and shouted, "Yes, red numbers!"

"Yes. Cheryl said they were red numbers," Danielle confirmed.

"I think I know where that is," Lily said. "Ian and I walked Sadie down there a few times. It's on the south side of town."

"Okay, so now we have a good idea where…where we might find…you know…" Danielle said. "Now, Cheryl, do you remember how you got to that shed?"

Cheryl shook her head. "No. I don't. But I have a question."

"What?" Danielle asked.

"When was the party? What's today's date?"

"It's Friday, July 11. You went missing a week ago," Danielle explained.

Cheryl glanced down at her dress and frowned.

"What is it?" Danielle asked.

Tugging at the hem of her pink dress, Cheryl looked at Danielle and said, "Are you telling me I've been wearing the same dress for a week? An entire week!"

"Well, I suppose so." Danielle shrugged. "But I don't see what that has to do with anything."

"Of course you wouldn't understand. Just look how you dress!" Cheryl let go of her hem and sat back in the chair.

"It won't always be like this," Walt explained.

"What do you mean?" Cheryl asked.

"This…" Walt snapped his fingers. The suit he had been wearing changed colors.

"How did you do that?" Cheryl asked in awe.

"Can we please discuss your wardrobe later?" Danielle said impatiently.

"I'd like to know where she took the necklace and why. And where is it?" Lily asked.

"Yes, I would like to know that too." Danielle looked at Cheryl. "I have a feeling that's what got you…well, to your current state."

"Maybe I'm still wearing it." Cheryl touched her throat. "Perhaps it is on…on the other me."

"I suppose that depends on what happened to you. Why were you in that shed? Did Adam take you there?" Danielle doubted the necklace was still on Cheryl. After all, it was what probably got her killed.

"Adam? Why would Adam take me there?"

"What's your last memory before the shed?" Danielle asked.

"I don't know; it's kind of fuzzy."

"Do you remember the open house?" Danielle asked.

"No. I said it's fuzzy." Cheryl squirmed in her chair.

"But you remember having the necklace," Danielle reminded her.

"Yes. But like I said, it is…"

"Fuzzy. Yes. You've mentioned that. Maybe I can refresh your memory. At the open house, you tried on the necklace, went to look at it in the mirror, and then left the house suddenly with Adam. According to him, you two drove to one of his beach rentals, where apparently he had too much to drink and you helped him to bed. When he woke up in the morning, you were gone with the necklace. They've been looking for you ever since."

"Okay…I guess I remember trying on the necklace. I wasn't going to steal it. Honest."

"Why did you leave with it?" Danielle asked.

"You got to wear it all day. I just figured it was my turn. But I didn't want to wear it around a bunch of old people at your open house, and I knew you wouldn't let me wear it out so people could see it. I figured I'd spend a romantic evening with Adam. I mean, come on, Danielle, imagine how sexy it would be to make love wearing just that necklace!"

"I suppose I can understand that," Walt said. "Was it?"

"Walt!" Danielle snapped.

"She really can be such a prude," Cheryl told Walt. "I don't know what you see in her."

"Please, let's stay focused," Danielle said impatiently.

"Fine…" Cheryl sighed dramatically. "It's getting a little clearer. I can remember some of it. Adam took me to the beach house. When he got there, he poured us each a glass of wine. I hadn't told him yet about the necklace."

"What do you mean, what hadn't you told him?" Danielle asked.

"He didn't know I had it. After I left the parlor, I took it off and slipped it in my purse. There was so much commotion with new people coming in the house that no one seemed to notice."

"So Adam didn't know you had the necklace?" Danielle asked.

"No. I wanted to surprise him at the beach house."

"Then what happened?" Walt asked.

"After Adam poured us the wine, I went to the bathroom. I was going to put the necklace on and then come back out and surprise him. I suppose I stayed in the bathroom for longer than I intended

—I kept looking at myself in the mirror. It was so pretty. And then I decided it would be more dramatic if…well…I simply walked into the bedroom wearing just the necklace."

"You took your clothes off?" Danielle asked.

"No! I was going to do that later, after we had some wine. So I put the necklace back in my purse and went to the living room. Adam's wineglass was empty. I didn't think anything of it, but then he started acting funny, like he was drunk. I mean on one glass, can you believe that? I helped him to his bed, although I don't know why I bothered. I should have just let him pass out on the couch."

"Then what did you do?" Danielle asked.

"That's when it gets fuzzy again. I can't quite remember how I got there—but I remember walking on the beach. It was dark. And then someone else was there."

"You obviously got as far as those huts. What do you remember about leaving the beach house?" Danielle asked.

"I remember putting the necklace back on. I remember standing on the back porch, looking down the beach. I could see the fireworks in the distance. And then…well, things get sorta spotty…"

"Spotty?" Danielle asked.

"It's like bits and pieces. Someone was there with me. I wasn't alone on the beach."

"Who was it?"

Cheryl shook her head. "I don't know. I don't remember." Cheryl sounded frustrated. "But it was someone familiar."

"A man or a woman?" Walt asked.

"I'm not sure. But someone who I wasn't afraid of. I remember that."

"Did you walk to the beach shack together?" Danielle asked.

"I think so…maybe…I'm not sure…" Cheryl stood up abruptly. "I don't like these feelings."

"What feelings?" Danielle asked.

"The feelings I get when I try to remember the rest of it. I just want to go home!" Cheryl began to cry again. She flopped back down in the chair and slumped over, her muffled sobs breaking into an occasional hiccup.

"I'm sorry, Cheryl, calm down. It'll be okay, I promise," Danielle said.

Cheryl jerked her head up and looked at Danielle. "Okay? I am dead, dead! How can I be okay?"

"Bad choice of words," Walt noted, shaking his head in disapproval.

"Thank you, Walt." Cheryl sniffed and wiped her eyes with the back of her hand. "At least you understand."

"Is Cheryl upset again? What's wrong?" Lily asked.

"I guess I need to take a course in afterlife sensitivity training," Danielle said with a sigh.

TWENTY-EIGHT

Danielle woke up the next morning to the sound of Lily vomiting in the bathroom down the hall. Groggy, she sat up and was surprised to find not just Walt sitting on the side of her bed, looking at her; Cheryl was sitting with him.

"Lily is sick," they said in unison.

"What's wrong?" Danielle rubbed her eyes and stumbled out of bed.

"I think she has the flu," Cheryl said. "The sound is grossing me out; you really need to do something about it."

"You should wash down her face with a damp cloth," Walt suggested. "The poor thing looks miserable."

"Oh, you're so sweet," Cheryl cooed, flashing Walt a smile.

Danielle rolled her eyes and silently made her way from the bedroom to the bathroom down the hall. She found Lily sitting on the floor in front of the toilet.

"Oh, poor Lily," Danielle said, turning on the bathroom light.

Lily flushed the toilet and then looked up at Danielle through red-rimmed eyes. She remained seated on the floor, leaning over the toilet bowl. Danielle grabbed a clean washcloth from the bathroom cupboard. After running it under cold water and wringing it out, she handed it to Lily.

"Thanks." Lily took the cloth and wiped down her face. "I think I have the flu."

Danielle noticed Lily already had a glass of water by her side. "When did you get sick?"

"I woke up about an hour ago with a killer headache. Started throwing up about twenty minutes ago. Sorry I woke you."

"No problem. Can I get you anything?"

"No. But I won't be able to go down to the beach with you today and show you where those beach huts are."

"That's okay, you take care of yourself. You can give me directions; I'll find it."

"You can't go alone. I mean, what if you do find…well, you know…Cheryl."

"That's sort of the point, isn't it?" Danielle leaned back against the bathroom counter and looked down at Lily.

"Yeah, but if you find her, what are you going to do?"

"I guess I'll call the police."

"How are you going to explain how you happened to find her?"

"I suppose I'll call in an anonymous tip."

"They can trace those things. And if she died of unnatural causes, which I imagine was the case, you certainly don't want them to think you had anything to do with it."

"I'll figure out something. Maybe I can get Ian and Sadie to go with me. I'll tell him I want to walk the beach from Adam's bungalow to the beach in front of his house—on the theory she tried to walk here. I know the authorities supposedly did that already, but if she is at that hut, they obviously didn't do a terrific job."

"I'm afraid Ian is going to Astoria today for another interview with Emma. He's taking Sadie with him. I imagine he left already."

"Well, I'll just have to go there alone."

"I'll go with you," Cheryl said from the doorway.

Danielle turned to face her cousin. "You? I don't even know if that's possible."

"I don't think she's bound to this house," Walt said.

"What do you mean bound to this house?" Cheryl looked from Walt to Danielle.

"Walt and Cheryl are here, aren't they?" Lily asked.

"Yes. They were in my room when I woke up. Wanted me to come check on you."

"Ah, that's sweet." Lily looked to the doorway where she assumed they were standing.

"Yeah," Danielle said dryly. "I've been hearing that a lot lately."

"You didn't answer my question," Cheryl interrupted. "What do you mean bound here?"

"Walt isn't able to leave the house. When he's ready to move on to the next level—wherever that is for him—it appears he can now do that. But while he chooses to be on this plane, it seems he's confined to Marlow House—inside the house, not the grounds."

"Next plane…you mean there is more than just this?" Cheryl asked.

"Certainly. I don't think this is your final destination. You sort of got derailed because of how you died, and before you can move on, you need to resolve some issues. At least that seemed to be the case for Walt, so I imagine that's what's going on with you."

"You really did see Grandma, didn't you?" Cheryl asked with a pout.

"Yes. She was the first spirit I ever saw."

"So she did love you more." Cheryl's lower lip began to quiver.

"It has nothing to do with who she loved more. Grandma didn't choose me to see her. Ask yourself, did you choose for me to see you?"

"No. You just saw me," Cheryl murmured thoughtfully. "Did you see Mom and Dad and Sean?"

"No. I never saw them. I never saw my parents or even Lucas."

"Well, I imagine Lucas probably wanted to avoid that meeting, considering what he did," Cheryl scoffed.

"My point is, I don't think I can choose—nor can the spirits choose. It just sometimes happens."

Lily began to throw up again. When she stopped, she said, "Would you guys mind taking your conversation elsewhere so I can puke in peace?"

"Sorry, Lily," Danielle said, stepping from the bathroom into the hall, shutting the door behind her.

"So does this mean there is a heaven?" Cheryl asked excitedly. "Will I see Mom, Dad, Grandma, and Sean again?"

"I don't know if there is a heaven exactly. I believe there is something more. Maybe it is heaven. I don't know. But I do believe you will see your loved ones again on the next plane, at least, that's what I've gathered from other spirits I've encountered."

"Why are you still here, then?" Cheryl asked Walt.

"What do you mean?" he asked.

"If you're confined to this old house when you have the option to move on to another place where you can see friends and family, why stay here?"

"I really have no one I care to see right now," Walt said with a shrug.

"But what about the other stuff?" Cheryl asked.

"Other stuff?"

"Well, what if the streets really are paved in gold?"

"Perhaps. But what do I need with gold streets?"

"Maybe you don't want to go, but I do. Okay, I'm ready." Cheryl closed her eyes and stood still for a few moments.

"It doesn't work that way," Danielle said.

"Danielle's right," Walt agreed. "There's something holding you here, or you wouldn't have returned to this house. My guess is you'll be able to go with Danielle to the beach shack, but I could be wrong. You might be confined here in the same way Angela is confined to the cemetery."

"Who is Angela?" Cheryl asked.

"Walt's wife. Angela is more under house arrest for not being such a good person."

"Oh crap, do you think I'm under house arrest too?" Cheryl slumped against the wall.

"Do you think you were a bad person?" Danielle asked with wry amusement.

"I don't think I was bad exactly…but I suppose I did some things my parents would not be proud of." Cheryl looked down at her feet.

"I think we need to take one thing at a time. First things first. We need to find your body and figure out what happened to you. I think when the time is right for you to move on, you'll know it," Danielle explained.

"Why are you being so nice to me?" Cheryl asked.

"You're my cousin," Danielle explained.

"Do you love me?"

"Love you?" Danielle shifted nervously from one foot to another.

"Yes, love me. We are family. Aren't you supposed to love family?"

"Do you love me?" Danielle asked.

"Certainly," Cheryl said absolutely.

"Then why did you make a pass at Lucas at our rehearsal dinner and then insist he was the one who did it?"

"Because I knew he was all wrong for you. I was right. You know it."

"Is that why you came on to all my boyfriends?"

"Oh, come on, Dani, if any of those boys were right for you, they wouldn't have been swayed by a little harmless flirting from me. But that doesn't matter now. What does matter, I always had your best interest at heart. Because I loved you and felt responsible for you."

"You felt responsible for me?"

"Certainly. You were just so…so…well, awkward. And I was… well, I was me."

"What in the world is that supposed to mean?" Danielle asked.

"Come on, Dani, we all knew you were jealous of me."

"I was never jealous of you!" Danielle was insulted.

"Don't get upset, Dani. I understood. That's why I felt so responsible for you. It couldn't have been easy on you, having to watch me in one beauty pageant after another—while you sat on the sidelines."

"No, it wasn't easy," Danielle said dryly.

"I think we need to focus on what's important now," Walt interrupted.

"Yes, of course. Walt is right." Cheryl smiled sweetly at Walt.

"I suppose we can agree on that. In this instance, Walt is correct. Let's focus on what's important now," Danielle said.

BY THE TIME Danielle dressed and braided her hair, Lily had taken a shower and returned to bed. When Danielle came to check on Lily and get directions to the beach shack, she found her sitting up in bed, eating a slice of toast. A cup of hot tea sat on her nightstand.

"You went downstairs?" Danielle asked as she pulled up a chair and sat next to the bed.

"No, Walt brought it to me." Lily smiled. "At least I assume it was Walt and not Cheryl."

"I don't think it was Cheryl. She hasn't figured out how to move things. In fact, I don't think she even realizes the possibility yet."

"If she's going with you to look for her body, don't you think that would come in handy if you ran into trouble?"

"Trouble?"

"If whoever she took that walk with murdered her and put her body into the shed, you certainly don't want to be alone and run into him. Having someone capable of tossing around a croquet set might come in handy."

"Yeah, I sorta thought about that. But this is Cheryl we're talking about. Do I really want her to know how to do all that? Just imagine if she had started tossing the furniture at us during her crying fit."

"You have a point. But please, be careful. Maybe you should just call in an anonymous tip for someone to check that beach shack."

"Didn't you say they trace those things?"

"Sure, but I bet there's a pay phone in town you can use."

"And probably some traffic camera ready to take my picture."

"Now you're just being paranoid, Dani."

"Maybe…" Danielle shrugged.

"Okay, so if you find her body, what are you going to do about it?"

"I've been thinking about that. If she is in the beach hut, then I'll have to go back with someone and pretend to accidentally find her. I think it would look better if I was with someone else if I do. If this is a twenty-four-hour bug and you're feeling better tomorrow, maybe we can rope Ian into taking us down along that stretch of the beach like I suggested earlier."

"Then just wait for him. Don't go today."

"No. I don't want to wait. I need to know if Cheryl's body is down there. And if it isn't, maybe walking along that stretch of beach will help trip her memory."

"Okay, Dani, but please, please be careful."

TWENTY-NINE

The closest parking spot Danielle could find was south of Adam's beach bungalow. Since Lily couldn't recall where the beach huts were exactly, they decided it would be best if they started at the bungalow and worked north.

It was a sunny morning with temperatures in the low eighties. There seemed to be far more people along this stretch of beach compared to Danielle's end of town, yet it scarcely compared to the crowds that gathered at Southern California beaches.

"Odd, I don't feel any sand between my toes," Cheryl said as she looked down at her bare feet.

"I just realized you aren't wearing shoes. You didn't have any shoes on when you returned to Marlow House."

Cheryl looked down at her feet again and wiggled her toes. "Hmm, you're right."

"Tell me, do you remember taking your shoes off?"

"Well…" Cheryl thought a moment. "I took them off at Adam's. I don't remember putting them back on. I certainly wouldn't have put them on when I walked on the beach."

"When the police found Adam the next day at the bungalow, nothing of yours was at the house—not your purse or shoes."

"Oh, I took them with me," Cheryl said.

"Are you sure?"

"Yes! I remember now," Cheryl said excitedly. "I wasn't about to stay at Adam's with him passed out. I didn't know how to get back to Marlow House exactly, but I figured if I kept walking north along the ocean, I would eventually get to the beach in front of Ian's house."

"I sort of figured that might be the case. I mean, about you finding your way back to Marlow House by going north on the beach."

"People are starting to stare." Cheryl giggled. "After all, you are talking to yourself."

Danielle glanced around. It was true; a few people they had passed were still staring in her direction. For the next few minutes, Danielle and Cheryl walked in silence. Danielle carried her purse in one hand and her shoes in the other.

"There it is!" Cheryl said, pointing to a beach house; its back porch faced the ocean.

"What?" Danielle asked.

"That's the house Adam brought me to. I remember now walking along this stretch of the beach. Up here." Cheryl pointed ahead.

"Can you remember anything else, like who it was you ran into that night?"

"No..." Cheryl shook her head. "But it was someone familiar... not someone I knew well, but someone I met here; I'm certain of that. Which means you probably know that person too."

They continued to walk farther north and the crowds dwindled until at last Danielle could comfortably talk to Cheryl without fear someone would think she was talking to herself.

"Look, it's getting a little rocky up ahead!" Danielle said. "Does any of this look familiar?"

"No, not really. But it was nighttime."

"You recognized the bungalow."

"That's only because Adam took me there the first day we met. We sat on the back porch for about an hour and talked. I thought he was really nice. Too bad he had to drink so much."

They walked a little ways more until finally they went around a bend and there they were—six beach shacks as Lily had described, each painted with a different red number, one through six.

"There they are!" Danielle exclaimed.

Some distance from the huts, over a hill that faced the ocean, Danielle spied a row of rooftops, their houses concealed by the hill.

A path leading from the houses to the huts wound around the grassy hill, and midway there was a wooden bench, faded and bleached from constant exposure to the elements.

"It looks like they store their beach stuff here, you know like chairs and surfboards," Danielle said. When her cousin didn't respond, she glanced back and noticed Cheryl had stopped walking and just stood quietly, staring at the small buildings.

"What is it? Aren't you coming?" Danielle asked.

"I can't." Cheryl stood frozen to the spot.

"What do you mean you can't?"

"It feels funny. I'm afraid," Cheryl whispered, her voice trembling.

"If you think about it, what can really happen to you? I mean… well, you're already dead."

"You aren't."

"I'll be okay. Doesn't look like anyone is around, and I seriously doubt whoever you were here with is lurking about."

"Okay, but I'm staying here."

"Fine. I'll see if I can have a look inside, and then we can get the heck out of here. Okay?"

Cheryl nodded her head in agreement.

The sound of ocean breakers crashing along the beach filled Danielle's head. There was no other human in sight, although she assumed the houses in the distance were probably occupied for the summer, and it was possible someone could show up on the beach at any minute. She needed to move quickly, especially if she didn't want to be seen. If Cheryl's body was in the shed, it probably wouldn't be a great idea to be seen poking around the area.

Danielle felt less brave than she acted. A sense of dread washed over her as she neared the shacks.

"Okay, let's hurry this up," Danielle mumbled to herself as she approached rustic hut three. She set her purse and shoes on the sand and looked around the hut, but there didn't seem to be any windows, just a door. The ill-fitting boards provided gaps, and she wondered if one might prove useful as a peephole.

When she put her eye to one, it was too dark inside to see anything. Then it hit her, the indescribable scent of decaying flesh. Danielle quickly glanced behind her to Cheryl, who stood a good distance away, her back now to her. Cheryl was no longer watching

Danielle; she gazed out to the ocean as if she could not bear looking at the beach shacks.

Danielle felt her own heart beating wildly, and for a brief moment she entertained the idea of just walking away—no, running—back to Cheryl and her car to figure out some other way to get the police to the hut. Yet she couldn't get herself to turn back now.

Instead of a keyed doorknob, a latch and padlock held the door securely shut. On closer inspection, Danielle discovered someone had already cut through the padlock, yet left it hanging on the latch, giving the impression the building was locked.

Reluctant to grasp the hut's latch for fear of leaving fingerprints, she remembered what Lily had said. *Now you're just being paranoid.* Slipping her hand under her blouse to use the fabric to shield her fingerprints, she gingerly opened the latch, leaving the broken padlock hanging. She opened the hut's door wide, letting in the sunshine.

Lifting the collar of her shirt upward, she used its fabric to cover her nostrils. The stench was sickening. Nervously, she peeked into the hut, but it was too dark to see inside when standing in the bright sunlight. Stepping into the dark space, she looked around and waited for her eyes to adjust to the dim lighting. Shafts of sunlight cut through the small space, finding their way in through the gaps between the wallboards. Looking around, she noticed a workbench with several surfboards propped against it. There were old beach chairs, several beach umbrellas and, in the corner by the door, a stack of children's beach toys—buckets, shovels, and a deflated beach ball.

Her eyes, adjusting to the lighting, darted across the dimly lit space as she took another step inside. Just as she did, she glanced down and saw them—a pair of women's bare feet, covered in dry sand, sticking out from under a pile of partially inflated rafts.

Danielle let out a little cry and fell to her knees, no longer thinking rationally as she shoved the rafts aside and uncovered the bloated body of her cousin, who lay lifeless on the wood floor, staring blankly up to the ceiling.

"Oh, Cheryl," Danielle murmured sadly.

Cheryl's once golden hair was now matted in dry blood from what appeared to be a severe head wound. While Danielle was no forensic expert, she guessed that someone had bashed Cheryl over her head with something hard.

Quickly glancing around the shed, she didn't see a likely weapon, at least, nothing with bloodstains. Cheryl wasn't wearing the Missing Thorndike, which didn't surprise Danielle. Looking around, she spied Cheryl's purse and shoes not far from the body.

While she didn't expect to find the necklace stuffed in Cheryl's purse, she felt compelled to look, just in case.

The necklace wasn't there.

"God, I hate leaving you here like this," Danielle whispered over her cousin's broken and lifeless body.

Cheryl's frantic screams interrupted the somber moment. "Dani! Dani! Hurry!"

With a quick jerk, Danielle turned toward the open door, but the silhouette of what appeared to be a man standing in the doorway blocked the sun.

"What the hell?" the man said, stepping into the hut.

Danielle looked up. She could now see his face. It was Bill Jones.

"What are you doing here?" Danielle blurted out.

"I am so sorry, Dani! I didn't see him coming until it was too late. Hurry up, run!" Frantic, Cheryl now stood at the doorway, anxiously hopping about from foot to foot.

"Is this the man, Cheryl?" Danielle asked in a steady voice as she kept her eyes on Bill and slowly stood up, preparing herself for physical combat if necessary.

"Who are you talking to?" Just as he asked the question, he looked down and his gaze fell on the dead body.

"I don't think so. He doesn't look familiar. But I'm not sure," Cheryl said in an uncertain voice.

Danielle's eyes darted around for a weapon. She spied a piece of pipe near the children's beach toys. Bill noticed her looking at the pipe. Together they lunged for it, each taking hold of an opposite end. Cheryl let out a scream and began yelling, yet her screams only distracted Danielle.

Bill jerked Danielle outside, away from the decaying body and into the sunlight. The two fell onto the sand, yet Danielle was no match for his strength. She found herself facedown in the sand, her arms jerked back forcibly, held in place by Bill's weight as he sat on her back. Spitting sand from her mouth, she raised her head slightly and looked up in time to see Bill raising the pipe over her head as if he were preparing to bash it in.

Cheryl let out another scream and the pipe went sailing into the distance. Surprised that she was still alive, Danielle could feel Bill shift his body.

"What are you going to do to me?" she asked, spitting out more sand.

"Call the police. Now just settle down," Bill said.

"Call the police? You mean you aren't going to kill me?" Danielle asked.

"Kill you? Why in the hell would I kill you? You're the one with the dead body, lady, not me."

"Oh, thank god," Danielle said wearily, letting her head rest on the sand. She closed her eyes and relaxed her body.

THIRTY

Danielle sat on the pathway bench next to Bill while Cheryl paced anxiously back and forth.

"Thanks for letting me up," Danielle said, shaking more sand out of her braid.

"Hey, I figured once I called the cops and told them what I found, you'd be more likely to take off than try to break my head open with that piece of pipe. You're their problem now, not mine." Bill pulled a pack of cigarettes from his shirt pocket.

"I wasn't going to hit you over the head with the pipe," Danielle insisted.

"It sure looked that way." Bill removed a cigarette from the pack and lit up.

"I just wanted to protect myself."

"I guess I understand. The body in there, that's your cousin, the missing girl, right?" Bill took a drag off the cigarette.

"Yes. Why did you come down here?" Danielle asked.

"Got a complaint from one of the renters. Said there was a nasty smell coming out of hut three. Figured it was a dead rodent or maybe a cat."

Cheryl stopped pacing and looked from Bill to Danielle. "Is he talking about me? Was I that smell?"

"Who owns these huts?" Danielle asked. She looked up to

Cheryl and gave her an apologetic nod. Cheryl frowned and resumed her pacing.

"Frederickport Vacation Properties."

"The hut's padlock was cut."

"Yeah, been that way all summer. I kept meaning to bring down a new one. First week of summer vacation one of the renters cut it off in a panic. His kids were screwing around. The son locked his daughter in the hut and then ended up dropping the key in the sand, couldn't find it. She was screaming her head off, so the dad figured it would be faster to cut off the lock instead of getting another key from us."

"So anyone could have gone in there," Danielle murmured.

"I have a question for you. How did you happen to be here? Judging by the condition of that body, it's obvious she's been in there a while."

"I was frustrated and decided to do my own detective work and retrace my cousin's steps. I ended up here."

"Retrace her steps? I don't remember anyone seeing her on the beach."

"I should have said possible steps. If Cheryl left Adam's as he says, I'd expect her to come back to Marlow House. After all, her car was there. Since she was new to town, the easiest way to find her way back in the dark would be by walking along the beach. At least, that's what I'd do."

"What made you go into the hut?" Bill asked.

"I don't know. The huts were between Adam's bungalow and my place. Thought I'd look around and see if I could find any clues. Any sign Cheryl had been in the area. When I noticed the lock was broken, I decided to look inside."

"You are a good liar." Cheryl laughed. "I have to say I am surprised! If I didn't know better, I'd actually believe your story."

"I better call Lily," Danielle said, reaching into her purse for her cellphone. "I don't want her to worry about me."

"Dani, are you okay?" Lily answered in a rush.

"Lily, I decided to retrace Cheryl's steps—if she had tried to walk from the bungalow back to Marlow House by the beach."

"Is someone there?" Lily asked.

"I came across some beach shacks. One was unlocked. Lily, I found Cheryl inside. It looks like she's been murdered."

"Who is with you?" Lily asked anxiously.

"Bill Jones, the one who works for Frederickport Vacation Properties—who owns the huts—happened to come by. He's called the police. They're on their way down."

"Are you okay?"

"Yeah, I think so."

"Did the body have the necklace?" Lily asked.

"No, but I didn't expect it would be here. I have to assume that's why someone killed her." She heard voices and footsteps coming from the pathway. Turning around, Danielle and Bill watched as close to a dozen or more police officers and responders made their way toward them. Among the officers were Joe and Brian.

"I have to go now, Lily. The police are here."

"Okay, Dani. Be careful." Lily hung up.

"You found her?" Joe asked when he reached the bench.

"Yes," Danielle said as she started to stand up.

"Please stay there, Ms. Boatman," Brian said curtly. "We'll get to you in a moment. Bill, come with us."

ALMOST THREE HOURS LATER, Danielle sat alone in an interrogation room at the Frederickport Police Department, eating a ham sandwich Joe had procured for her. She was ravenous and wanted to go home. Her head ached from all the questions. She hadn't seen Cheryl's spirit since they had left the beach. Danielle wondered if Cheryl had returned to Marlow House, stayed with her body, or perhaps she had moved on to the next plane now that her body had been found.

The door opened and in walked Brian.

"I see you got something to eat," Brian said as he tossed his notepad on the table and took a seat across from Danielle.

"I would rather have gone home to get something to eat. When can I leave?"

"Just a few more questions." Brian picked up the notepad and opened it. "You don't seem very upset at finding your cousin's body."

"Everyone deals with these things differently." Danielle knew the lack of tears was going to be a problem. "But I cared enough to try to find her."

"Her or the necklace?"

"I really don't care about the necklace, I never did." Danielle was beginning to think the Missing Thorndike should be renamed the Cursed Thorndike.

"Maybe not the necklace but the million or so bucks you'll get when you sell it."

"That will be kind of hard to do now."

"There is always the insurance money." Brian smiled.

"None of that matters. The only thing that matters right now is finding whoever killed my cousin."

"I can see how much it matters to you, considering the way those tears are flowing."

"Okay, I will admit Cheryl and I were not close. We've never been. And frankly, sometimes she irritated the heck out of me. But I never wanted anything bad to happen to her."

"I understand she was contesting your aunt's estate. With her out of the picture, that takes care of that problem, doesn't it?"

"I don't think she had a claim in the first place. Do you seriously think I had something to do with my cousin's death? Do I need to hire an attorney?"

"I don't know, do you? You had a motive," Brian reminded her. "With her out of the picture, you don't have to share your inheritance."

"I think the killer's motive is fairly obvious—the Missing Thorndike. A dozen or more people saw her leave Marlow House with the necklace. Joe was there; he knows I was still at Marlow House when she took off."

"So what do you think she intended to do with the necklace? Why steal it with so many witnesses, especially if she expected to claim half ownership to it?"

"I've given that a lot of consideration…" It wasn't a lie; she had thought about it a great deal. But the conclusion she drew was not hers, it was Cheryl's version of the story. "My cousin wasn't a jewel thief. She was irresponsible and flighty, but I don't think she intended to sell or keep the necklace. She was borrowing it for the night as a lark."

"A deadly lark."

"I don't think she realized how foolish it was to be running around with that thing on."

"You wore it to the open house."

"I wore it to get publicity for my grand opening. I didn't think anyone would try to steal it with so many people around, and Joe was there."

"Do you think Adam is responsible for her death? You were pretty emphatic he was responsible for her disappearance. I understand his company owns the hut where she was found."

"I sort of doubt it." Danielle shrugged. She still didn't like Adam, yet she didn't want to falsely accuse him of the crime. "I would expect him to put her body in the ocean, not in a hut his company owns. Especially considering anyone could go into it because of the broken lock."

AFTER DANIELLE WAS FINALLY ALLOWED to go home, Brian sat with Joe, discussing the case.

"You don't seriously think Danielle was involved in her cousin's murder?" Joe asked.

"Joe, you're too close to the case. You're not being objective."

"We're not that close. Sure, Danielle is a friend, but I'm not opposed to arresting a friend if they break the law. And especially if I believe they murdered someone."

"Even a woman you're dating?"

"Danielle and I have only gone out a couple times. Hell, I haven't even kissed her yet."

"Why not? Maybe she's not really interested in you—maybe she's just using you?"

"No. The reason is I haven't tried to kiss her yet. You keep forgetting; I was there. I met her cousin. I have no doubt she took off with that necklace and ran off with Adam."

"I asked Danielle if she thought Adam was responsible for her cousin's murder, and she said no," Brian said.

"Really? That surprises me considering how she went on about him after Cheryl went missing."

"I agree. Plus, I think her rationale for his innocence is a little weak," Brian noted.

"What was that?"

"She said if he killed her, she would expect him to dump her body in the ocean, not in a shed he owned."

"I don't suppose you pointed out we're pretty sure Cheryl was murdered in the shed, not taken there postmortem."

"No, I didn't say anything. As far as I'm concerned, we have two prime suspects, Adam and Danielle."

"Okay, give me your theory on Danielle for a suspect."

"The motive is there, obviously. After she went missing, you didn't stick around Marlow House, so it is possible Danielle left, right?"

"Sure, but none of us knew where Cheryl went."

"How do you know? We know Cheryl went down to the bungalow with Adam the first day she met him. Maybe she said something to her cousin. Maybe Danielle had a good idea all along where Cheryl and Adam took off to."

"But you forget the wine. Someone drugged the wine."

"Yeah, about the wine. Who was the target, Adam, Cheryl, or both of them? We know it was a bottle from the party. According to Adam, Cheryl took it from the table in the side yard. He said those bottles had been opened and lightly re-corked."

"Are you suggesting Danielle drugged the wine?"

"She could have seen her cousin take it. It's possible she got the bottle from Cheryl's hiding place, drugged it and put it back in the bushes. Makes Cheryl and Adam more manageable once she gets to them."

"You're making a lot of far-fetched assumptions. And you're forgetting, I was with her the entire time."

"You never left her side?"

"Only to use the bathroom. Sometimes I was in the next room. But she never went outside without me."

"Maybe she had an accomplice. I don't know; I'm just saying it's possible she was responsible."

"Let's say you're right. Explain to me how Danielle just happened to have Rohypnol on her? Not something you normally have around the house," Joe asked.

"Maybe she intended to use it on Cheryl all along but in another scenario. Danielle is the one who mentioned dumping the body in the ocean. Maybe she intended to take her cousin down to the beach some night, enjoy a little wine. And then when Cheryl passes out, drag her down to the ocean and get rid of the body."

"You have a fertile imagination, Brian," Joe scoffed.

"You never saw anything between them that might suggest Danielle would be capable of something like this?"

"What, you mean bashing her cousin over the head? Of course not…" Joe paused a moment as if he were remembering something.

"What is it?"

"Oh, it's nothing really." Joe shook his head.

"Come on, Joe, what did you remember?"

"Before the party Cheryl accused Danielle of hitting her." Joe moved restlessly in his chair.

"Any indication the story was true? What did Danielle say?"

"We were all right there. Didn't see what happened exactly, they were behind us. I know Cheryl was grabbing at the necklace, wanting to try it on. Next thing I know, Cheryl is on her butt and claiming Danielle smacked her. Danielle said she tripped. I figured if it really happened, it was more a knee-jerk reaction on Danielle's part, considering how Cheryl was all over her."

"You think she did hit her?"

"Cheryl's cheek was bruised. I suppose it could have happened if she slipped, but it was probably from being hit and then falling."

"Danielle didn't fess up?"

"No. She kept insisting Cheryl fell, that she didn't hit her. I figured it was a possible scenario, and no one saw what happened."

"Who was there?" Brian asked.

"Danielle's friend Lily, who's staying with her for the summer. Ian Bartley, he's the author, the one who wrote the article about the Missing Thorndike—and he's writing the book about Eva Thorndike's life. And Joanne Johnson."

THIRTY-ONE

Clarence Renton sat at Lucy Diner's lunch counter, reading the current edition of the *Frederickport Press*. The waitress behind the counter refilled his coffee cup and said, "Can you believe it? A murder in Frederickport."

"It certainly looks that way," Clarence said as he folded the paper and set it on the countertop. He picked up his now full mug and took a sip of coffee.

"I wonder if that necklace will stay lost for another hundred years. It really is a shame, that poor woman getting killed," the waitress said.

"Foolish running around wearing something that valuable."

"When it first went missing, I heard she stole it from her cousin. But now I'm hearing she just borrowed it and intended to bring it back. Hey, didn't I read you were the one that handled that estate?"

"Yes. Brianna Boatman was my client for years. Her mother was the one who inherited the property from Walt Marlow."

"Did you know the woman who was killed?"

"I met her briefly. Brianna left her estate to the murdered woman's cousin."

"So she really didn't have claim to the necklace? The one who was killed, I mean."

"I don't think so. But it's all a moot point now."

"Well, it really is a shame. I hope they catch the killer quick. I don't like to think there are people like that running around here."

"I imagine there are people like that in every community."

"You're just saying that because you're a lawyer and meet all kinds of crooked people."

Clarence smiled and said, "I'm not a criminal lawyer. But I have to admit, a few of my corporate clients are a bit crooked." Giving the waitress a quick wink, he added, "But please don't repeat that."

The waitress laughed and playfully swatted his arm. The cook rang a bell, signaling food was up. She turned from Renton, grabbed the plate from the pass-through window, and then set it in front of him.

"Thanks," Clarence said as he picked up his fork. Taking a bite of his egg, he looked out the window to his left.

"Can I get you anything else?" the waitress asked, still hovering.

"Have any salsa back there?"

"Sure." The waitress walked to the nearby cooler, grabbed a salsa-filled soufflé cup, and set it next to Clarence's plate. "I heard Adam Nichols was a suspect. I know Adam can be a little slick—always reminded me of a car salesman—but I can't imagine he'd kill anyone."

"He was the last one seen with her," Clarence said.

"According to the newspaper article I read, Adam swears she didn't have the necklace on her. But you know what?"

"What?" Clarence asked.

"If they find that necklace, they'll find the killer," the waitress said.

"I suppose you're right." Clarence pulled the lid off the plastic cup and doused the remainder of his eggs in salsa. The waitress started to walk away when he asked, "Hey, do you know what's up with the jewelry store across the street? I noticed a for rent sign on the building."

"Damnedest thing—last week Sam comes in here, tells me he's decided to move. Says he wants a change. Right out of the blue. Next thing I know his store is cleaned out and the building's owner has that for rent sign up. I guess he was pretty pissed, because Sam didn't give him a thirty-day notice."

"I thought Sam owned that building."

"No, sold it last year. I think he needed the money," she said in a whisper. "Sold his house too. Been renting back since then."

"Too bad. That jewelry store has been a fixture in this community since before I moved here. Surprised he didn't try to sell the business. Wonder what he's going to do?"

"I don't know. But he already left town. Sam told me he was leaving by the end of the summer, but he must have figured why wait? Heard he pulled out this morning."

"Interesting…" Clarence murmured.

MARVIN BURROWS nervously tapped his right foot as he waited impatiently in an office at the Frederickport Police Department. Glancing down at the right sleeve of his suit's jacket, he flicked off a minuscule piece of lint. He was straightening the sleeve when the door opened.

"Mr. Burrows, sorry to keep you waiting," Brian said when he entered the room.

"Is it true what they said in this morning's paper? Did you find Cheryl? Is she dead?"

"I'm afraid so, sir." Brian took a seat at the desk in front of Marvin.

"I don't understand; why didn't someone call me?"

"I'm afraid it's been a little hectic around here since we found her yesterday."

"Hectic? My client has been murdered and you tell me it was a little hectic so you couldn't bother to take two seconds to call me?" he said angrily.

"I am sorry, sir. We are doing everything we can to find whoever murdered your client."

"This is awful…just awful…" Marvin shook his head.

"Had you known her for a long time?" Brian asked.

"Yes. I was her parents' attorney. It was tragic, she lost them both, along with her brother, aunt, and uncle in a plane crash when she was practically still a teenager. Left the poor girl devastated."

"The aunt and uncle you mentioned, were those Danielle Boatman's parents perhaps?"

"Yes. I've always felt Ms. Boatman was rather bitter about the accident. Cheryl's father was the pilot. The girls were never close after that. I always suspected it was because Danielle resented Cheryl, blaming her in some way for her parents' death."

"It was hardly Cheryl's fault."

"No, but the sins of the father, so to speak," Marvin said.

"Did the girls have other family, aside from the aunt who left Danielle Marlow House?"

"Cheryl does. She has an aunt and uncle, plus several cousins who will be devastated at the news. As for Danielle, I understand Cheryl was the only family she had, yet she wanted nothing to do with her. Such a shame. As for the aunt's estate, I don't believe for a moment she intended to leave it entirely to Ms. Boatman. Had the woman not been suffering from Alzheimer's, she would have surely left it to both of them. I suspect Ms. Boatman did a little manipulating there."

"Will you continue to pursue the issue?"

"You mean continue to contest Brianna Boatman's will? What would be the point now? Cheryl is dead."

"I don't claim to understand how these things work, but wouldn't Cheryl's heirs be entitled to her share of Brianna Boatman's estate if Cheryl really did have a legitimate claim?"

"Yeah, right. I don't think that's going to be an issue."

"What do you mean?"

"Cheryl left her entire estate to Danielle Boatman. An estate that is now worth in excess of ten million dollars. I don't think she has any interest in pursuing a case against herself."

"You're saying Danielle Boatman is Cheryl's heir? Didn't you say Cheryl had other relatives that cared about her—while she and Danielle weren't close?"

"I said Danielle didn't care about Cheryl. But obviously, Cheryl cared about Danielle. Unwisely, if you ask me. As far as I'm concerned, there's only one person who had a motive to kill Cheryl, and that was her cousin Danielle Boatman."

After Marvin finally left the police station, Brian gave Joe a call and asked him to stop in. They needed to discuss the murder.

"Did the attorney say Danielle was aware of the inheritance?" Joe asked after Brian recounted his conversation with Marvin Burrows.

"He didn't know. Apparently, Cheryl had other cousins she was closer to, so I'm not sure Danielle would assume she was in her cousin's will, much less be her sole heir. You met Cheryl; do you think she's the type to keep something like that secret?"

"I don't know." Joe shrugged. "But I really can't believe Danielle would kill her cousin for an inheritance."

"Ten million is not chump change."

"No, it's not. Damn." Joe shook his head.

Another officer opened the door and poked his head in. "Hey, Millie Samson from the museum is here, I think you guys need to hear this."

Five minutes later, Joe and Brian sat with Millie Samson in the interview room. By the way she was fidgeting, they could tell she was anxious to tell her story.

"What is this all about, Millie?" Joe asked.

"I was working as docent in the museum this morning when I get this phone call from a woman. I didn't recognize her voice; she spoke in a whisper. I think she was afraid someone would hear her. She says she has some information about the murder, and I need to get it to the police right away."

"Why didn't she just call us?" Brian asked.

"I could tell she was afraid. I don't think she wanted you to trace her call. I see on TV how you do that."

"So what did she want you to tell us?" Joe asked.

"She said Adam Nichols killed Cheryl Hartford and took the Missing Thorndike, and you'll find the necklace in his office. It's in a green vase on his bookshelf."

"How would she know that?" Joe asked.

"She said she saw him put something in the vase when she walked by his office. She was curious, and when he left, she looked inside the vase. She immediately recognized the necklace from the pictures in the newspaper. She's afraid for her life because that woman was already killed for the necklace. So you can't tell anyone how you got the information. You better hurry before he moves it."

When Millie left five minutes later, Joe looked at Brian and asked, "What do you think?"

"If the call was legit, means someone who works for Adam called Millie. After all, who else would still have access to the office after he left?"

"But why call Millie? If an informer gives away her place of employment, why would she care if we traced the call? The anonymity ship has already sailed. I think only two women work in that office; it shouldn't be too difficult to figure out which one called Millie," Joe said.

"Or it's a prank call," Brian suggested.

"Or the killer trying to throw us off."

"In that case, I doubt we'll find the necklace in the vase, because I seriously doubt the killer will give up the necklace just to implicate Adam."

"True. But we need to follow up on this."

"I agree. How about you get a search warrant while I run out to Marlow House."

"I could go to Marlow House," Joe suggested.

"Come on, Joe, you know as well as I do I should be the one interviewing Danielle Boatman, not you."

"All right, but I hope I find that necklace at Adam's."

"I wouldn't hold your breath."

THIRTY-TWO

Danielle stood quietly at the library window and looked outside. A breeze was blowing, rustling the leaves of the flowering bushes along the perimeter of the yard while sending the tree limbs into a gentle sway. The lawn needed trimming and the yard seemed desolate when she considered how it looked on the fourth, with the white lawn chairs and tables set up, her guests milling around and enjoying the refreshments while a few tried their hand at croquet. That day had not gone exactly as she had planned.

"Do you think she's gone for good?" Lily asked when she walked into the library.

Danielle turned from the window and looked at Lily. "You mean Cheryl?"

"Yes." Lily sat down on the sofa.

"I don't know. Maybe. After they took her body away, I looked around and didn't see her. I wondered if she stayed with her body or came back here. But if you think about it, there's no reason for her to really stick around now."

"How are you doing?"

"I think it's starting to sink in. Cheryl is really dead."

"I'm sorry, Dani."

"Yeah, me too." Danielle walked over to the sofa and sat next to Lily, propping her feet on the coffee table. "She could sure be a pain in the butt." Danielle sighed. "I think I might actually miss her."

"Does it help knowing…I mean…"

"That there is something more after this?" Danielle asked.

"Yes."

"I suppose so. But I'm not really sure what that something is. And it's not like I can summon up my departed loved ones whenever I feel like a little chat."

The doorbell rang. Lily stood up and said, "I'll get it."

Danielle nodded and closed her eyes, leaning back on the sofa.

When Lily answered the door, Brian was standing on the front porch. He was in uniform.

"Hi," Lily greeted him. "You're Joe's friend Brian, right?"

"Yes. I'm here to see Ms. Boatman on official business."

"Sure. I'll take you to her. She's in the library."

Brian followed Lily down the entry hall and to the library.

"Dani, Brian is here to see you. He says it's official business," Lily announced when they entered the library.

Danielle opened her eyes and got to her feet. "Hello, Brian. Has there been any news?"

"I was wondering if we could talk alone?" Brian asked.

"Umm…sure…" Danielle looked at Lily.

"I'll be in the kitchen if you need me," Lily said as she left the room, closing the double doors behind her.

"Why don't you sit down." Danielle pointed to the chair across from the sofa. When Brian took a seat, she sat back down on the sofa. "So what is this all about?" Danielle asked.

"At the party, after Cheryl took off with the necklace, what did you do?"

"What did I do? I hung around here. I still had guests and people were still coming. I couldn't very well leave."

"So your cousin takes off with a million-dollar necklace and you don't go after her?"

"Joe did that; you can ask him."

"When did your guests finally leave?"

"Everyone was gone by the time it was dark. I sort of planned it that way, because I figured most would want to leave to go watch the fireworks show."

"What did you do then? Did you go watch fireworks?"

"No. I really wasn't in the mood for fireworks, considering Cheryl had taken off with the necklace."

"So you stayed here all night?"

"Yes."

"Do you have any witnesses?"

"Lily was here."

"For the entire night?"

"She went over to Ian's for a while."

"Where is that?"

"Across the street. What is this all about anyway?"

"I understand you hit your cousin before the party."

"I did not hit her. She grabbed for the necklace and slipped."

"According to witnesses, she claimed you hit her."

"Well, she was wrong. I didn't."

"Joe said her face was bruised."

"Joe said that?"

"Yes."

"Well, I don't know how it got bruised, but I didn't do it."

"I understand you haven't taken any reservations yet for the B and B."

"No, with Cheryl missing…and now with her death…I think I want to give it some time. Maybe open next season."

"Or not at all?"

"I'd think you'd understand why I'd want to postpone the opening."

"I certainly do. Inheriting over ten million dollars probably doesn't make you too anxious to move forward with your plans. Why be an innkeeper when you have all that money?"

"What are you talking about?"

"You're Cheryl's heir. She left everything to you. How fortunate for you."

"No, I don't believe that. Cheryl had other relatives; she wouldn't leave it to me. And even if she did, her estate isn't worth ten million dollars."

"What do you think it's worth?"

"When her parents died, I heard the estate was worth five million."

"Five million is still quite a fortune, isn't it? I bet you'd never have to bother turning this place into an inn."

"Everyone saw Cheryl leave that night. Even if I wanted to find her, I had no way of knowing where she was. You honestly think I would be able to track her down faster than Joe?"

"Perhaps you knew all along where she was going."

"How would I know that?"

"Maybe she mentioned the bungalow to you before that night. It's my understanding Adam took her there the day they met."

"And if she did mention it, would she really use that as a hiding place, knowing it would probably be one place I'd look—especially since she took off with Adam?"

Brian considered her words for a moment and then said, "Perhaps it started out as a publicity stunt."

"What are you talking about?"

"You're good at grabbing attention for your inn. Maybe you cooked this up with Cheryl. She would run off with the necklace; it would stir up the press like when you initially found it. But then you started thinking about all that money and figured this would be a good time to really cash in."

ADAM SAT AT HIS DESK, trying to focus on the invoices before him. It was a difficult task considering he couldn't stop thinking about Cheryl. He didn't notice his assistant standing nervously by his office doorway while several police officers stood behind her. He looked up when she cleared her throat and said, "The police are here."

Adam set his pencil on the pile of invoices and watched as Joe Morelli and two other officers, one male and one female, filed into his office. Joe held a piece of paper in his hand. He lifted it over his head and said, "We have a warrant to search your office, Adam."

"Should I be calling my attorney?" Adam asked, still sitting behind his desk.

"I suppose that depends on what we find." Joe tossed the warrant on Adam's desk and gave a little nod to the female officer. She went directly to the green vase sitting on the bookshelf. Adam watched as she lifted the vase down from the top shelf and looked inside.

Giving Joe a nod, she dipped her gloved hand into the vase and said, "It's here." Lifting the Missing Thorndike from its hiding place, she held it up for all to see. Instead of the glittering piece Joe remembered Danielle putting on her neck, it was now splattered in dry blood.

"What the hell?" Adam stood abruptly, his eyes riveted on the bloody necklace in the officer's hand.

Joe reached back and grabbed the handcuffs from his belt. He stepped to Adam and said, "Adam Nichols, you are under arrest for the murder of Cheryl Hartford…" Adam stood numbly as Joe pulled his hands behind his back and fitted them in the handcuffs. "You have the right to remain silent. Anything you say can and will be used against you in a court of law. You have a right to an attorney. If you cannot afford an attorney, one will be appointed for you…"

THE POLICE CHIEF looked down at the sealed plastic bag sitting on his desk. Inside it was the Missing Thorndike. Dry blood dulled its shine. He shook his head and said, "Would have been a hell of a lot less trouble if Boatman would've just kept the damn thing locked up in the bank until she sold it."

"I'm really sorry about this, Chief," Joe muttered. The two officers who had accompanied him to Adam's office stood by his side.

The chief looked up at Joe and said, "So you say he didn't try to stop you?"

"No. In fact, he didn't seem a bit concerned about the warrant."

"I guess we need to get it over to the lab. They're going to love this. We better get Hayman over here."

"Hayman?" Joe asked.

"We'll need to verify it's the real Missing Thorndike before we send it over there. When they're done with it, I really don't want them sending back a piece of costume jewelry and insisting that's what we sent over."

Joe pointed to the makeshift wire attaching the clasp to the necklace. "I can't verify the diamonds and emeralds are real, but that is definitely the necklace Danielle was wearing when Cheryl took it. The chain broke before the party and I added that wire."

"I've no doubt it's the Missing Thorndike, but I want to follow protocol on this one." The chief picked up the plastic bag and placed it in the evidence box. Sealing the container, he marked the tape. "I'll take it to lockup myself. Call Hayman and get him over here. The sooner I get this out of here, the better."

DANIELLE WAS ABOUT to ask Brian to leave when his cellphone rang. He curtly excused himself to answer the call. Disgusted with Brian's accusations, Danielle left him alone in the library. She found Lily in the kitchen.

"Did he leave?" Lily asked.

"No, he got a call. The jerk."

"What happened?"

"He thinks I killed Cheryl."

"You're kidding me."

"I wish I was. Do you know what he told me?"

"What?"

"I don't know if it's true. Not really sure how he would know. But according to him, Cheryl left me everything. Apparently, she was worth considerably more than what her parents left her."

"How much are we talking?"

"Ten million."

Lily let out a low whistle. "Wow."

"I tell you what, I wish people would stop making me their heir. It's starting to be a real pain in the butt."

"I thought you were happy about Marlow House."

"That was before the Missing Thorndike. It's been nothing but trouble. And if Brian Henderson has his way, my most recent inheritance is going to get me locked up. I wonder, do they have the death penalty in Oregon?"

"I don't think you need to worry about that quite yet," Brian said from the doorway.

Lily and Danielle quickly exchanged glances, wondering how much he had heard of their conversation.

"What do you mean?" Danielle asked.

"It seems the Missing Thorndike has once again resurfaced."

"Where?" Lily and Danielle chorused.

"We got a tip this afternoon that Adam Nichols had the necklace stashed in his office. Seems you were right all along, Ms. Boatman. Adam Nichols killed your cousin for the necklace."

Stunned, Lily and Danielle walked Brian to the front door and watched him make his way down the front walk toward the street, where he had parked his car. After they shut the door, they looked at each other.

"I don't believe it. It really doesn't go along with what Cheryl told me," Danielle said.

Cheryl suddenly appeared, shouting, "That's because it isn't true!"

"Cheryl! Where have you been?" Danielle asked.

"Is Cheryl here?"

"Yes," Danielle told Lily. She turned to her cousin and asked, "I thought you'd left for good."

"So did I. But it seems everything is screwed up here. I can't leave now!"

THIRTY-THREE

"Where have you been?" Danielle asked Cheryl again after they went into the library.

Before she could answer, Walt appeared. "So you're back. Couldn't find the light?"

"I didn't intend to come back, but I really had no other choice, did I?" Cheryl flopped down onto the couch as if exhausted.

"The last time I saw you was when the police arrived at the beach. But the next time I looked, you were gone."

"I had to see where they were taking me. And might I suggest, if you ever have the opportunity to view your own autopsy, don't." Cheryl cringed.

Lily started to sit on the couch when Danielle called out, "No, Lily, Cheryl is sitting there."

"I tell you what," Lily said, standing up straight. "I'm going into the parlor to read. These one-sided conversations sorta drive me nuts. When you're done, come in and give me a recap of what's happening."

"You watched your autopsy?" Danielle asked after Lily left the library.

"Not all of it. Rather pisses me off to think someone would bash in my head like that."

"I know the feeling," Walt said.

"There is one thing I do know; Adam did not kill me."

"How can you be so certain?" Danielle asked. "You said you can't remember much after you left the bungalow."

"I've been able to remember more about that night. I remember leaving the hut—after—well, after I died. I didn't understand what was happening. I panicked. Instead of returning here, I went back to Adam's. He was right where I left him, snoring away. I tried to wake him up, but of course, he couldn't hear me. Everything was right where it was before I left the bungalow—his shoes, clothes, cellphone, keys, everything. I don't believe he ever woke up and came to the beach and killed me and returned to the bed. No. It wasn't him; that I'm certain of."

"Can you remember anything more about being on the beach… before you were killed?" Danielle asked.

"After you found my body in that beach hut, things started to come into focus," Cheryl said.

"Like a fuzzy picture getting clear?" Walt suggested.

"Yes." Cheryl sat up and looked at Walt. "You understand, don't you?"

"Very much so." Walt sat on the couch's arm.

"What else do you remember?" Danielle asked.

"I remember feeling really annoyed at Adam for drinking so much. I was mad at him for ruining the evening. I started to put my shoes on, but then realized I wasn't sure how to get home from his house, and I sure didn't want to call you for a ride. I decided the easiest way to find my way back here was to walk along the beach. So I picked up my shoes and purse and slipped out the back slider of the bungalow."

"I wish you had just called me," Danielle said.

"So do I," Cheryl said with a sigh. "I remember standing on the back porch. I could hear the waves breaking on the shore. The moon was up—not a full moon, just a sliver, but its reflection shimmered along the ocean. I remember thinking how lovely it looked. In the distance, to the north, I could see the fireworks. I stood there a while watching and trying to figure out how long it would take me to walk down to the stretch of beach by Ian's. I remembered his place was just past the pier. And then someone was there. I'm not sure if he came from down the beach or walked around the house, coming from the street."

"It was a man?" Walt asked.

"Yes. I don't know why, but his face is still blurry to me—I just can't quite figure out who he is. I do remember asking him what he was doing there. It surprised me to see him standing in the dark on the beach…behind Adam's house."

"What did he say?" Danielle asked.

"He said he was walking down to the fireworks show. He asked me where Adam was—another reason I know it was not Adam who left me in the beach hut. I told him Adam had passed out from drinking too much wine. He asked me what I was going to do now. I told him I was going to walk back to Marlow House."

"So this is someone you knew…who knew you?" Danielle asked.

"Yes, but I just can't wrap my head around who he was." Cheryl sounded frustrated.

"Then what?" Walt asked.

"I remember him saying I'd be smart to go back to Marlow House right away, because the police were looking for me, and they thought I stole the necklace."

"Did you have the necklace on?" Danielle asked.

"Yes. He was looking at it. I remember that. I told him I hadn't stolen it." Cheryl looked at Danielle. "I knew you would be mad at me for taking it, but I thought you would understand I only borrowed it. I wasn't afraid of being arrested."

"Did you ever consider calling me?" Danielle asked.

"No. My night with Adam didn't go like I wanted, but I wasn't ready to come back here yet. He—the man on the beach—said we might as well walk together, since he was going in that direction anyway. He suggested I grab something for us to drink for our walk. I went inside and took a couple of beers from the refrigerator."

"And you have no idea who he was?" Danielle asked.

"No. However, I do know I didn't find him particularly attractive. But I trusted him. I remember he insisted on opening my beer for me. I thought that was rather old fashioned and gentlemanly; I remember that. We walked along the beach, and I started getting really sleepy. He said he knew where some beach chairs were kept and suggested I sit down for a minute and rest. I was so tired. I just wanted to sit down and go to sleep, so I said okay, anything so I wouldn't have to keep walking. I remember going into that hut, but after that…after that, everything is black. My next memory is leaving the shack and going to Adam's."

"He must have hit you over the head and taken the necklace," Danielle said.

"I suppose…damn, why did I have to do something so stupid?" Cheryl slumped back into the sofa. Closing her eyes, she flung her right wrist over her forehead and let out a dramatic sigh.

Danielle walked over to the sofa and looked down at her cousin. "I have another question for you, Cheryl. This doesn't have anything to do with your death."

Cheryl opened one eye and looked up at Danielle. "What?"

"Did you really leave me your entire estate?"

Cheryl closed her eye and was silent a moment. Finally, she said, "Yes."

"Why? We didn't even like each other."

Cheryl sat up abruptly and looked at Danielle. "That is an awful thing to say! How can you talk that way about me? I'm dead!"

"Come on, admit it. You and I have never been close. Just because we didn't particularly like each other, it doesn't mean I didn't love you."

"You love me?" Cheryl sounded hopeful.

"I suppose I did…do. So why, Cheryl—why did you leave me your estate? And how in the world did it get so…so large?"

"Well, if you must know, I always felt guilty."

"Guilty? About what?" *The times you hit on my boyfriends? Teased me? Called me a liar?*

"I know you could have sued my father's estate after the accident. I've no doubt you would have won. I really did think you were going to sue, and when you didn't, I started feeling guilty."

"If that's true, then why in the world would you contest Aunt Brianna's will? Her estate was not even a fraction of what you inherited."

"Exactly," Cheryl said confidently, nodding her head to punctuate her point.

"I don't get it." Danielle sat on a chair facing Cheryl.

"Well, if I was willing to give you everything I owned, I figured it was only fair that you share Aunt Brianna's estate with me. I never could understand why you were being so greedy about it."

"Cheryl, I had no idea you had me in your will, and anyway I would only get your estate if you died. And I could very well have died before you and never seen a penny from your estate."

"Well, you didn't. I died, and now you are a very rich woman. Don't you feel just a teeny bit guilty for being so stingy?"

"Oh, brother," Danielle mumbled. She took a deep breath and asked, "Okay, so how did your estate double?"

"Don't ask me." Cheryl shrugged. "Daddy's business manager handles all that. But we have more important things to worry about right now."

"You mean about who killed you?" Danielle asked.

"That, and you have to prove Adam was not responsible for my death."

"Do you realize the police have two suspects?" Danielle asked.

"Adam and who else?" Cheryl asked.

"Me."

"You?" Cheryl frowned.

"Yes. Right before you showed up, I was beginning to wonder if Officer Henderson was about to arrest me. He seems to think I'm a prime suspect—at least, until he received that phone call that the necklace had been found in Adam's office. He's the one who told me I was your heir—which puts me at the top of the suspect list."

"Well, I can't help that," Cheryl said impatiently. "I mean, I have the right to leave my money to whomever I want. But I can't control the police if they want to get all suspicious about it."

"I understand that but—" Danielle began.

Cheryl interrupted by saying, "You aren't going to let Adam go to prison for something he didn't do, are you?"

"No, I didn't say that. I just wanted to point out that according to some officers on the local police department, if Adam didn't do it —I did."

"Well, pooh. What about that handsome cop you were so cozy with at the party? Surely he isn't going to let them arrest you."

"Yes, Danielle, what about him?" Walt asked.

"Joe? Well, I haven't seen much of Joe this past week."

"Are you saying he's abandoned you in your time of need?" Cheryl asked incredulously.

"I'm not saying that exactly. But he has a job to do, and I guess he needs to remain impartial while he does it. I can understand—I suppose," Danielle said weakly.

"Well, I can't!" Cheryl snapped.

"Neither can I," Walt agreed.

I don't really understand either, Danielle thought.

THIRTY-FOUR

It was past 8 a.m. when Joe arrived at the police station on Tuesday morning. When he got there, he found one of the officers leading a disheveled-looking Adam Nichols from lockup to the interview room. The chief stood outside his office door, drinking a cup of coffee. Spying Joe, he waved him over.

"I'm surprised Nichols is still here," Joe said after he walked to the chief. The two men glanced to the now closed door of the interview room.

"His attorney's from Portland. He couldn't get ahold of him last night," the chief explained. "He finally did this morning. The attorney's supposed to be here in a little while."

"Has the necklace been sent over to the lab yet?" Joe asked.

"No. Still trying to get someone qualified to check out the stones. I just assumed we'd use Sam," the chief said.

"I had no idea he was planning to close his store and move from Frederickport," Joe said.

"I talked to a couple of the shop owners in the area. I guess he'd been talking about closing down for some time. You know, he sold that building a while back, his house too."

"It still surprises me. He grew up here. That store's been a regular fixture for years. I talked to him for a while on the fourth at the open house. He didn't say anything about leaving."

"I'd heard around town the store wasn't doing that great," the chief said.

"That's too bad. Sorry to see him go. So what are you going to do now?" Joe asked.

"I talked to someone in Astoria. They'll be here after lunch. And then I'd like you and Carpenter to take the necklace to the lab."

"Excuse me," the woman who worked at the front desk interrupted.

"Yes?" the chief asked.

"Danielle Boatman is here to see you," she explained.

The chief glanced at Joe and then asked her, "Who does she want to see, Joe or me?"

"Well, I suppose either one. I didn't realize Joe was here. She asked to see him, and when I told her he wasn't here yet, she wanted to know if she could talk to you."

"Bring her in," the chief said, taking a swig of his coffee.

IT HAD TAKEN a great deal of convincing for Danielle to persuade Cheryl to stay at Marlow House and not follow her to the police station when she went to check on Adam.

"If you want me to go, you have to let me go alone," Danielle had insisted. "It's too distracting to have you in the background talking to me."

At the police station, Danielle was led to the inner offices. She was surprised to find Joe standing with the chief. She had been told Joe hadn't yet arrived at the station that morning.

"I understand Adam has been arrested for the murder of my cousin," Danielle began.

"Morning, Danielle." Joe greeted her with a smile. "I guess you were right all along."

"I don't think Adam killed my cousin," Danielle said.

"Excuse me?" Joe frowned.

"She left with him; the necklace was found in his office," the chief explained.

"I don't understand," Joe said. "You were the one convinced Adam had something to do with your cousin's disappearance."

"Is he still here, or has he been let out on bail?" Danielle asked.

"He's in the interview room, waiting on his attorney," Joe said.

"Can I see him?" Danielle asked.

"I'm afraid that's not possible—"

"No, that's okay," the chief interrupted Joe. "Let her see him for a minute if she wants. His attorney isn't going to be here for a while."

WHEN DANIELLE ENTERED the interview room, she found Adam sitting alone at the table. It looked as if he hadn't slept for hours. He wore the same dress shirt and slacks he'd had on when they had arrested him the previous day, yet now the shirt was wrinkled, the collar unbuttoned. He had obviously been arrested without a comb, and he needed to shave.

"You're the last person I expected to see," Adam said, shifting uncomfortably in the hard chair.

"How are you doing?" Danielle asked as she took a seat across the table from him.

"My attorney is working on bail. I'm hoping I can get out of here today. Worried about my grandmother."

"Does she know?"

"I haven't talked to her yet. But this is a small town; I can't imagine some busybody hasn't been over there already, filling her in on the juicy details."

"If you want, I'll check on her," Danielle offered.

"Why? I know you don't like me."

"I care about your grandmother. Plus, I don't think you killed my cousin."

"I sure wish the local police shared that belief."

"How do you think the necklace ended up in your office?"

"My guess is the killer put it there to frame me."

"But why use a necklace worth a million dollars to do that?"

"I sort of thought maybe you'd have the answer to that." Adam leaned forward, his elbows propped on the table. He studied Danielle's face.

"Me? Why would I know?"

"Well, I can only think of one reason the killer would use that necklace to frame me—if she knew she would be getting it back."

"Are you suggesting I killed my cousin?"

"Funny how a person has a lot of time to think when you get locked up."

"Umm...you haven't even been here twenty-four hours."

"Well, it's also funny how fewer than twenty-four hours in here can seem like a hell of a lot longer."

"I don't believe you killed Cheryl, but I didn't kill her either."

Adam leaned back in his chair. "I've been asking myself, how is it I passed out after drinking just one glass of wine? I've never been a lightweight. I know Joe confiscated the wine and wineglasses from the beach house. Pretty sure he had them tested; of course, no one has shared the results with me. That's one thing my attorney's working on. I want to know what was in that wine."

"Joe had the wine analyzed? I didn't know that."

"Guess he isn't quite the pal you thought he was, is he?"

"Are you saying the wine may have been drugged?"

"Here's what I think happened. You and your cousin cooked up this little publicity stunt. Have the necklace disappear and then reappear. She's convinced she owns a share of the Thorndike and Marlow House, so she's willing to go along with your little game. But you have other ideas, don't you? I heard you inherited her estate. This is a small town; things like that get around quick. You figured out how to get rid of your cousin, frame me, and get the necklace back—and your cousin's money."

"Are you serious? Just how did I drug the wine?"

"Maybe Cheryl was in on that; I don't know. I haven't worked it all out yet. But I'm pretty sure you killed your cousin."

Danielle stood up, shaking her head. "I came here to help you, dammit!"

"Well, that is mighty big of you, considering you created this mess. But I don't need your help, lady. I suggest you get yourself a good lawyer; I think you're going to need one."

Speechless, Danielle turned and left the room.

"WELL, THAT WAS INTERESTING," the chief said. He stood with Joe in an office next to the interview room, looking at Adam through the two-way mirror. Danielle had just stormed out of the room. "Adam makes a convincing argument."

"I have to admit he does. He sure seemed sincere in there."

"I've known Adam most of his life. He's never been in any real trouble."

"You sound like Brian," Joe said.

"Brian's been here a lot longer than you," the chief reminded him.

"I just find it hard to believe Danielle had anything to do with her cousin's murder."

"How well do you really know the girl?"

"I guess not that well." Joe shrugged.

"There was a hell of a lot of money at stake, especially considering her new inheritance with Cheryl out of the way. If you think about it, Danielle Boatman seems to be falling into all sorts of money these days."

"If she's guilty, then why come to see Adam? Why tell him she thinks he's innocent?" Joe asked.

"Maybe she just wanted to see what he was thinking. Had he been more receptive to her offer of help—then it would be easier for her to gaslight him. Make sure he gets convicted of her cousin's murder. That way she gets off free and clear, with someone else going to prison for Cheryl's murder. Now she knows he's onto her. I'm curious to see what she'll do."

"You sound as if you believe Danielle killed Cheryl, not Adam," Joe said.

The chief shrugged. "Just playing devil's advocate."

An officer peeked his head in the room and said, "Adam Nichols's attorney is here. Should I take him on in?"

"Go ahead." The chief turned from the window looking into the interview room. "I guess our little show is over. Too bad they don't let us listen into client-attorney discussions; it would sure make our jobs a hell of a lot easier."

"SORRY I'M LATE," Ted Zimmerman said when he walked into the interview room.

"I just hope you can get me out of this damn place."

"I'm afraid I have bad news, Adam."

"What?" Adam sat up straighter.

"I checked on those tests you asked me about. The wine was drugged with Rohypnol. It's a date-rape drug."

Adam slammed his fist on the tabletop and grinned. "I knew it!"

"Don't get too happy. It seems Cheryl had Rohypnol in her system when she died. They never checked your blood, did they?"

"No. What does this mean?"

"It means the police are building a nice little case against you. They're convinced you drugged Cheryl, hid her body in one of your beach huts, and stashed the necklace in your office."

"Why in the hell would I put her body in an unlocked beach hut I own?"

"I didn't say they thought you were a smart killer, just a killer. They're taking the necklace to a lab. I guess it had some blood on it. If it turns out to be Cheryl's, then that would prove she had it on when she was killed."

"If I can prove someone else put that necklace in my office, will it help my case?"

"Definitely, but how do you intend to do that?"

"I have a hidden security camera in my office. Do you know if the police found it?"

"Not that I know of. Are you saying you had your office bugged?"

"Not bugged exactly. I wasn't recording the sound. It's like a nanny cam but no sound. It sends the video to a computer I keep in the spare bedroom at my grandmother's. I need to get over there and check out that computer. The camera should have recorded whoever put the Missing Thorndike in that vase."

"Why didn't you say something before?"

"Because I didn't particularly want a bunch of cops going through my personal computer. But frankly at this point, I don't really care if they know about the porn sites I occasionally visit. I don't want my next date to be with a dude named Bubba."

"How would someone have gotten into your office?"

"Back door's usually open during the day. Someone could easily slip in that way without the girls in the front office seeing. We'll just have to see what the video tells us."

"Do you have any idea who it'll be?"

"Oh, without a doubt. I know exactly who put that necklace in my office. Danielle Boatman."

THIRTY-FIVE

"I have to admit, I've been dying to have a look at the Missing Thorndike," Aaron Michaels, the jeweler from Astoria, said after they led him into the interview room. Officers Morelli and Henderson stood in the room with the chief. On the desk was the necklace, still in its plastic bag.

The moment Aaron glanced down at the bloodstained stones, his face went ashen. "I guess that was a poor choice of words, considering the circumstances."

"This definitely is not the Lucky Thorndike," the chief noted, handing the jeweler a pair of latex gloves.

The men were silent as they watched Aaron remove the necklace from the bag and inspect the stones. Immediately, the jeweler started shaking his head, as if he didn't understand what he was seeing.

"This isn't the Missing Thorndike," Aaron said, returning the necklace to the bag. "Those stones are fake."

"Fake?" the chief asked.

"As far as fakes go, they're pretty nice. Quality costume jewelry. But this necklace doesn't have a single diamond or emerald in it. The gold is real. The piece is obviously an antique—even the fake gemstones are old. This necklace is worth something for its antique value alone. But over a million? No."

"I don't understand," Joe muttered. "This is the necklace

Danielle and I took out of the safety deposit box. It's the one she wore to the party. This is the Missing Thorndike."

"How can you be so sure it's the one Danielle wore to the party?" Brian asked.

"Because of this." Joe pointed to the wire he had used to reattach the latch to the necklace.

"Maybe it is the same one," Aaron suggested. "Maybe the Missing Thorndike had fake stones all along."

"When they found the necklace, Sam Hayman appraised it," the chief said. "Claimed the stones were real."

"Well, if Sam said they were real, then someone must have switched out the stones since then. Sam would easily recognize these as fake," Aaron said.

"Could Sam have been wrong…could you be wrong?" Brian asked.

"You're welcome to get a second opinion. Frankly, the guy at your local pawnshop will be able to tell you these stones are fake," Aaron said. "As for Sam being wrong. Only if he intentionally lied. But why would he?"

"I don't think Sam lied," Joe said. "I know the insurance company sent out their own appraiser before insuring the necklace."

"I certainly don't think the insurance company's appraiser would confuse fake stones for diamonds and emeralds," Aaron said.

BRIAN AND JOE pulled up in front of Marlow House late Tuesday afternoon. They were just getting out of their car when they noticed Marvin Burrows, Cheryl Hartford's attorney, coming through the front gate. Carrying a briefcase, the attorney seemed preoccupied as he made his way down the walk toward the street. He got into his vehicle, which was parked in front of their car.

Brian stood by the police car and watched Burrows drive away. "That's Hartford's attorney, isn't it?"

"Yes. Wonder if it is official." Joe slammed the car door shut.

"What do you mean?" Brian and Joe made their way up the front walk to Marlow House.

"Cheryl's estate and Danielle's inheritance," Joe said.

"If Danielle can avoid getting arrested for her cousin's murder, then she'll become a very rich woman."

"For the time being, we have someone arrested for that crime," Joe reminded him.

"Yes. For the time being."

Five minutes later, Joe and Brian were seated in the parlor with Lily and Danielle. Walt and Cheryl were also there, but neither lawman could see them.

"Is Adam still in jail?" Danielle asked after the two men sat down.

"He got out on bail this afternoon," Joe explained. "But we've come to talk to you about the Missing Thorndike, not Adam."

Danielle couldn't help but notice Joe's normally friendly demeanor was absent. *He might as well be a stranger*, she thought. *He is no friendlier than Brian.*

"Okay," Danielle said in a quiet voice. "What about the Missing Thorndike?"

"The chief wanted to have a jeweler verify the stones were real before we sent it to the lab."

"Why would he want to do that? We've already had it appraised, twice," Danielle said.

"We have to maintain the chain of evidence," Brian explained. "When we turn the necklace over to the lab, we want to make sure we get the same necklace back."

"Oh, you mean if someone at the lab switched out the stones and put in fakes?" Lily said.

"Yes." Brian nodded.

"I suppose that makes sense." Danielle still couldn't figure out why they were here.

"The necklace we found in Adam's office was the same one you wore to the open house," Joe explained. "The problem is, the stones of the necklace we found are fake."

"What does he mean fake?" Cheryl screeched. "Did I get murdered over fake diamonds?"

"Excuse me?" Danielle looked from Joe to Brian. The way they stared at her, she had the feeling they expected her to explain the fake stones.

"We had the necklace looked at. The gemstones are fake," Brian said.

"Are you sure it's the necklace Cheryl took? That might explain why the killer was willing to leave it in the office to frame Adam. It wasn't the Missing Thorndike; it's a fake. The killer has the real necklace," Danielle said.

"All I know, it's the same necklace you had on," Joe told her.

"How do you know that?" Lily asked.

"If you'll remember, the necklace broke before the party, and I had to fix it with a piece of wire. It's the same necklace."

"That doesn't make any sense." Danielle shook her head in disbelief. "It was appraised twice. How could that be? What did Sam Hayman say?"

"We didn't talk to Sam," Joe said.

Danielle frowned. "I assumed that's who looked at the necklace."

"No. We had to get someone from Astoria. Sam's gone," Brian explained.

"Gone, what do you mean gone?" Danielle asked.

"He's left town," Brian said.

"Left town? What about his store?" Lily asked.

"I guess he's been struggling for some time. He sold his commercial building a while back and his house," Joe explained. "But it doesn't matter, because the person who looked at the necklace is more than qualified. We aren't saying the stones weren't real when they went into the safety deposit box. But sometime between then—and when you put on the necklace, the stones were switched."

"That's impossible. I seriously doubt Steve Klein or one of his employees switched out the stones. And I know it didn't happen here. The killer must have murdered Cheryl, taken the necklace, switched the stones and then put the necklace with the fake gemstones in Adam's office," Danielle said.

"The only problem with that is the blood," Brian said.

"What are you talking about?" Danielle asked.

"Oh god…blood…they're talking about my blood…I think I'm going to be sick…" Cheryl groaned.

"You can't get sick," Walt reminded her. "You're dead. We don't get sick."

"Are you sure?" Cheryl asked.

Walt nodded.

"We spoke to the lab before we came over here, and it looks like the blood is Cheryl's. Not a hundred percent yet, but fairly certain. Cheryl was killed with the necklace on—the necklace she took from you, the one Joe wired together. Her blood is all over it," Brian said.

"Oh my god, I did get killed over fake stones!"

"This doesn't make any sense." Danielle stood up and began pacing the room.

"I told you the stones were fake," Walt reminded her.

"But they had to have been real. The insurance appraiser would never have made a mistake like that," Danielle said.

"We agree they were real when you had it appraised." Joe didn't understand Danielle was talking to Walt, not him.

"Did you switch out the stones before the party?" Brian asked.

"Excuse me?" Danielle stopped pacing and faced Brian.

"It would be understandable. It's not uncommon to keep the expensive stuff locked up while wearing fake doubles. After all, who at the party would be the wiser? Of course, if the necklace gets stolen and you try to make a claim on the insurance while you have the real gems locked in your safe, then you might have a problem," Brian said.

"Oh my god, is that what you did?" Cheryl asked.

"No, I did not swap out the stones," Danielle said, staring past Brian to Cheryl.

"Maybe you could let us see in your safe?" Brian suggested. "I mean, you don't have to let us; we don't have a search warrant or anything. But it might clear a few things up for us."

"I'm not really sure what all this has to do with my cousin's murder," Danielle said angrily. "If I had swapped out those stones—which I didn't—it wouldn't really have any bearing one way or another on my cousin's murder."

"We do need to figure out when those stones were switched. It does have a bearing on the case," Joe said in a gentle voice, sounding much kinder than before. "If we know you didn't change the stones, then maybe the killer did. Those missing diamonds and emeralds could lead us to your cousin's killer."

"If that was the case…" Danielle considered the possibilities. "Then you're suggesting Cheryl removed the necklace, someone switched the stones, and then she put the necklace back on, and then someone bashed in her head?"

"Bashed in my head? Oh, Dani, please! Must you be so graphic?" Cheryl moaned.

"Did you have anything to do with the stones being switched?" Walt asked.

"Absolutely not!" Cheryl insisted. When Walt continued to stare at her as if he didn't believe what she was saying, she crossed her finger over her chest and said, "I'm telling the truth, cross my heart and hope to die, stick a needle in my eye."

"Need I remind you…" Walt began.

Cheryl stomped her foot and disappeared.

Danielle was so preoccupied with the exchange between Walt and Cheryl that she didn't realize Joe was saying something to her. Finally Lily touched her arm and said, "Dani, just show them."

"What?" Danielle looked at Lily.

"Show them what you have in the safe. What will it hurt?" Lily said.

Danielle looked over at Joe and Brian, who were staring at her. She imagined they wondered where she had just zoned out to.

"Fine," Danielle said. "Come with me. It's upstairs in my bedroom."

The two men followed Danielle and Lily upstairs to Danielle's room. They watched as Danielle removed a piece of paneling from the wall to expose the safe. Without saying a word, she turned the combination lock to the right, then the left, and then the right again before swinging the safe's door open. She stood to one side so the two men could look inside the small compartment. The safe was empty.

"Well, at least you haven't put the stones in the house safe," Brian murmured.

"Are you insinuating I have them somewhere else?"

"No. I'm just saying the only thing you've proved is that you didn't put the gemstones in your wall safe."

"Will there be anything else?" Danielle asked tersely.

"No, I think that's all for now," Brian said.

As they walked back downstairs, Joe whispered to Danielle, "I hope you understand; I'm just doing my job."

Danielle paused on the stairway and faced Joe. Brian and Lily continued to walk down to the first floor, leaving Joe and Danielle alone on the stairs—alone except for Walt, who stood nearby listening.

"Do you think I killed my cousin?" Danielle asked.

"We've arrested Adam Nichols for the murder," Joe said.

"That doesn't really answer my question. Your partner clearly does not like me. And I'm beginning to think that you don't either."

"Danielle, this has nothing to do with me liking you or not. I'm simply doing my job, and to do that I have to remain impartial."

"Yeah…well…whatever…" Danielle started back down the stairs.

"We noticed your cousin's attorney was just leaving here when we drove up," Joe said as he followed Danielle.

"Yes, he was. I guess your partner was right. I'm a very rich woman now that my cousin is dead," Danielle said dully. "Lucky me."

THIRTY-SIX

Lily stumbled into the kitchen on Wednesday morning, rubbing sleep from her eyes. There hadn't been time to comb her hair; the aroma of the fresh brewed coffee was too seductive. Still wearing her Hello Kitty pajama bottoms and red tank top, she made her way directly to the pot of coffee sitting on the counter.

Danielle looked up from where she sat at the kitchen table, drinking her coffee and reading the morning paper. "You were out late last night. Did you have a good time?"

Lily sipped the coffee she had just poured herself before answering. "Grabbed a burger down by the pier and then spent the rest of the night at Ian's, talking." Lily brought her mug of coffee to the table and sat down.

"Just talking?" Danielle teased.

"Yeah, just talking." She set the mug on the table and glanced around. "Are we alone?"

"You mean Cheryl and Walt?"

"Who else? Don't tell me we have other spirits hanging around here."

"I've only noticed two. And yeah, we're alone." Danielle glanced around the room. *I think we're alone*, she thought.

"I told Ian about the gemstones being fake," Lily said.

"What did he think?"

"He agreed they must have been removed after Cheryl left

here." Lily lowered her voice to a whisper and said, "He seems to think Cheryl must have been in on it and was double-crossed."

"How so?"

"Ian said that if the necklace had the real diamonds and emeralds in it when Cheryl took it, then she—and whoever she was working with—switched out the stones. She intended to return here with the necklace, trying to pass off the fake stones as the real ones. But when she put the necklace back on, with the fake stones, she was double-crossed when her partner in crime hit her over the head. Ian said he probably didn't kill Cheryl just for her half of the take, but because she was a witness."

"The only problem with that scenario is that Cheryl insists that isn't what happened. And I believe her."

"I know…but do spirits always tell the truth?" Lily asked.

"No, I don't think so. But I do believe her. After all, the buyer was supposed to arrive after the weekend, and he would've spotted the fakes. All eyes would be on Cheryl, who had the necklace last."

"I thought that too. But Ian reminded me that Cheryl was trying to stop the sale of the necklace, and maybe she thought you would postpone the meeting with the buyer until after the estate was settled. By that time, she wouldn't be a prime suspect because there would be significant distance between her and the Missing Thorndike."

"You're also forgetting Cheryl was already a wealthy woman. There was no reason for her to suddenly embark on a new career as a jewel thief."

"I know, but some people do things like that for the thrill."

"True." Danielle sipped her coffee.

"Ian also thought it was bizarre that Sam Hayman has disappeared. He was surprised the police aren't looking into that. But I told him maybe they were but just didn't tell us."

"Sam hasn't disappeared, he moved. So what?"

"Don't you think it odd? Sam has been living in this town his entire life—he is the one who appraised the necklace for you—he was at the party—and then poof—he ups and moves about the same time they find poor Cheryl's body?"

"And if someone wanted to switch out the stones, he would certainly know how to do that," Danielle murmured. "I wonder if he was the one Cheryl met on the beach that night. She said he was someone familiar—someone she thought she had met here."

The landline began to ring. Lily got up from the table and answered the phone. "Hello, Marlow House."

"Lily, I tried calling your cellphone." It was Ian.

"Oh, I left it upstairs. You're up early. What's going on?"

"I've been up for a couple hours. I couldn't stop thinking about what we were talking about last night. I found something interesting. Can I come over? I'd like to show it to you and Danielle."

"Sure, I guess. Give me a minute to get dressed."

"Hey, you don't have to dress for me," Ian said with a chuckle.

Fifteen minutes later Ian was sitting in the parlor of Marlow House with Lily and Danielle. Before he arrived, Lily had slipped into a pair of shorts and a clean tank top, and had combed her hair. Danielle had already been dressed for the day, wearing denim shorts and a blouse, when Lily found her in the kitchen that morning.

"After Lily told me about the stones being fake, I kept thinking about how you initially insisted they were fake when you first found the necklace," Ian told Danielle. "I woke early this morning thinking about it, and I remembered something I'd seen when researching for the Thorndike story. So I got up and started rummaging through the boxes I brought with me. I found this."

Danielle took the slip of paper Ian handed her. On closer inspection, the yellowed and crumpled piece of paper appeared to be a receipt from a Portland jewelry store—dating back to the weeks prior to Eva Thorndike's death.

"I don't understand." Danielle looked from the paper in her hand to Ian. "What is this?"

"It's a purchase receipt for diamonds and emeralds—purchased by Eva Thorndike's father from a Portland jeweler," Ian said.

"What does this mean?" Danielle looked back to the paper.

"It didn't click when I first saw it—I didn't realize this had anything to do with the Missing Thorndike. And maybe it doesn't. It could just be a coincidence. After all, the Thorndikes were wealthy, and this wasn't the only receipt I came across that showed they had extravagant tastes."

"I still don't get it." Danielle shook her head. She felt stupid. *What is Ian implying?*

"This purchase receipt is for gemstones—diamonds and emeralds, to be exact. It's the precise number of diamonds and emeralds and karat sizes as the stones in the Missing Thorndike." Ian pointed to one line in the receipt. "And if you see there, the jeweler charged to have the diamonds and emeralds set. There is no mention of the Thorndikes purchasing a setting to put the diamonds in."

"So her parents figured out the stones were fake," Walt said, appearing in the room. "They were the ones who replaced the stones."

"I have a question for you," Danielle asked Ian.

"What?"

Danielle waved the receipt in the air and asked, "How in the world did you ever get ahold of this?"

"I guess Lily never told you how I happened to start writing about Eva Thorndike."

Danielle glanced from Ian to Lily and back to Ian. "No."

"I mentioned I was working on the story with my sister, Kelly."

"Yes, I remember that." Danielle nodded.

"Kelly is also a writer. She freelances for several of the smaller newspapers, writing local interest and historical pieces. She's also a bit of a yard-sale addict. She even writes a blog about her finds. A couple years ago, she went to one of those sales where they auction off old trunks and suitcases that haven't been opened by the auctioneers. Gives the sale a bit of mystery and surprise. You never know what you're really buying."

"Like a dead body," Lily smirked.

"No, that would smell," Ian said with a grin.

"Is it really necessary to speak so cavalierly about those of us who have departed? Please get on with your explanation," Walt said, knowing full well only Danielle could hear him. Danielle glanced over to Walt and smiled.

"She purchased a trunk, and when she brought it home and opened it up, it was stuffed with personal papers, letters, and receipts from the Thorndikes. Kelly wasn't quite sure what she had on her hands, so she called me over. The rest is history."

"So you got a book out of the trunk," Danielle said.

"Pretty much." Ian grinned.

"It sure looks like her parents replaced the fake stones," Danielle said.

"Okay, stop there," Ian interrupted. "I agree this is fascinating that her parents happen to purchase the identical stones needed for the Missing Thorndike, but what makes you so certain it once had fake stones—I mean, before now."

"It's hard to explain..." *Impossible is more accurate*, Danielle thought.

"Was there something else about the receipt you wanted us to see?" Lily interrupted. "I'm not sure why you felt it was so urgent for us to see this. I mean it is interesting and everything, but..."

Ian pointed to a signature at the bottom of the receipt.

Squinting her eyes, Lily brought the piece of paper closer to her face and tried to make out the handwriting. "Jacob Hayman," she read aloud.

"That's Samuel Hayman's grandfather," Walt said. "He's the one who started the store—he's the one who appraised the necklace for Eva."

"Hayman. I was wondering, could that possibly be any relation to Samuel Hayman, our missing jeweler?" Ian asked.

"That's Sam's grandfather," Danielle explained. "He's the one who opened the jewelry store in Frederickport—the one that just closed down."

"I have no idea what any of this means—if it means anything at all—but I had to show you," Ian said.

"Lily mentioned you thought it was odd that Sam left, and the police don't find that suspicious."

"Yes. Especially since it looks like someone switched out those stones while Cheryl had the necklace. That's not something just anyone can do. You'd have to know what you were doing. I'm surprised Sam isn't on the top of the police's suspect list."

"No, that would be me," Danielle said.

WHEN DANIELLE WENT to the police station to talk to Joe later that day, she was annoyed to find herself led to the interview room with both Joe and his partner, Brian Henderson.

"I was wondering," Danielle asked Joe, "have you found Sam Hayman yet?"

Brian looked at Danielle. "I didn't know he was lost."

Danielle glared at Brian then looked back to Joe. "You aren't looking for him?"

"I'm not really sure why we would be," Joe said apologetically.

"Are you seriously saying you haven't for a moment considered Sam Hayman as a suspect?"

"What motive would Sam have to kill your cousin?" Brian asked. "He didn't stand to inherit ten million bucks."

"Brian, please," Joe lightly reprimanded.

"Well, let's see," Danielle said impatiently, looking back at Brian. "I'd say getting away with diamonds and emeralds worth over a million dollars is a good motive. We have a jeweler who was at the open house, and he spent a great deal of time there chatting with Cheryl. He certainly knows how to set stones; after all, that's what he does for a living. Oh, and when it comes to reselling those diamonds and emeralds, I think he'll know how to do that too. After all, that is his profession. Have I left anything out? Oh, I know, he just happens to have up and moved from a town he has lived in all his life—closed his store overnight—and leaves. Leaving the necklace in Adam's office was a nice touch, to throw off the cops." Danielle stood up abruptly.

"Are you saying Samuel Hayman stole those gems and killed your cousin?" Brian asked.

"I am seriously beginning to doubt the overall intelligence of the Frederickport Police Department." Danielle turned and abruptly left the room.

"Not sure about the overall intelligence of our department," Joe said to Brian. "But I sure feel stupid."

THIRTY-SEVEN

Brian and Joe found Joanne Johnson at her home on Wednesday afternoon. When she opened her front door, she seemed surprised to find the two officers standing on her front porch.

"Joe, Brian, what's going on?" Joanne asked.

"We wondered if we could have a few moments of your time to ask you some questions about Marlow House and the Fourth of July party," Brian said.

"Certainly, come on in." Joanne opened the door wider and showed the two officers to her living room. They declined her offer for something to drink, wanting to get immediately to their questions.

"We were wondering if you remember seeing Sam Hayman at the open house," Brian asked.

"Why, certainly. You remember, Joe. You were there." Joanne glanced from Brian to Joe. "I don't understand, I thought Adam had been arrested for the murder of Danielle's cousin."

"He has, but we're trying to tie up some loose ends and we wanted to see if you remember anything…anything in particular about Sam and the party," Joe explained.

"Well, let me see…" Bringing the tip of her index finger to her chin, Joanne stared off across the room. "I do remember that when he was talking to Mr. Renton, I thought it was rather funny."

"What was funny?" Joe asked.

"It was one of those moments where someone is staring at someone—in this case Mr. Renton and Sam were staring at Cheryl and Adam, who didn't know they were being watched. And here I was, watching them all. Of course, maybe someone was watching me watching them." Joanne let out a short laugh.

"What were they watching that was so interesting?" Brian asked.

"Cheryl and Adam were by the wine table, talking. Mr. Renton and Sam were standing under the trees, watching the pair. I noticed Cheryl swiping a bottle of wine from the table. It looked like she was trying to conceal it in her arms. She runs out toward the gate and sticks it in the bushes. I look over at Renton and Sam, they're watching the whole thing, laughing. Of course, Cheryl thinks she's being very sneaky and doesn't think anyone sees her."

"Did you ever see Sam talking with Cheryl?" Brian asked.

"Yes. Not long after Cheryl put the bottle in the bushes and returned to Adam, Sam walked up to them. They all went inside together. I really didn't notice Sam until later, after he left and then came back."

"What do you mean he left?" Joe asked.

"Well, I assumed he was leaving the party. A lot of people came for just a short while, looked around, had something to eat then left. But he came back about thirty minutes later. Not really sure where he went." Joanne shrugged.

"So you never saw him again with Cheryl?" Brian asked.

"No…but I just thought of something."

"What's that?" Joe asked.

"When he returned, he entered through the side gate. I thought it was odd, because I noticed him crouching by the bushes where Cheryl had put the bottle of wine. At first, I thought he was going to take the bottle for himself, but when he stood up, he didn't have it. I guess he was just looking at the bottle for some reason."

Joe and Brian exchanged glances.

"What did he do then?" Joe asked.

"He walked back to the house. I believe he stopped to talk to someone. I went back into the kitchen, and I don't remember seeing him again that day."

"DID SAM LEAVE the party to get some Rohypnol to put in the

wine?" Joe asked Brian after they got back into their car and headed to the station.

"It does make me wonder. But where in the hell did he get Rohypnol?"

"We know someone drugged the wine. If Sam was with Adam and Cheryl at the party, perhaps they told him where they were going. Maybe he figured they would both drink the wine and pass out; then he could steal the necklace. But something went wrong, so he ended up killing Cheryl."

"But that would mean he knew Cheryl intended to take off with the necklace," Brian said.

"Maybe Cheryl and Sam were in on it together all along, and Adam was just a patsy."

"There is one way to find out," Brian began.

"Find Sam?" Joe suggested.

"Exactly."

SAM HAYMAN WASN'T difficult to find. If he was trying to hide, he hadn't done a very good job at it; his credit card activity led the police to the motel where he was staying on the outskirts of Portland. The local authorities cooperated, understanding that time was of the essence. If Sam had the stolen gems on him, he probably wouldn't have them for long.

The jeweler seemed genuinely surprised to find the police at his motel door with a search warrant on Wednesday evening. Sam was even more surprised when they found where he had hidden the diamonds and emeralds from the Missing Thorndike—tucked in a plastic pouch and hidden in the bottom of his can of Metamucil.

As they transported Sam back to Frederickport, he kept insisting, "I didn't kill her, honest! She was alive when I left her!"

SAM HAYMAN SAT ALONE at the table in the interview room when Joe walked in and shut the door behind him.

"He sure looks nervous," the chief observed as he stood with Brian in the small office, watching the scene unfold through the two-way mirror. "I can't believe he's waived his rights to see an attorney. Thought Sam was smarter than that."

"All the way back here he kept insisting he was innocent," Brian said.

"Innocent? How does he explain having the missing gemstones on him?"

"I guess we're about to hear…"

"YOU KEEP SAYING you didn't kill Cheryl Hartford. Can you explain how you happen to have the diamonds and emeralds from the Missing Thorndike?"

"Okay, I admit I took them. But I didn't kill her. You know me, Joe. I'm not a murderer."

Joe sat down across the table from Sam. "I never thought you were a thief either, Sam. So tell me what happened."

"I grew up hearing about the Missing Thorndike. My grandfather was especially fascinated with the necklace and the mystery of its disappearance." Sam paused a moment and stared at his hands; they fidgeted nervously on the table.

"Go on," Joe urged.

"When they found the necklace and brought it to me, Danielle Boatman thought the stones were fake. She was surprised they were real. I didn't think much about it at the time, but it got me to thinking of my grandfather and his fascination with the necklace."

"Is this the grandfather who originally started your store here?"

"Yes. There was an old trunk in the store's storage room that belonged to my grandfather. I never really looked in it before; it was just filled with old papers—or so I thought. But finding the necklace sort of renewed my interest in him, so I decided to go through it. I wasn't really looking for anything in particular. To be honest, it was no more than idle curiosity."

"What did you find?" Joe asked.

"A large envelope. It was kind of bulky. When I opened it, I found what looked like diamonds and emeralds. Oh, I got excited at first, but I soon realized they were fake—though impressive fakes. My grandfather used to leave notes about some of his more memorable clients. I guess the Missing Thorndike was the most memorable for him."

"Are you saying he originally sold the Thorndikes the necklace?"

"No. According to my grandfather's notes, Eva Thorndike brought the necklace to his store in Portland. She'd been recently abandoned by her husband, and she feared he'd removed the real gems and replaced them with fakes. It turned out she was right. They were fake."

"I thought you said the necklace had real diamonds and emeralds when you first looked at it?"

"It did. Apparently, her parents found out; they'd discovered my grandfather's appraisal in her belongings. She was sick by that time. They wanted to replace the imitation diamonds and emeralds with real ones, but they didn't want a scandal. I guess they figured if they hired grandfather to replace the stones, he'd keep the story of their son-in-law's betrayal to himself. I mean, they were going to pay someone to replace the diamonds and emeralds anyway. They just figured they would use my grandfather to ensure it was all confidential."

"What does any of this have to do with you stealing the stones?"

"I started thinking—how I wish I had looked in that trunk before Danielle Boatman brought me the necklace. She thought they were fake. How easy it would have been for me back then to simply put the fakes back in—the ones my grandfather kept—and she never would have known. No one would have."

"I thought Ian and Lily initially brought the necklace in."

"Well, they did. But still. Danielle was the owner. She thought it was fake."

"When did you decide to switch the stones?" Joe asked.

"Not until that night. When I was with Cheryl and Adam, I overheard them talking about taking off later and spending the night in one of his bungalows."

"How did you know she'd have the necklace with her?"

"She sort of told me—when we were alone. I knew she was planning to take it for the night. She made me promise not to tell anyone. Said she was going to bring it back in the morning, and since she owned half of it, it was no big deal."

"Why would she tell you?"

"I think she was bragging."

"So you drugged the wine?" Joe asked.

Samuel's eyes widened. He looked at Joe. "How did you know?"

"I'd like to know where you got the Rohypnol."

"Sometimes I can't sleep…" Sam stammered.

"You can't legally buy it in this country. Where did you get it?"

"When I was in South America last year. It's legal down there."

"When did you decide to drug the wine?" Joe asked.

"After Cheryl told me she was going to take the necklace and Adam made it clear where they were going to be, I started having fantasies about taking it from them. But I didn't want to hurt anyone. Then I remembered the wine—and the Rohypnol. I thought it would be easy."

"What happened?" Joe asked.

"I went home and got the drugs. When I came back, I put it in the wine. I figured when they got to the bungalow, they'd drink it and pass out. I could just take the necklace. I never really planned to switch out the stones."

"What went wrong?" Joe asked.

"I brought the fake stones with me, the ones my grandfather had taken from the necklace. I brought them along for good luck—but a heck of a lot of good they did me…"

"From what Adam tells us, he drank the wine, but Cheryl didn't."

"I parked my car down the beach, not far from where you found Cheryl's body. I didn't want anyone to see my car parked near the bungalow. So I walked down from the beach. When I got to the bungalow, Cheryl was cold sober. I didn't mean for her to see me. I was going to come in by the back door. But she was there on the porch, carrying her purse and shoes. I asked where Adam was. She said he'd passed out, and she was walking home."

"Cheryl had Rohypnol in her system."

"Yes. I offered to walk her home and suggested she get something for us to drink. I thought she'd take the wine, but she grabbed a couple of beers."

"So you managed to drug the beer?"

"Yes."

"And then you realized she would probably remember seeing you when she woke up without the necklace, and she'd start pointing the finger at you."

"No! That's when I changed my plan. I figured I would have to switch the stones when she passed out. That way when she woke up, she'd assume she still had the necklace. I had the tools I needed in the car to switch the stones, and I figured I just had to get her to that hut."

"How did you know the hut was unlocked?"

"I didn't. I figured one of them would be open. If not, it wouldn't be too difficult to break in."

"But after you made the switch, you realized they would eventually discover the stones were fake, and she'd start pointing the finger at you."

"Who would believe I was walking around with the exact amount of fake stones—of the necessary size and color—to make such a switch? I couldn't see any way they could trace the fake stones to me. Anyway, I knew there was always a chance she wouldn't even remember seeing me when she woke up the next morning."

"But she didn't wake up, did she?"

"I swear she was alive when I left her. She wanted to sit down; the drug was really starting to take hold. I managed to get her in the shed right before she passed out. I left her there, went to my car to get my light and the necessary tools, and returned to the shed and switched out the stones. I left her there wearing the necklace."

"Why didn't you just take the necklace, if you thought she might not remember seeing you anyway?"

"I couldn't be sure. And anyway, I didn't want people to start looking for the necklace."

"Didn't Danielle have a buyer arriving a couple days after the party? He'd know they were fake."

"Yes, but Cheryl said Danielle was going to have to call the buyer and cancel, because as long as the estate was being contested, she had no right to sell the necklace."

"But someone smashed in her head and took the necklace with the fake stones."

"I know. But it wasn't me."

THIRTY-EIGHT

Danielle stepped out on her front porch to get her newspaper on Thursday morning and was greeted by Joe Morelli.

"Joe," Danielle said in surprise. She glanced around to see if he was alone. "Where's your partner?"

"Brian? Probably on his way to work. I was wondering if we could talk a moment."

Glancing at Joe's uniform, Danielle asked, "Is this official business?"

"Unofficial official business."

Danielle looked at him a moment before answering. Finally, she said, "Sure, first, let me get…"

"This," Joe asked, handing her the newspaper. She had been so startled to find him standing on her front porch that she hadn't noticed what he was holding.

"Thanks." Danielle took the paper and then led the way into the house. She took Joe to the parlor. After tossing the newspaper on the desk, she sat on a chair and motioned for him to sit on the couch.

"I wanted to let you know we arrested Sam Hayman last night. He was staying in a motel outside of Portland. He had your diamonds and emeralds with him—the ones from the Missing Thorndike."

"He killed Cheryl?" Danielle asked.

"He says he didn't."

"Of course he does."

"He admitted to stealing the gemstones but insists Cheryl was alive when he left her in the hut." Joe went on to tell her Sam's account from that evening.

"What now?" Danielle asked. "Are you charging him with murder or theft? Do you believe him?"

"I have to admit, he sounded sincere, but the chief is hoping the DA agrees to press charges. He believes we have our man."

"What about Adam?" Danielle asked.

"We're dropping the charges against Adam. Even if Sam is telling the truth and someone else killed Cheryl after he left her in the hut, it couldn't have been Adam. Sam's version vindicates him. Adam was the one who drank the drugged wine. I'm pretty certain he was out all night, considering how much he consumed and his condition the next morning."

"You never mentioned the wine had been drugged," Danielle said.

"Adam told you he suspected the wine had been drugged."

"Did Adam tell you that?" When Joe didn't immediately answer her question, Danielle said, "You were listening, weren't you? You listened in on our conversation at the police station."

"That really doesn't matter now."

"It does to me," Danielle said.

"Why were you so convinced Adam was innocent?"

"I guess you can call it a hunch," Danielle lied. "You say you aren't convinced Sam killed Cheryl. Who do you think did? Whoever it was obviously knew the necklace was a fake, since they didn't have a problem using it to frame Adam."

Joe studied Danielle, a somber expression on his face. "Or maybe they were confident they'd get it back after the police found it. Or maybe they didn't care, since it was insured."

Danielle stared at him in disbelief. She couldn't believe what he seemed to be implying.

"Wow, Brian isn't the only jerk." Danielle stood up. "I think you should go now."

"Danielle, I like you." Joe stood up. "I don't think you intended to kill Cheryl. But I think after I left that night, you decided to go looking for her. Maybe she mentioned something about Adam's beach house. You started walking down the beach, hoping to find her. You saw her go into the hut with Sam, and when he left, you found her unconscious. Maybe it had nothing to do with Cheryl's money—she just made you so angry, you couldn't help yourself."

"You believe I killed my cousin?"

"I don't think you meant to. But I saw how angry she made you. Even now you refuse to admit what you did—what I saw with my own eyes. The way you hit her so hard she fell down, or how in a fit of rage you dumped all her things into her suitcase, ruining her clothes."

"You didn't see me do either of those things," Danielle said.

"I was right there when she fell. No, I didn't see you actually push her, but her face was bruised, you were the only one standing close to her, and Cheryl herself claimed you hit her. And unless Joanne is lying, you're the only one who could have thrown all of Cheryl's things in that suitcase."

"You need to leave now." Danielle walked to the door.

"I want to help you, Danielle. But I can't do that if you aren't prepared to take responsibility. I don't think it was premeditated, and considering your mental state…"

Danielle paused at the doorway and faced Joe. "Please. Leave."

Letting out a weary sigh, Joe walked to the front door. Before leaving, he turned and faced Danielle. "I believe Sam's story. Maybe the chief doesn't, but I do. I wish you could understand, but I can't let a man go to jail for a murder he didn't commit. If you would only meet me halfway, it would go a lot easier on you."

"Goodbye, Joe," Danielle said, holding back her tears.

WALT FOUND Danielle twenty minutes later, curled up in a fetal position on the center of her bed, crying inconsolably. It took him five minutes to calm her down, and it wasn't until his right hand brushed her forehead, gently pushing back her hair from her face, did she quiet. Blinking away the tears from her eyes, she looked up at Walt.

"I could feel your hand touch me," she whispered in awe.

"It's only an illusion," he said with a gentle smile. "I've been practicing harnessing my energy."

"That felt nice, like you're really here."

"I am really here," he told her.

"You know what I mean…like you are…"

"Please don't say it," Walt asked.

Alive.

Wiping away the tears with the back of her hand, Danielle sat up in the bed.

"Can you tell me what happened?" Walt remained seated on the mattress next to her.

"Where's Lily?" Danielle asked.

"Last I checked, she's still sleeping."

"And Cheryl?" Danielle asked.

"I haven't seen her since last night."

"Where does she go?"

Walt shook his head. "I don't know. But tell me what happened."

Danielle took a deep breath and then proceeded to tell Walt about her conversation with Joe.

"I'm so sorry, Danielle," Walt said after she finished. "Do you think he could actually convince them to press charges against you?"

"I don't know. I sort of doubt it. It's so circumstantial, and Sam was caught with the stolen gems. I think Joe was playing good cop, bad cop—taking both roles—trying to get me to confess."

"He hurt you, didn't he?"

"Yes. And the thing is, he has no idea how he hurt me. I honestly believe in some twisted way he thought he was being my friend, trying to help me. It…well, it reminded me of Lucas."

"Your husband? How is that?"

"When I told Lucas about…my gift…he pretended to believe me, because he really couldn't find it in himself to believe I might actually be able to see ghosts. So he thought he was being supportive by pretending. It's just like Joe. Joe was trying to be supportive too, but the bottom line is—just like Lucas, he doesn't believe in me. Doesn't trust me."

"Did you like Joe a great deal?"

"I don't know. He seemed like a nice enough guy." Grabbing her pillow, Danielle rolled over, her back to Walt as she curled up into a ball, hugging the foam bundle. "Heck, it's not like we even kissed or anything."

ADAM HADN'T BEEN BACK to his office since the arrest. He spent most of his time at his grandmother's house, going through the computer, hoping to discover who had slipped the necklace in the vase. The task would have been easier had he known what he was actually doing. When he initially installed the camera in the office, he never imagined it would one day save him from going to prison.

He couldn't recall the last time he had slept. When he finally left Marie's house and headed back to his place, he considered calling his attorney, Ted Zimmerman, and letting him know what he had discovered. He wasn't sure how to proceed, and it was too important to screw up and make the wrong move. But first, first he needed to get some sleep. He imagined that once his head hit the pillow, he would finally get the rest he needed. It didn't matter that it was almost noon.

To Adam's surprise, Ted Zimmerman was waiting in his driveway when he pulled up to his house.

"I was going to call you, but I wanted to deliver the news in person," Ted said excitedly when Adam got out of his car.

"What's going on?"

"They dropped all the charges." Ted beamed.

"I don't understand. What happened?" Adam stood with his attorney in the driveway.

"They've arrested someone named Samuel Hayman. Do you know who that is?"

"Sam? You're kidding. Sam owns the jewelry store here in town. Or at least he used to. Sam, are you sure?"

"They caught him red-handed with the stolen jewels. He was holed up in some little motel near Portland."

"That can't be right," Adam murmured.

"Why, was he a friend of yours?"

"I've known Sam forever. He's older than me, but we both grew up in Frederickport. I can't believe it. It doesn't make sense."

"I thought you'd be dancing with joy over the news."

"Well…naturally I'm thrilled they dropped the charges. But what happens if something comes up and they decide Sam isn't the one? Will they come back after me?"

"It looks like Sam's testimony put you in the clear. He admitted to drugging the wine. Claimed you were out cold when he got to the house and Cheryl took off with him."

"Are you saying Sam confessed to murdering Cheryl?"

"No. But he did confess to drugging Cheryl, then replacing the gemstones with fakes and leaving her in the hut, still wearing the necklace with the fake stones. You drank the drugged wine and Cheryl didn't, according to Hayman. So even if he's telling the truth, and Cheryl really was alive when he left her, you couldn't have been the one to kill her. You were out cold."

"I thought you told me they found the same drug from the wine in Cheryl's body."

"Hayman confessed to putting some of it in a beer Cheryl drank after she left the bungalow."

"So this means I really am in the clear?"

"It sure does. How about we celebrate? Let me take you out to lunch."

"Thanks, Ted, I appreciate the offer. But the only thing I want to do right now is take a shower and go to bed. I'm exhausted."

"I can understand that."

"There is something else I need to discuss with you about the case. But that can wait. I don't think I've gotten two hours' sleep since I was arrested. All I want to do is crash. But can you do me one favor?"

"Sure, what do you need?"

"Call my grandmother, and let her know the charges have been dropped. Tell her I'll give her a call when I wake up."

"Sure, no problem."

THIRTY-NINE

Brad Miller stood in front of the Frederickport Police Department, debating if he should go in or not. His friends were going to kill him, but he knew he didn't have another choice. Once he walked in the door and told his story, he knew the cops would round up the other guys. His friends would be pissed, but none of them would lie to the cops.

Ten minutes later, Brad found himself alone in the interview room, waiting to talk to an officer. He was relieved when Joe Morelli walked in. Joe had dated his older sister last summer, and for a cop, he was cool.

"Morning, Brad," Joe said as he walked to the table, offering the teenager his hand. Nervously Brad accepted the brief handshake but remained seated. After Joe released Brad's hand, he sat down at the table across from him. "So what's this about? They told me you had some information about the Hartford murder."

"I know I should have come in before, but we figured we really didn't know anything, and well…we just didn't want to get involved."

"We?" Joe asked.

"Well, me and some of the guys."

"Where are these guys? Why aren't they here with you?"

"They don't want to come in. We all kind of agreed not to say anything."

"Do they know you're here?" Joe asked.

"No. But Mom was reading the newspaper this morning about Sam Hayman getting arrested. And well, I knew I had to come in, because Sam didn't murder that woman."

"Why don't you start at the beginning and tell me what you know."

"Me and some of the guys were supposed to be at the fireworks show, but we got sort of bored, so we took off. Started walking down the beach. After a while we got tired, so…we, ahh…well…" Brad moved restlessly in his seat.

"What is it?" Joe asked.

"Well, sometimes we sort of borrow the surfboards they keep in the beach hut where you found that woman. We always put them back, I promise."

"You were going to surf at night?"

"No. But Kevin remembered seeing some chairs in there, and we were going to borrow a couple. It's not like we were breaking in or anything, that hut isn't locked."

"So what happened?"

"When we got there, we saw Sam taking that woman into the hut. By the way she was walking, we figured she was drunk. At the time we didn't know who it was; it was pretty dark. But then he left and ran up the path."

"What do you mean he left?" Joe asked.

"Right after he helped her in the hut, he took off. We were sort of debating if we should go check it out, to see if she was passed out or something. But he came back carrying this little bag, you know, like a briefcase."

"Did he go back in the shed?"

"Yeah, he was in there for quite a while. And then he left again. I decided to follow him to see where he kept going. But this time he got into his car and drove off. I recognized him. It was Sam who owned the jewelry store."

"What about the woman?"

"She was still in the hut, so we decided to check to see if she was okay."

"Was she dead?" Joe asked.

"No. We checked her pulse. I could smell beer on her, figured she was drunk and had passed out."

"What was her hair like?"

"Her hair?" Brad frowned.

"Did you notice any blood? Whoever killed her hit her over the head. There was a lot of blood."

"No. There wasn't any blood. Nothing like that."

"Are you sure? It would have been dark in that shed," Joe said.

"We had flashlights."

"So what did you do?"

"We figured we'd just leave her there. Let her sleep it off. Thought she'd be safe in the shed; was no reason to get involved. I mean, we really weren't supposed to be in there, so didn't see a reason to get in trouble."

"You just left her there?" Joe asked.

"Yeah." Brad shrugged.

"Did you pile the rafts on her body?" Joe asked.

"What do you mean?"

"When they found her, she was supposedly buried under a pile of rafts."

"No, that would be lame. Why would we do that? We just left her, promise."

"Then what did you do?"

"We took off. Went back to the firework show. But she was alive when we left her, honest."

"I'm going to need the names of your friends, the ones who were with you that night."

"I'D LIKE you to interview the other boys first," the chief said after Joe updated him on the case. The two sat in the chief's office.

"I know Brad Miller, and I believe him," Joe said.

"Yes, I know. But before we do anything, we need to talk to the other witnesses. However, it does look like you were right; Sam probably didn't kill Cheryl Hartford."

"That only leaves one other suspect—Danielle Boatman," Joe said.

"I have to admit I'm surprised you've taken that turn. Got the impression you were rather fond of the girl."

"I was—I am. This isn't easy for me, but I have a job to do, and frankly, I can't see where it could be anyone else. She's the only one with a motive. Even if someone happened to find Cheryl in that hut, there would be no reason to kill her. Why would they? They could simply take the necklace and leave her there, considering the amount of drugs in her system."

"Before we bring any charges against Boatman, we'll need more —much more. Arresting a different person every other day for Hartford's murder doesn't make us look very competent. Before we file charges, we need something more substantial."

CARRYING TWO CUPS OF COFFEE, Danielle Boatman showed Clarence Renton to the back patio. She set the mugs on the patio table. "I really appreciate you coming over this afternoon," she said. "I would have been happy to stop by your office."

"No problem. I had a few errands to run today anyway." He took a seat at the patio table.

"I thought it would be much nicer to talk out here," Danielle said as she sat down on the chair across from him.

"Is your friend Lily still staying with you?"

"Yes, but only for a few more weeks. But she's not here right now. She went with Ian to Astoria. He's working on a story about Emma Jackson's life."

"Yes, they mentioned that at your party. I understand you aren't taking guests yet?"

"No. Things are just too confusing right now for me to open for business."

"So what is it you wanted to talk to me about?" Renton asked.

"I was hoping you might be able to recommend a criminal lawyer. I know you don't do criminal law."

"Criminal lawyer? What for?"

"I think I might need one. Joe Morelli seems to think I murdered my cousin."

"I thought Sam Hayman was arrested for her murder. They found the missing jewels on him. At least, that's what it said in today's paper."

"I know. And they arrested Adam first but let him go. Now they have Sam. But yesterday Joe was here, and he told me he didn't believe Sam killed Cheryl. He thinks I did."

"A little strange for him to say that to you if they intend to charge Sam with the murder."

"I agree. I barely got any sleep last night. When I woke up this morning, I decided the smart thing to do was to go ahead and hire a lawyer now, just in case. I know you aren't a criminal lawyer, but I was hoping you could recommend someone."

Inside the kitchen, Walt Marlow watched Danielle through the window.

"What are you looking at?" Cheryl asked as she appeared in the room.

Walt glanced over at Cheryl. "Where have you been? I thought you'd moved on."

"I keep trying, but it's like someone is tugging on me to return, like I'm still needed here." Cheryl walked to the window and looked outside. She could see Danielle sitting at the small patio table with a man. The man's back was to her; she couldn't see his face. "Who's Dani with?"

"It's her attorney. She wants to find a criminal attorney and hopes he can recommend one."

"What does Dani need with a criminal attorney?" Cheryl asked, still watching her cousin.

"She's afraid they might charge her for your murder."

"What? That is ridiculous. Dani didn't kill me…Although, she did knock me on my butt," Cheryl said with a sigh.

"About that," Walt said as he cleared his throat.

"About what?"

"Danielle didn't hit you."

"What are you talking about?" She reached up and touched her once injured cheek. "I have a bruise to prove it…or at least I did…I mean my other self did…But I forgive her."

"It wasn't Danielle, it was me."

Cheryl stared at Walt. "You?"

"I didn't mean to hit you." Walt shrugged. "But you were grabbing at the necklace, and I just meant to push you away. I'm sorry."

"Hmmm…" Cheryl frowned. Glancing back out the window, she said, "You really need to show me how you do that."

They were silent a few moments when Walt finally said, "I wish I could hear what they're saying."

"Why are they outside, anyway? She knows you can't hear her when she's on the patio."

"I think that is exactly why she's outside," Walt grumbled. "Said something about me being too distracting when she's trying to have a serious conversation with someone."

"Well, I can go outside," Cheryl said.

"No, it would be better if you just stay here with me."

"Oh poop, when have I ever made the better choice?"

"That's probably the reason you got yourself killed."

"Perhaps. But the nice thing about being dead—they can't kill you again!" Cheryl laughed and then moved through the kitchen wall to the back patio. Glancing back to the window, she noticed Walt's look of disapproval. In response, she stuck out her tongue then turned to her cousin and the attorney.

Danielle was listening to Mr. Renton list the various criminal attorneys he knew, along with their pros and cons, when she noticed Cheryl standing behind him. She wanted to tell Cheryl to go back into the house so she could concentrate on the conversation.

"Hello, Dani, I'm back!" Cheryl said cheerfully. "I'm here to help you. I won't let them charge you with my murder, I promise."

"Excuse me, Mr. Renton, could you repeat that. I'm afraid… well, I didn't quite get it," Danielle said. Glancing over his shoulder, she narrowed her eyes at Cheryl.

"Oops, sorry, Dani. I'll be quiet, promise," Cheryl said sheepishly as she walked around to Dani's side of the table so she could listen to what Mr. Renton was saying. When Cheryl turned to face the attorney, she froze. Unable to move, Cheryl's eyes widened as she took in the face of Clarence Renton. It all came back to her—she remembered.

"Zimmerman is a good man, but he's representing Adam, so I think…" Clarence continued to talk, unaware of Cheryl's presence.

"It's him! He's the one who killed me!" Cheryl shrieked.

Cheryl's accusation so startled Danielle that before she had time to consider her words, she blurted out, "You murdered my cousin?"

Clarence Renton immediately stopped talking. He looked at Danielle, who continued to stare at him, her eyes wide with a hint of fear. "What did you just say?" he asked in a soft voice.

"Oh my god, it is him!" Cheryl said excitedly, jumping up and down. "I remember now. Sam took me into that shed, and I was so sleepy. I just remember closing my eyes and lying on the floor. But then I was standing up, looking down at my body—oh my god—there was so much blood! And someone was standing next to me; it wasn't Sam, it was Clarence Renton. He was holding a flashlight. It was covered with blood. I could hear him cursing, saying he didn't have a choice. He took the necklace off my neck, covered my body with some rafts and then left me there, all alone in that dark shed."

"You killed my cousin, why?" Danielle asked, still stunned.

"Umm…I don't think you should be asking him that," Cheryl said nervously. "You need to run, Dani. Please, Dani!" Cheryl continued to hop around nervously.

Clutching the handle of his coffee mug, Renton glared at Danielle. Without answering her question, he jumped up and flew across the table. Swinging the heavy ceramic mug in her direction, coffee flying, he hit Danielle squarely on the temple, sending her backwards in the chair, landing on the patio.

"No, Dani, No!" Cheryl cried, jumping up and down. Waving her arms, she tried to push Clarence away from her cousin, but her attempts were futile. Inside the house, Walt stood helpless at the window, the palms of his hands against the glass. He watched in horror as Clarence Renton leaned down to Danielle's unconscious body.

FORTY

Walt stood inside the house and watched Clarence drag Danielle's lifeless body toward the kitchen door.

"Do something!" Cheryl shouted, now standing in the house next to Walt.

"I can't do anything until he gets inside. But when he does…" Walt watched as Clarence opened the door. He tugged Danielle's body inside the kitchen, dropping it on the floor. When Clarence went to close the door, Walt leaned down beside Danielle. "She's still breathing," he told Cheryl.

"What are you going to do about him?" Cheryl pointed to Clarence, who now stood over Danielle.

"I'm sorry I have to do this," Clarence said aloud. "If your cousin hadn't come, none of this would have happened."

"Do something!" Cheryl continued to jump up and down.

"Be quiet, I want to hear what he has to say. There will be plenty of time to deal with him. I won't let him hurt Danielle anymore." Walt watched Clarence.

"We'll have to make this look like an accident. I'll carry you up the stairs and let you take a nice tumble," Clarence said.

"That's what Roger was going to do to me," Walt said.

"Who's Roger?" Cheryl asked.

"My brother-in-law." Walt didn't take his eyes off Clarence.

"Gee, nice brother-in-law…I wonder why Mr. Renton says none of this would've happened if I hadn't come. What did I do wrong?"

"Aside from stealing the necklace? Being annoying?" Walt asked.

"Sometimes you can be mean." Cheryl said with a pout.

"Hush, I want to hear what he has to say."

Hooking his arms under Danielle's armpits, Clarence began to drag her unconscious body backwards, toward the kitchen door leading to the hallway. The effort taxed his overweight body, his breathing labored from the exertion.

"Damn, you feel like a ton of bricks," Clarence moaned. "If your damn cousin hadn't come nosing around, threatening to look into your aunt's will, I wouldn't have to do this. But maybe this will work out for the best." Clarence smiled. "Yes, it really might. O'Malley Trust won't just be getting the rest of your aunt's money —it will be getting your cousin's. Damn, I couldn't have planned this better if I tried!" Clarence laughed as he dragged Danielle into the wide entry hall leading from the front door to the stairs.

Walt had heard enough. Clarence didn't see it coming, the bronze statue that floated from the library, hovering over the attorney's head. Just as Danielle came to, the statue dropped, crashing down on Clarence's skull, sending him sprawling unconscious on the entry hall floor.

Rubbing her sore forehead, Danielle sat up and looked around. Clarence was sprawled on the floor next to her, either unconscious or dead; she wasn't sure. Jumping to her feet, she looked around frantically. The moment she spied Walt and Cheryl, relief washed over her. "What happened?"

"Your attorney tried to kill you," Walt said angrily.

"Is he dead?" Danielle looked down at the man by her feet.

"I don't think so," Walt said as the bronze statue rose from the floor, hovering again over the attorney's head. "But I can take care of that."

"No!" Danielle cried out.

BRIAN HENDERSON and Joe Morelli stood on the front porch of Marlow House. Joe was just about to ring the bell when he heard a woman frantically cry out, "No!" Without hesitation, he and Brian rushed inside.

Danielle Boatman stood in the middle of the hallway, her hands raised in the air as she held a bronze statue. On the floor was a man; who it was Brian and Joe couldn't tell. But it was obvious to them she was about to hit the helpless man a second time.

"Don't move!" Brian and Joe called out simultaneously.

Danielle hadn't heard anyone come into the house—she had been so intent on stopping Walt from killing Clarence Renton. Looking to the voices, Danielle found herself staring down the barrels of two guns. She almost dropped the statue, but she managed to stop herself, terrified one of the men would shoot her.

"Put it down slowly," Joe ordered.

"I'll take care of this!" Walt said angrily.

"No, Walt, please. Let me handle this, please," Danielle begged, slowly lowering the statue to the floor.

Holstering their guns, the officer's rushed forward, Brian pulling Danielle's arms around her back as he handcuffed her wrists while Joe leaned down by Clarence's side, checking his vitals.

"It's Clarence Renton. He's alive," Joe announced before calling for an ambulance.

DANIELLE SAT ALONE in the interview room, her head throbbing. She had asked for a couple aspirin, but so far, no one had bothered to give her any. On the way to the police station, Cheryl had sat in the back of the police car with Danielle, telling her what Clarence had said while she was unconscious. When they arrived at the station, Cheryl disappeared. Danielle didn't know where she had gone.

"You're lucky you didn't kill him," Joe said when he entered the room and sat down across the table from Danielle. "I just talked to the hospital; they tell me he's going to be okay."

"He tried to kill me," Danielle said angrily. "But I guess you don't care about that."

"Why would your attorney try to kill you?"

"Well, gee, why would I try to kill my attorney?" Danielle snapped. "Look at my head; can't you see where he hit me?"

Joe leaned toward her and looked where she pointed at her temple. "It looks a little red but nothing like the number you did on poor Clarence."

"Poor Clarence? He tried to kill me!"

"Clarence was just trying to help you. Just like I am. Let us help you, Danielle, before anyone else gets hurt."

"What are you talking about?" Danielle leaned back in her chair and looked at Joe. She remembered the first time they had met. It seemed like ages ago—yet it had only been weeks. She thought he was so handsome back then—with his wavy dark hair and friendly brown eyes. They didn't look friendly now. He looked at her with pity—as if she was somehow broken.

"I know Clarence was just trying to convince you to get some help. He suspected you killed Cheryl, and when he tried to talk to you about it, you became enraged and attacked him."

"He told you that?"

"He told Brian. Brian talked to him after he regained consciousness."

"He's lying. He killed Cheryl."

"Please stop, Danielle. You aren't helping yourself."

"And you aren't listening to me!" Danielle said angrily.

"We did a little digging in your background," Joe said.

"So? I've never had any problem with the law."

"No, but you do have a history of mental illness."

"What are you talking about?" Danielle felt sick. She knew very well what he was talking about.

"Brian and I heard you—you said *No, Walt, please. Let me handle this, please.* Who did you think you were talking to?"

"I wasn't talking to anyone," Danielle lied, shifting nervously in her chair.

"I know your parents were concerned about you. You claimed to hear voices—see things that weren't there. They tried to get help for you. I'm trying to help you now."

"Oh god," Danielle groaned. "You think I'm crazy. That crazy me killed my cousin."

"Like I said, I just want to—"

"Help me, yes, I know. You keep telling me that. But if you sincerely want to help, listen to what I have to say."

"Okay. Go ahead." Joe leaned back in his chair and studied Danielle.

"I believe there was something funny about my aunt's estate."

"Funny?"

"My aunt left most of her money to her favorite charities—one in particular received the bulk of her estate—O'Malley Trust. I never questioned it."

"I thought you were the sole heir to your aunt's estate," Joe said. "I thought that's why Cheryl was contesting the will."

"No, I just inherited a small portion of it, Marlow House and a little money. But like I said, most of Aunt Brianna's money went to O'Malley Trust. I never thought anything about it because I never expected to inherit anything in the first place. I was just thrilled to get Marlow House."

"Are you suggesting Clarence Renton did something illegal?"

"I had no idea Aunt Brianna had Alzheimer's during her last year. She'd write every few months. The letters weren't as long as they used to be, but I didn't think anything about it."

"Cheryl found out your aunt had Alzheimer's?"

"Yes. I had no idea. Cheryl believed Aunt Brianna wasn't competent when she made her last will—that she'd never leave her out of it. At the time, I assumed if Cheryl was successful at proving her claim, the only thing that would happen—I'd have to give her half of my inheritance. But I was wrong."

"What do you mean?" Joe asked.

"The court wouldn't just look at what I inherited from my aunt, they would look at the nonprofits she left money to—especially O'Malley Trust. I have a feeling if you look into O'Malley Trust, you'll find Clarence Renton profits in some way. He didn't want Cheryl pursuing her case. He needed her out of the way for good."

"Why kill you?"

"Because I figured it out, and I foolishly let him know. He was going to kill me, just like he killed Cheryl. Plus, with me dead, O'Malley Trust would inherit my money—Cheryl's money."

"Why would they?"

"After my aunt's inheritance, Mr. Renton encouraged me to make a new will. My husband had recently died, and in my previous will, everything went to him. When I couldn't decide who I should leave my estate to, Mr. Renton suggested I leave it to my aunt's favorite charity—O'Malley Trust. He said I could always change it later when I decided what I wanted to do. At the time it seemed like a nice gesture."

Brian popped his head in the door for a moment, telling Joe the chief wanted to see him. Joe excused himself and left Danielle alone in the room. She looked up at the mirror on the wall and wondered if they were watching her.

"WELL, WHAT DO YOU THINK?" the chief asked when he met Joe and Brian in the hall outside of the interview room.

"I think she believes what she's saying," Joe said.

"Does that mean you don't think she killed her cousin?" the chief asked.

"I think she's a sick girl," Joe said sadly. "You didn't hear her back at Marlow House."

"It was kind of strange," Brian agreed. "She obviously thought she was talking to Walt Marlow. And then there was the way she was preparing to bash in Clarence's head. I mean, hell, he was already unconscious."

"How in the world did you find out about her mental health issues?" the chief asked.

"Mostly from Cheryl Hartford's attorney. Apparently, Cheryl told him when Danielle was a child she insisted she could see ghosts. Her parents sent her to a psychologist for about a year. The doctor is retired now. When I called him, I wasn't surprised he'd refuse to talk about her case, but he inadvertently confirmed she'd been his patient."

"So what do you think we should do?" the chief asked.

"I think she needs a psychological evaluation," Joe said.

ADAM WOKE to the sound of his cellphone ringing. Sitting up in his bed, he glanced at his alarm clock. He had been sleeping off and on for almost twenty-four hours. Yawning, he reached for the phone from his nightstand. It was his grandmother.

"Hi, Grandma," Adam said lazily, leaning back in the bed.

"Adam, where are you?"

"In bed." Adam yawned again.

"What, are you sick?"

"No, but I've been a little sleep deprived this past week. Just catching up."

"Well, you need to get right out of that bed and do something!"

"Do something? What are you talking about, Grandma?"

"About poor Danielle Boatman. You have to help her. She would never do such a horrible thing. This would break my dear friend's heart."

"What dear friend?" Adam sat up in the bed and scratched his head. *What is she talking about?*

"Brianna O'Malley, of course! Danielle needs our help. She's practically family."

"Why does she need our help?"

"Because she's been arrested! I heard through Joyce Pruitt, whose next-door neighbor's niece is dating a boy who works at the police station. They're arresting Danielle for the murder of her cousin!"

"Danielle didn't murder Cheryl."

"I know that. That's why you have to do something!"

SLUMPED OVER THE TABLE, her head resting on folded arms, Danielle closed her eyes. She felt as if she had been in the interview room for hours. She wanted to call an attorney, but she had no idea who to call, and the idea of using a public defender didn't appeal to her. They told her she could make one call. She wanted to call Lily. Lily and Ian would help. The only problem, she didn't know Lily's number. It was programed into her cellphone—her cellphone that was still sitting in the kitchen at Marlow House. The fact was, she didn't know anyone's phone number by heart; she could barely remember her own. When she got out of this mess—which she hoped to God she would be able to do—she vowed to memorize a list of important numbers.

The door to the interview room opened. Danielle looked up and was surprised to find Adam Nichols standing at the doorway. Brian stood behind him.

"Adam wanted to see you. We thought it would be okay," Brian said. Adam walked into the room. Brian left and shut the door, leaving Adam alone with Danielle.

"Why are you here?" Danielle asked, sitting up straight in the chair.

"My grandmother wanted me to come. She was worried about you." Adam sat across the table from Danielle.

"How did she know I was here?"

"Small town." Adam shrugged.

"Gee, the last time we were here, the situation was sort of reversed, huh?"

"I suppose you're right." Adam grinned. "This place sucks."

"I must say you're much more cheerful than the last time I saw you."

"Finally caught up on my sleep. Not so grumpy."

"Are you here to gloat?" Danielle asked.

"I know you didn't kill Cheryl."

"I have to warn you," Danielle interrupted.

"What?"

"They're probably listening to us." Danielle nodded toward the mirror.

"Oh, that, yeah, I know."

"You know?"

"Why sure. Everyone in Frederickport knows about the two-way mirror." Adam laughed. "Heck, don't you ever watch TV?"

"So why are you really here?"

"I want to help. I confess, I would have come even if Grandma hadn't called me. And I would have come sooner, but I didn't know you had been arrested. I've been sleeping. Felt great, by the way. Slept like a baby." Adam glanced to the mirror and gave it a little wave.

"Are you just here to tell me you think I'm innocent?"

"If you killed your cousin, that means you're the one who left the necklace in my office. Whoever killed Cheryl tried to frame me."

"I didn't leave that necklace in your office."

"Oh, I know that. You see I have this nifty little hidden camera in my office. You know all about hidden cameras, don't you?" Adam gave Danielle a wink and pulled his keys from his pocket. On his key chain was a USB memory stick. He unhooked the stick and set it on the table between them.

"WHAT'S HE DOING?" the chief asked as he stood with Brian and Joe in the office next to the interview room, watching Danielle and Adam.

"I don't know. Looks like one of those portable memory sticks," Brian said.

"WHAT'S THAT?" Danielle asked, looking down at the memory stick.

"It's a little footage captured from my security camera. Shows the killer with the Missing Thorndike. At least the Missing Thorndike with the fake stones and poor Cheryl's blood all over it. Pretty good camera, I must say. I'll have to leave it a five-star review over on Amazon. Great shot of the killer's face and no mistaking the necklace. Clear as day, Clarence Renton hiding the Missing Thorndike in my office."

Before Danielle could respond, Joe and Brian rushed into the room. Brian snatched up the memory stick.

Adam leaned over the table and whispered to Danielle, "Don't worry. If they screw it up and erase the stick, I saved it to the cloud."

FORTY-ONE

Inside the kitchen of Marlow House, Ian and Lily prepared Sunday breakfast. Sitting alone on the back patio with Sadie sleeping by her feet, Danielle felt pampered by her two friends. Since she had returned from the police department late Friday, Lily had been her protective champion, clucking around like a fierce mother hen.

Danielle had slept most of Saturday. When she finally woke up on Sunday, she remembered what Adam had said about sleeping all day after the charges against him had been dropped. She had to admit, Adam Nichols was starting to grow on her. For a sleazy guy, he could be sweet.

Enjoying her second cup of morning coffee, Danielle closed her eyes and leaned back in the chair. She could hear the birds chirping in the trees overhead and in the distance the waves washing up on the beach. When she heard the unmistakable sound of the back door to the kitchen opening, she assumed Lily was about to call her in for breakfast.

"I'm sorry, Dani, he insisted on seeing you." Lily sounded annoyed.

Danielle opened her eyes and looked to the kitchen door. Joe stood with Lily on the back porch. "What, am I under arrest now?"

"I just wanted you to know Clarence Renton confessed." Joe

stepped off the porch onto the lawn. Danielle noticed Ian standing in the doorway, listening.

Danielle sat up straight in the chair and set her coffee on the table. "Really? What did he confess to? I know Sam confessed but just to the theft."

"He confessed to everything. You were right about O'Malley Trust; it was a scam. He set it up after your aunt got sick. Apparently, your aunt always intended to leave you her entire estate. She never mentioned Cheryl, even before she got sick. So I don't think she ever intended to leave her anything in the will. Until Cheryl showed up, Clarence had no idea there was another niece. He killed your cousin. We found the flashlight he used; it was in his trunk. It still had Cheryl's blood on it and was covered with Clarence's fingerprints."

"I guess for an attorney he wasn't terrific about covering his tracks," Danielle said dryly.

"I don't think he ever thought he'd be a suspect. And when we started questioning him and showed him Adam's video, he remembered he never got rid of the flashlight. He just broke. Told us everything."

"How did he know Cheryl was in that shed?" Danielle asked.

"Apparently, he was with Sam when Adam mentioned where they were going after the party. When she took off with the necklace, Clarence thought that was his opportunity to get rid of Cheryl. People would think she was killed for the necklace. He didn't know exactly where the beach house was, and by the time he found it, Cheryl was with Sam, walking back to Marlow House."

"He found her in the shed after Sam left her?"

"Yes. There were also some teenagers at the beach. Clarence stayed in the shadows, watching. After Sam and the teenagers took off, Clarence went into the hut and found Cheryl unconscious. He killed her and took the necklace."

"Someone said a woman called in the tip about the necklace in Adam's office," Danielle said.

"Sounded like a woman," Joe said. "But it was Clarence, disguising his voice."

"Well, thank you for telling me," Danielle said politely.

Joe glanced back at Ian and Lily, who continued to stand behind him. "Do you think I could talk to Danielle alone, just for a minute?"

Lily looked over to Danielle, who gave them a little nod. With a grunt, Lily grabbed Ian by the hand and went back into the house, slamming the door behind her.

"I wanted to tell you how sorry I am," Joe said, taking another step closer.

"I suppose you were just doing your job," Danielle said with no emotion.

"I never wanted to hurt you, Danielle."

"I believe you." Danielle smiled sadly. "I really do."

"Do you think…well, maybe we could start over?"

Danielle looked at Joe a moment, studying his hopeful expression.

"No…I don't think so," Danielle said at last.

"You said you believed me."

"There is no point," Danielle said sadly. "You had absolutely no faith in me—not a shred."

"That's not true," Joe insisted. "I care about you."

"You believed Sam when he said he didn't murder Cheryl, and he had stolen the diamonds and emeralds."

"And I was right. Sam didn't kill her," Joe said weakly.

"And neither did I. Yet you were convinced I murdered my cousin."

"I was just trying to do my job. I am sorry. You need to understand."

Danielle pointed to the house and said, "Lily in there, she's my best friend. I know that no matter what, she'll always be there for me. And if I was to tell her some insane story—oh, I don't know—maybe like Walt Marlow's ghost haunts this house—she wouldn't think I was crazy, or she wouldn't pretend to believe. She just would, because she has faith in me. Even Ian didn't doubt me, and I've known him for about as long as I've known you. I'm sorry, but I don't have room in my life anymore for people who don't have faith in me. Caring is simply not enough."

"ARE YOU OKAY?" Lily asked from the doorway after Joe left.

"Yeah, I'm fine." Danielle smiled at Lily.

"Breakfast is almost ready."

"Okay, I'll be right in."

Lily gave her a little nod and went back into the house, closing the door behind her.

"I guess I was wrong about Aunt Brianna," Cheryl said as she appeared on the patio.

"How long have you been listening?" Danielle asked.

"I heard what Joe said." Cheryl paced back and forth in front of Danielle. "I guess she really didn't love me."

"She didn't know you."

"I suppose." Cheryl stopped pacing and faced Danielle. "I'm sorry I made such a mess of everything."

"I'm sorry how things turned out. You being—well…"

"Dead, you mean?" Cheryl asked.

"Yeah…" Danielle smiled sadly.

"I guess it was going to happen eventually. Would have been nice to have more time, but I have to admit, I'm curious about what's around the corner."

"Are you leaving?" Danielle asked.

"Yeah, I think so. I'm done here. Time to move on, I suppose."

"I have a funeral to plan. Thought you might stick around for that, give you a chance to see all your friends before you move on."

"Nah," Cheryl said with a sigh. "At one time I would probably have been all over that—a party where I'm the focus of everyone's attention. All those tears, just for me." Cheryl flashed Danielle a smile and said, "But no. I think I really am ready to move on."

"I'm sorry we weren't closer," Danielle said.

"Me too. I'm sorry I was such a brat. I shouldn't have hit on Lucas. And look, I did it again!"

"What do you mean?"

"I've obviously messed up another one of your relationships!" Cheryl sounded sincerely remorseful.

"Are you talking about Joe?"

"Yeah, I mean, he is a good-looking guy, and I think he really liked you."

"Maybe you were right all along," Danielle said.

"Right about what?"

"You said if a guy could be swayed so easily, he probably wasn't worth it."

"I never hit on him. I promise, not once," Cheryl insisted.

"Oh, I know, I don't mean that. But it was easier for him to imagine I might do something so horrible as to kill you, than to try to find some way to prove I was innocent."

"In fairness to Joe, you guys really didn't know each other that long. Maybe you should give him another chance."

"No, I don't think so." Danielle shook her head. "I suppose I have this fanciful notion that when I someday meet the right guy, he will inherently have faith in me—or at least give me a chance before he's ready to have me committed or imprisoned."

"You'll find someone, Dani," Cheryl promised. "Someone who is worthy, someone who won't let you down."

FROM INSIDE THE KITCHEN, Walt watched Danielle and Cheryl through the window. He couldn't hear what they were saying, but he had a good idea they were saying goodbye. Unlike him, Cheryl was ready to move on, and there was really no reason for her to stay.

In the background, he could hear Ian and Lily talking as Lily set the table for breakfast. They discussed Joe Morelli, who had left just minutes earlier. From what they were saying, Joe wouldn't be seeing Danielle again, at least not socially. Walt felt partly relieved to know Danielle was no longer interested in the handsome police officer—which made him feel guilty.

Walt noticed Cheryl was no longer wearing the pink dress she had worn to the open house. Instead, she wore a long pale blue dress. Its full skirt fluttered around her ankles. He watched as Cheryl raised her right hand in a wave—and then her image gradually faded into the landscape until she was no longer visible. Cheryl had moved on.

THE GHOST WHO WASN'T

Return to Marlow House in

The Ghost Who Wasn't

Haunting Danielle, Book 3

When a local heiress goes missing, Danielle discovers it's not always possible to distinguish the living from the dead. To complicate matters, it seems Danielle is not the only one who communicates with spirits. Her new guest claims to hear Walt. But something's not quite right with Marlow House's newest medium.

Danielle must move quickly before her best friend joins the spirit world.

NON-FICTION BY

BOBBI ANN JOHNSON HOLMES

Havasu Palms, A Hostile Takeover

Where the Road Ends, Recipes & Remembrances

Motherhood, a book of poetry

The Story of the Christmas Village

BOOKS BY ANNA J. MCINTYRE

Coulson's Wife

Coulson's Crucible

Coulson's Lessons

Coulson's Secret

Coulson's Reckoning

UNLOCKED HEARTS

Sundered Hearts

After Sundown

While Snowbound

Sugar Rush